PRAISE FOR
FRIENDS WITH BOATS

"Fun, addictive and indulgent. Everything you'd want in a beach read."

—**KAREN ALPERT,** *New York Times* Best-Selling
author of *I Heart My Little A-Holes*

"The absolutely perfect beach read! *Friends with Boats* has everything—
sex, intrigue, violence, summer fun in the sun, girl-fights, tennis, country
club parties, and about a gallon of pricey Chardonnay. Not to mention
those monied friends, with boats. Author Alexandra Slater takes the
trope of the Cape Cod novel, turns it on its head, and then gives it a
good spanking. Think *Heathers* meets Richard Russo's *Old Cape Magic.*
Friends with Boats is the ultimate guilty pleasure!"

—**JAMIE CAT CALLAN,** Author of *Parisian Charm School*

"*Friends with Boats* is the perfect sexy, summer beach read. I read it from
start to finish in one sitting!"

—**LAURA WINTERS,** Publisher of *Hingham Anchor*

FRIENDS WITH BOATS

ALEXANDRA SLATER

FRIENDS WITH BOATS

RIVER GROVE
BOOKS

Published by River Grove Books
Austin, TX
www.rivergrovebooks.com

Distributed by River Grove Books

Design and composition by Greenleaf Book Group and Brian Phillips
Cover design by Greenleaf Book Group and Brian Phillips
Cover images copyright *Marish*. Used under license from Shutterstock.com

Publisher's Cataloging-in-Publication data is available.

Print ISBN: 978-1-63299-676-3

eBook ISBN: 978-1-63299-677-0

First Edition

For L.T., James, Caroline, London, & Farah
and
My parents, Bill and Phoebe

PROLOGUE

Falmouth, Massachusetts
September 2019

When the text came in early that morning, Sadie knew that something was terribly wrong. She rolled over in bed, fumbled for her cell phone, put on her glasses, and felt an immediate sense of dread: Mack Taylor's pickup truck had hit a telephone pole on Route 151 and Currier Road in the early morning hours and rolled over. The truck was totaled, and an ambulance had taken him to Falmouth Hospital. Details to follow.

Sadie panicked. She had caused that accident. Not directly, but she had wished him dead at the Farewell to Summer Fling at the golf club the night before. In fact, all three of them—Sadie, Charlotte, and Ada—had wished Mack dead. Through the early morning brain fog, Sadie thought about how she had gone up to the bar to get her third glass of Whispering Angel. This was when Mack approached her from behind. She could feel the warmth of his muscular body behind her as she slowly inhaled the familiar smell of salt air mixed with pine.

But there was nothing left to say. Ever since Mack arrived back home on Cape Cod, the summer had been an absolute disaster for the four of them. He reached over Sadie's shoulder to grab his Moscow mule in the chilled copper mug. She sensed Mack was desperate to engage, as he kept turning his head toward her, but she avoided eye contact, especially with her husband, Chip, there. She slowly backed up and headed to the ballroom where the ten-piece swing band, Stage Door Canteen, played. Charlotte flailed her arms about and above her head on the dance floor, along with Caroline Wall and the other ladies from tennis. Ada, on the other hand, sat at a table with four empty chairs around her. She picked at the bouquet of peonies and hydrangeas while her husband, Ben, caroused with Chip by the window.

But when Mack entered the room, Sadie felt the tension escalate. All three women glanced over at him. He surveyed each one of them. Mack took a final swig of his drink, steadying the cup on the table, and dashed to the center of the dance floor. Since she knew he hated dancing with a passion—he had been her date at prom and at her older sister Mimi's wedding—Sadie guessed the night was not going to end well. Mack was clearly on another bender, verifying the rumors about his fall from grace. It was a fall that was a long time coming and one he brought on himself.

But getting into a deadly car crash? He didn't deserve that. Or did he?

Chapter One

MEMORIAL DAY

Four Months Earlier
Memorial Day Weekend, 2019

SADIE

Sadie Cooper loved organization, to-do lists, and her family, but this weekend on Cape Cod, she was unhappy with all three. Winter clothes had to be packed in bins, the deck furniture needed a power wash, and the boat had to be moved to the mooring before friends and family arrived. It was the beginning of the roller-coaster ride called summer on the Cape, bookended by Memorial Day and Labor Day. It was both exciting, as the restaurants and ice cream shops opened for the season, as well as daunting because life as Sadie knew it year-round was over. For the next few months, it would be beach days, traffic, boating, barbecues, and summer people. Prepping for this was draining—mentally and physically.

The kids would soon be out of school, up in her grill all day, and she hadn't taken one minute for self-care. Her mousy brown hairline was smattered with wiry grays, and her nails were jagged without polish.

At 45, Sadie didn't recognize her shape anymore. The thought of wearing a bathing suit was cringey, and she'd fallen off her diet every weekend. She would start the week with good intentions, logging her food into the Weight Watchers app, drinking eight glasses of water, and eating no carbs. But by the weekend, her plans all went to pot, and she failed to log in that third glass of chardonnay (3 points) and the bagel (9 points). Thankfully, her husband, Chip, never body-shamed her and would still initiate having sex several times a week, even if she wasn't into it. It wasn't that she was no longer attracted to Chip, but more that she wasn't attracted to herself. She felt fat and squishy. And unless they were going to do it in the dark, missionary style, forget it.

Sadie walked downstairs to check on the kids. They were older now, so they spent a lot of time on their phones and devices. She lamented the days when Tina would ask her to play with American Girl dolls, and Charlie would give her a big bear hug. Nowadays, he'd shoo her away if she went in too close for a squeeze, and Tina was busy messaging her friends or on social media.

"Mom, I don't want carrots in my lunch. They're slimy. I want chips," Charlie said, picking out the carrots and tossing them across the room into the sink.

"Can you please just get up and throw those out?" Sadie huffed. "And you can't exist on snacks. You need some sort of fruit or vegetable in your lunch. Pick one, bottom shelf of the fridge." Charlie shuffled over to the Sub-Zero fridge and riffled through the fruit.

"Here, I'll have an apple," he said, handing it to her. "But I don't want the skin on it."

Sadie rolled her eyes and reached for the apple peeler. She had just stopped cutting his meat, but she was still peeling his fruit and cutting off the crusts for him. She knew she should let him be more independent, but Charlie was her tow-headed big baby. Tall for his age with whitish blond hair, you couldn't miss him in a crowd. Actually, both of her babies were coddled. She couldn't help herself. When they called, she came. It made her feel needed. She didn't have a job, so she was the mom. This was her job.

"Mom, I can't find my charger! Did you steal it?" Tina circled around the room, in her crop top and leggings. She began lifting things and tossing them about.

"First of all, Tina, I don't have to steal something that *I* bought. And, secondly, no, I haven't seen it. I thought we talked about no screen time this morning. You are supposed to be studying for your tutor. I am not paying for you to sit around and text your friends. This is so you can do well on the exams. Unless you want to live at home for the rest of your life and not go to college."

She knew this would motivate Tina to study. She wanted out.

"Fine, Mom! I am . . . ah! I just need my charger," Tina whined, storming off upstairs. Sadie couldn't remember the last time she and Tina had hung out and talked. When she was young, Sadie couldn't catch a breath from her. Tina was like Sadie's shadow until she turned eleven, when she transformed into caring only about her friends and her phone. Sadie was sick and tired of having to threaten to take Tina's phone away if she glanced at it throughout dinner or scrolled Instagram during family time. Family time was reserved for Sundays, when the football game was on, and Sadie and Chip insisted that everyone sit together to watch the first quarter. The family's tradition was to eat nachos and wings while watching the game.

Chip was camped at the kitchen island, eating a leftover pastrami sandwich and flipping through the *In Touch* she picked up at Windfall Market earlier in the week.

"I haven't even had a chance to read that yet!" Sadie said. "Just don't get mustard on it or dogear any of the pages."

"Relax, hon," Chip said. "I'll buy you a new one if you really want."

"That's not the point."

"Well, I'm not five, so no need to worry about condiments on your magazine." He continued to flip through the pages, and with every turn,

Sadie felt more unnerved. She had few things that were *just hers* in this house, and her celebrity trash reads were one of them. He knew she liked to have first read, but he did it anyway, perhaps out of spite. Sadie grabbed a La Croix grapefruit seltzer from the fridge and headed back upstairs, forgetting why she had come down in the first place.

"Where are you going?" Chip asked.

"To switch our clothes over for summer and get this house ready for the storm ahead called summer," she chided. "Can you go to Target and get me some more plastic bins?"

"Ugh, hon, I'm not going over the bridge today. It's Friday."

Chip was referring to the Bourne Bridge, the connector between Cape Cod and the mainland. Weekends, particularly on holidays during the summer, were a nightmare with bottlenecked traffic as everyone was trying to get onto the Cape. All locals knew it was a no-no. You stayed put on Fridays, Sundays, and holidays.

"Fine, then go to Walmart?" she pleaded.

"You know how I feel about Walmart."

"Chip? I really don't care about the social injustices of Walmart employees right now. I'm totally stressed. My entire family is coming for the weekend, and you know there will be some sort of drama. And have you sorted through your sweaters and chosen which ones we are donating to the Falmouth Service Center?

"Did you see that Scarlett Johansson might be pregnant?" Chip replied, still flipping through *In Touch*.

Sadie stormed up the stairs and grabbed her phone. There was a Facebook notification on it, a friend request from Mack Taylor, her ex-boyfriend from years past. She felt a jolt of excitement and quickly accepted, followed by a thorough stalking of his page. She knew he'd gotten married, because she had googled him periodically, particularly late at night after she'd had an argument with Chip. But he seemed to no longer be with his wife. His profile picture was just one of him on his boat, and the other photos on his page were of him tagged by his three daughters at various graduation parties and dinners. She wondered if he was reaching out to check in on her status, to get a feel if she was single too. Sadie went to her profile page and spruced it up, deleting unsavory photos of herself and removing tags that made her look depressed. She wanted to appear light and happy. Isn't that what all men wanted anyway? Light and happy? She was anything but; however, Mack didn't need to see that. And, in fact, she was feeling lighter and happier already now that he had reached out. She wondered if she should send him a private message but decided that might be crossing the line, something she had a proclivity for.

Sadie dropped the phone and went to the mirror. She turned to the side and sucked in her tummy. The pregnancies had left stretch marks, despite the copious amounts of coconut oil she'd glazed over her body, and then there was the permanent fold of skin she couldn't get rid of no matter how hard she tried. Sadie stepped in closer, pushing her face inches from the glass and turning her head side to side, inspecting it. Her fair ivory skin was just the right hue to illuminate her sympathetic eyes. She used her two index fingers to lift her furrowed brow and pull back her crow's feet, wondering if she should explore Botox. Her side-swept bangs concealed the tiny mole on her forehead she disliked, and her ski jump nose was peppered with tiny freckles from the springtime sunshine.

Sadie decided to try on the size 6 black sheath dress she had bought at Maxwell to see if it still fit. She put it over her head, slid her arms through the sleeves, and got stuck. Her arms waved above her head before she could wriggle out of it. Sweating, she threw it onto the elliptical machine.

That was it, Sadie decided. Not Botox, but that she was going to message Mack. *What's the harm? He's an old friend!* Surely, she could send an innocuous private message. If Chip did that, she wouldn't care. Right?

So nice to hear from you! Long time, no see! How are you doing??

She stared at the message, pausing momentarily, and then hit send. Once the "Read" receipt arrived, she eagle-eyed her phone, pacing as the word bubbles of an impending message showed. Then it came:

I'm great! How are you? Got some news: heading back to the Cape to start a cool new resort! Would be fun to catch up when I get there!

Mack Taylor was irresistible to women. Aside from his good looks—blond, blue-eyed, built, and tall—he was also smart and charming with a privileged background and bank account to match. Wherever Mack went, women would follow. He was the definition of a chick magnet. He didn't even need a puppy. No, he just had to walk into a room and women flocked to him, like bees to pollen.

Mack came from a wealthy family, inheriting money from his grandfather's successful trash disposal business. His grandaddy Joe was a blue-collar man raised in New London, Connecticut, and he had started the disposal business from scratch. He was ambitious to a fault, having grown up around privileged Connecticut College students and boarding school kids from Groton. It drove him to succeed and compete, eventually ending up at Yale, but unfortunately his ambition and passion hadn't passed on to Mack. Instead, Mack was the kind of man who was handed everything and squandered it. It's not that Mack wasn't intelligent. He was. He, too, had graduated from Yale—thanks to Grandaddy Joe's legacy—and before that he was on the dean's list at Exeter. However, things came too easily to Mack, between his looks and his money, so he never had ambition or drive. He was essentially a slacker and the "President of the Lucky Sperm Club," or so his friends said.

Sadie remembered the first time she met Mack's parents at his winter home in Connecticut when she was eighteen. Summer on the Cape had ended, and it was time for the annual Taylor Labor Day party: banquet, bocce ball, croquet, and swimming. Sadie dressed to impress, wearing a long white cotton dress with a blue sash, as this was the big introduction to his family as his official "girlfriend." Upon her arrival, Sadie walked through the archway onto the sprawling back lawn overlooking a river. He was standing next to his parents and turned around, moving closer toward her with his arms outstretched.

"Wow," he said. "You're a smoke show. I love that dress."

It was one of Sadie's treasured memories, which is why she'd kept that dress. It hung untouched in the far-right end of her closet. She wondered if she should try it on again, just to see how it would feel. She walked to the closet, pushed the hangers together, and there it was. The blue sash had faded a bit but still had some shine. Sadie held it up to her body. After she shimmied into it, she looked in the mirror. It was tight, but with a little work, she could fit back into it. She was feeling like her old self, for just a moment.

Chapter Two

MODELING AND MUDSLIDES

CHARLOTTE

Charlotte opened the freezer door, reached behind the lemon popsicles, and pulled out a half-eaten frozen Milky Way. She folded down the brown silky wrapper with the distinctive green writing and gently rested her top and bottom teeth on it. She wanted to savor this bite as long as she could. She put her tongue on the bottom of the solid frozen chocolate exterior, leaving it there for a moment of gustatory delight. She then bit down, and a hard square chunk broke off in her mouth, the nougat in the center congealed. She sucked on it, like an ice cube, tasting the milk chocolate as it slowly melted. When she got to the secondary layer of caramel, the sweet sensation made her tingle and savor it.

But that was long enough.

Charlotte ran to the sink, pulled out the trash can from beneath, and spit it out. She just wanted a taste, not the calories, as the magnet on her fridge read: *A Moment on the Lips, a Lifetime on the Hips*. There was also a photo of her from her days as a swimsuit model as "thinspiration," to keep her tight and lean. A reminder of what she once was—thin and beautiful.

At age forty-six, 130 pounds and five foot eight, Charlotte Simms was still lean and a head-turner. Her silky, straight blonde hair fell at the middle of her back. Like a pendulum, it swayed back and forth as she walked, just as it had when she strutted the catwalk during Fashion Week. Charlotte had been modeling since freshman year at New York University, when she was discovered in Washington Square Park by a talent scout. She was seated on a bench next to the old men playing chess, slurping a frozen Diet Coke, and reading *The Odyssey* when he approached her and handed her his Elite business card.

"You ever considered modeling?" he asked.

Charlotte nearly spit out her soda. "Please tell me you're joking," she said, looking up from her book. "Nice try, but I'm taken." Truth was, she wasn't taken at all, but she thought better than to fall for some lame line by a psycho in Washington Square Park. Her best friend Sadie had warned her of these druggies and sex addicts just days before when she packed up from her summer on Cape Cod.

"Well, I would ask you out, but I'm married. No, you have something. Think about it and give me a call if you change your mind," he said, walking off under the tall white arch in the park. Eventually, mainly out of curiosity, Charlotte reached out from her dorm room landline. She was suspect that "Charlotte says Moo" could ever model. But, before she knew it, she booked a J.Crew catalog shoot and a Scope commercial. Her modeling career took off, and she was on buses, in magazines, and even in Times Square. But it was her bathing suit spread in the *Sports Illustrated* Swimsuit Issue, 1992, that she was most famous for.

Charlotte was a classic American beauty, like Christie Brinkley and Farrah Fawcett. She had spreads in *Vogue*, *W*, *Self*, *Glamour*, and *Cosmopolitan*. She traveled the world on photo shoots to Monaco, St. Barth's, Rome, Capri, Paris, and Santorini. That life was exhausting but exhilarating—even when she had to lie in a bikini in the sand in below-freezing water in Antarctica. However, once the millennium rolled around, her modeling career tanked. The heroin-chic look was in, and All-American was out. Kate Moss and Christy Turlington were ubiquitous on magazine covers, sullen and starved. Charlotte's curves, blonde hair, and winning smile only got her bookings in commercial catalogs like Talbots and Ann Taylor. Eventually, Elite dumped her for one of those younger, thinner models.

"You had a good run," her agent said. "Most models never even make it to *Sports Illustrated*. Just walk away gracefully and go have some kids and settle down. You deserve it!" That was the last thing Charlotte wanted to do: get married and have kids. She was twenty-eight and living the single life in her Soho loft apartment on Spring Street. She spent days shopping and working out obsessively, and evenings partying late into the night, doing lines of cocaine and ecstasy before hitting the club scene with other models. She was handed drinks for being hot and never waited in line outside. The velvet rope was always open for her gaggle of gals because their hotness made the party *relevant*. They were like expensive decorations that ignited a dim room.

But being regarded as beautiful was all new for Charlotte. She had grown up a rather plain girl. In fact, when she was in grade school, her long blonde hair was mousy brown, and her body was somewhat squat, like SpongeBob SquarePants. Her bulky stature was the cause of much consternation, particularly when it came to her middle school social status. Boys like Patrick Conlon, whom all the girls fawned over and took turns dating, ignored her, unless he poked fun at her—as was the case with the infamous note that circulated about the school bus one gray, wintry day. The note was scribbled in ink and folded like origami when it was tossed over the seat to Charlotte on the school bus:

"Roses are red, violets are blue, Winnie's a slut, and Charlotte says moo."

Since the day Charlotte opened that note with her pink painted fingers, she loathed her body. She was a cow. A heifer. Her "moo" was an emotional albatross, and eventually, became a cry for help when she restricted her eating to apples washed down with Diet Coke for a year in high school. When she went to the emergency room crippled over in pain, thinking she was having appendicitis, the physicians explained to her parents that she had extreme gas from too much fiber ingestion and was malnourished. She needed to seek treatment for an eating disorder. After being shipped off to Renfrew in Arizona for several months, she returned home. But she never fully recovered from her body dysmorphia. She would always restrict her calories, spitting out tastes of food, like she had that morning with the frozen Milky Way.

Charlotte's body issues had recently become an issue in bed with her husband, John, too, who was frustrated that she would not have sex with the lights on—just with the bathroom door slightly ajar to shed a sliver of light. She also refused to be on top, as she couldn't help but stare at her stomach rolls, balking at the sight of her thighs.

"I can't believe how disgusting I look," she'd proclaim, right as he was about to climax.

Charlotte often felt more at ease when having sex if she wore a wig like she was someone else. She had an extensive collection of styles, and each wig had a name that corresponded with a character she was playing. There was Marilyn, for the short Marilyn Monroe platinum blonde wig, and there was Tammy for the redhead, who also spoke with a slow Southern drawl. John enjoyed it at first, for the variety. It was like he could cheat on his wife without really cheating. But soon the wig charade grew old, and so did she. Charlotte sensed John's wandering eye and couldn't help but wonder if he was cheating for real.

John and Charlotte had met at the Chart Room in Cataumet on Cape

Cod when they were in their late twenties. She was the thinnest she'd ever been, at the height of her modeling career. It was July, and Charlotte and Sadie clamored for the Chart Room's famous mudslides. They were a delicious milkshake of liquor: frothy, creamy, and thick. Slurping one down on an Adirondack chair on the outside patio, surrounded by broken white clamshell terrain, Charlotte spotted John. He was wearing a Wianno Club visor and was badly sunburned, like he'd been boating all day.

"I want that one," Charlotte said, pointing him out.

"Visor?" Sadie asked.

"Yep," Charlotte said, "Dare me to go talk to him?"

"Do I even need to?" Sadie laughed.

Charlotte sashayed over to John in her Zara short denim skirt and white tank top.

"Hi there," she said, chewing on the side of her thin red straw like she was Olivia Newton John at the end of *Grease*. John glanced up and smiled at her from his chair. He was dressed in Nantucket red shorts and an old Dartmouth T-shirt. "Did you go to Dartmouth?"

"I did!" John said. "Did you?"

"No." Charlotte smirked. "But I wish I had. Then I would have met you sooner." She flashed her big smile and tossed her hair behind her shoulder, a signature flirt move. John laughed. Her bravado masked her inner turmoil and insecurity. She loved male attention and affirmation, solidifying that she was worthy, because the truth was, no matter how many magazines covers she was on, she was still the girl that went "moo."

"Is that so?" John said. "Well, let's make up for some lost time. Have a seat." He glanced across the table at his buddies for approval. "Are you here by yourself?"

Charlotte motioned over to Sadie to join them. "No, my friend Sadie's here with me. We were dying for a mudslide," Charlotte said, holding up her empty cup. A tiny gnat flew by her face, and she shooed it away. One also bit her on the leg.

"I can see that," John said. "Let me get you and your friend a round."

"That'd be great," Charlotte said. "They remind me of a Frosty from Wendy's, except you get a good buzz."

"Maybe too much so. These bad boys can put the hurt on you in the morning," John said, taking the last sip of his and motioning for the waitress to come over. "Can we have another round? And two for these ladies as well."

Sadie joined them at the table. She sat next to John's frat buddy, taking one for the team. Charlotte spotted the plastic cup filled with goldfish crackers on the center of the wooden wagon wheel table. *One hundred and ten calories and seven grams of fat for one serving*, she thought. Maybe she'd just have a few sips and switch to vodka.

"So, do you summer on the Cape, or are you from here?" John asked. Using the word "summer" as a verb irked Charlotte. It sounded so affected and privileged. However, she was indeed a summer person, not year-round, so she let it slide.

"We spend the summers here," Charlotte said. "In Woods Hole."

"Cool beans," John said. Charlotte didn't see how that had anything to do with beans, and she liked her beans hot, not cold, but she let that slide too . . . because he was hot.

When the mudslides were gone, the sun was setting. The ducks that ran around the clam shells retreated to the harbor, and families took copious amounts of posed photos that would likely end up as holiday cards.

"Well, thank you for the drinks," Charlotte said, rising. "I'd say I'll call you, but I don't know your name or your number!"

"It's John." He chuckled. "And all you had to do was ask." He grabbed the damp cocktail napkin with the blue script and a boat on it and wrote his phone number down using the waitress's pen. "Can I have yours?"

"Nope. I'll call you," she said, grabbing the napkin, folding it, and tucking it into the back pocket of her skirt. She would wait a few days to make him sweat a little. By Wednesday, she thought, she would give him a call.

Now, as Charlotte stood in her kitchen, peering at the chewed-up frozen Milky Way in her trash can, she reflected on her decision to marry John. It had been ten years. Ten long years of him working nights and weekends and stonewalling her. She felt so alone, like the young girl on the bus reading the note. She wished she could talk to that girl now, tell her that she loved her, and make her feel safe. "You are wonderful, Charlotte," she murmured to herself. If only she believed it.

Chapter Three

REKINDLING ROMANCE

ADA

Ada peeled into Turning Point Dance Studio Saturday morning in her evergreen Range Rover to drop off her twelve-year-old daughter, Lilly, at ballet. The other Falmouth moms turned their heads at the sound of her screeching tires as they chatted outside the building. She was late—again.

"Mom, I think I forgot my ballet slippers," Lilly called from the back seat. She yanked everything out of her backpack, lobbing it onto the car floor with the candy wrappers and old McDonald's shake cups. "Whatever. I'll just borrow a pair."

"I told you, Lilly, that you have to start being accountable for things. You can't expect me to remember everything for you. I have my own stuff to worry about."

"Like what?" Lilly sneered. Ada peered at her through the rearview mirror. Lilly had become that salty teenager everyone had warned her about when she complained of her toddler antics. "Just wait till she's a teenager," they'd say. She didn't believe them. Until now.

"Lose the sass," Ada called out.

"Whaaat?" Lilly whined, her braces' rubber bands stretching up and down.

"Nothing. Just hustle and get out of the car," Ada said. "And don't forget to put your hair up in a bun!" Lilly gave her the thumbs-up as she ran toward the studio. Ada contemplated whether she should park and talk to the other moms, but she didn't feel like hearing about their blissful marriages, their dinner parties she and Ben were not invited to, or the addition so-and-so was building in her new house. When Ada had something positive to share, she would get out. For now, she was in the thick of things at work, with more than three grants to write, desperate for funding, and a marriage that was on romantic life support. How the hell she could both spark her marriage *and* work on a fifty-page grant till the wee hours of the morning was the golden question. She had no answer.

Ada and Ben had a disconnect with their schedules not aligning. After fifteen years of marriage, their jobs and the kids took precedence. And, they hadn't had sex in ten months and six days . . . but who was counting? Life became hectic, and it wasn't all her fault. Ben was completely capable of chauffeuring the kids around town himself. Between lacrosse practice and ballet, Ada basically lived out of her car. Then there was work, because, well, *someone had to make the money.* Ben's work as a general contractor wasn't consistent. He had all of three jobs this winter, and he'd only lined up two big ones for the summer. Ada didn't want to be resentful, but it wasn't fair that she had to work *and* do all the driving. Truth be told, Ben had offered, but her working mother guilt took over and she seized the opportunity to be with her kids outside of work, even if it was in the car.

This was Ada's controlling side. She wondered if she should start going back to therapy, or maybe try couple's therapy. But once you started going to couple's therapy, it was only a matter of time till you got a divorce. That's what everyone said. It was like the last-ditch effort to say *we tried* before moving on to what seemed like greener pastures.

Ada was committed to her marriage. Divorce was not an option. Her parents had divorced when she was six, and she hated the back-and-forth between their houses. Whether she forgot to bring her beloved stuffed elephant, Ellie, or left her sneakers and soccer clothes behind, it was a hassle. More than anything, she hated always missing one parent. She never felt complete. She recalled the months leading up to the divorce. Her father slept on the couch, and her mother slept in the bedroom. She wasn't quite sure why they never touched or held each other, but she could feel the ice forming between them.

I can't let that happen to me, Ada thought, driving away from ballet. *No, I will do everything I can to make this work.* So, she set a goal of having a romantic night with Ben. *Tonight, we will have sex,* she thought. She'd go to KMhudson in Mashpee Commons after ballet and buy some sort of saucy lingerie. Red lace, maybe? No, too trashy, and it wasn't Valentine's Day. How about a classy thong? That was an oxymoron. What about a camisole intimate? *Eww, gross,* she thought. She hated the word "intimate," but that was exactly the problem. She and Ben didn't have intimacy anymore, physical or otherwise. It was like she had lost her best friend.

Not forever. Tonight, was the night! She would commit herself to this . . . sex. Lilly would be sleeping over at Tina's house, and Henry was traveling with his lacrosse team to Canada. So, it was the perfect time to reignite the spark they used to have when they dated as seniors in college.

Ada drove down Thomas Landers Road and headed toward Mashpee, giving a few of the parents a coy wave on her way out. She was deactivating from Facebook too. That's it. Social media was done. She was going off the grid. It stressed her out too much and made her feel like a failure that she wasn't extolling her love for her husband or posting pics of her perfect children riding on a boat or anchored on Bassetts Island. Or those Isagenix cleanse pics where everyone stopped eating and drinking and lost weight. Forget it. That was not an option. She'd rather just drink coffee all day and not eat.

Ada's phone rang. It was Ben.

"Hey," she answered, "I just left Lil. I'm heading to the Commons."

"Oh, what are you doing there?" Ben asked.

"Just getting a birthday present. I forgot Lil has a birthday party to go to tomorrow. I'll probably run into Marshall's or something, too. Do you need socks?" She hated that she was talking about socks.

"I'm good," he said. Ada sensed the heavy air and knew he wanted to say something. *She* wanted to say something, but they had trouble talking about anything anymore. She remembered when they used to talk for hours about life and dreams over cocktails on the back porch at night. They would toast, making sure to stare into each other's eyes so as not to get jinxed and have bad sex for seven years. But she guessed they may have missed a night since they were certainly on a dry spell now.

"I'll see you later?" Ada asked. "Maybe we can take a walk to the beach and watch the sunset?"

"Yeah, I'll be home," Ben said. "Sounds nice."

Ada drove off down Route 151, going over the grocery list for Roche Bros. in her head: heirloom tomatoes, avocadoes, baguette, corn chips and salsa, light bulbs, and trash bags. The list slowly morphed into how she would save her marriage: have sex three times a week, wear matching lingerie, shave daily, work out, hide love notes . . . What else? Oh, remind herself why she fell in love with Ben in the first place.

Chapter Four

A LITTLE BIRD TOLD ME

SADIE

As Sadie rushed into Uptown Body for Power Pump class, Scarlett Crane grabbed her forearm.

"Hey, lady," Scarlett cooed. She was dressed in head-to-toe Lululemon yoga attire. Sadie, on the other hand, wore Athleta. Scarlett was like a walking fashion label with glossy lips and perfect hair. Not one stray gray to be found—which reminded Sadie that she needed to call Headlines for a single process color appointment for Friday before the Oyster Harbors Club cocktail party.

"Hey! I was wondering if you'd make it today," Sadie said. Scarlett wasn't a regular at Uptown Body, like Sadie. Sadie went to Power Pump class every Monday, Wednesday, and Friday morning at nine. She wondered if Scarlett's attendance had anything to do with the news circulating about the town that Mack was coming back to the Cape. Scarlett, after all, was the town gossip. She meant well, but Sadie knew better than to tell her anything. "Telephone, Telegraph, Tell-a-Scarlett," her friends would say.

"I almost didn't make it," Scarlett huffed. "I've just been so busy between golf at the club, the kids' birthdays, and different cocktail parties that I just needed to *rest*."

Sadie tried not to laugh at Scarlett's self-proclaimed exhaustion from these various leisure activities. Then, she realized her life wasn't any more compelling. She had been so wrapped up in raising the kids, volunteering for the hospital, and redoing the house that she put herself last. Going to the gym was about all she could manage to squeeze in. She had committed to building some muscle and losing her bat wings. A tank top dress was in her future, minus the shawl or cardigan.

"Sooooooo . . . a little bird told me that your old high school flame is headed back to town. The one and only Mack Taylor?" Scarlett sang, raising an eyebrow.

"Well, it was actually in college . . . but I think so? Who told you that?"

"Which part, honey? The birdie, or the part about your ex coming to town?"

"I guess . . . both?" Sadie's fair skin itched, as usual, when she spoke with Scarlett. The woman was like poison ivy.

"Well, a lady never reveals her sources, but let's just say *word on the street* is he's divorced, good-looking, and he can treat a woman right! I know several ladies lining up to claim him as we speak."

"Seriously?" Sadie felt a surge of envy and shame. "Well, I don't know what his deal is, but yes, he reached out to me and is coming in early June to start a high-end resort, kind of like Chatham Bars Inn, but here in Falmouth." Sadie purposely dropped that Mack had reached out to her, putting a stake in the ground on her territory.

"Well, I will have to stay tuned then," Scarlett chimed. "Interesting he reached out to you first," she said with a wink and scooted along to class, her yoga mat dangling over her shoulder.

Sadie walked into Power Pump and wondered which of these women had their eyes on Mack. She lay her mat down on the hardwood floor next to Ada's and went to grab two five-pound weights and an aerobic step. She waved to Tiffany, Nicole, and Amy, and lay down on her mat, closing her eyes, thankful for the break.

"Hey girl," Ada said, stretching out on her mat. Sadie opened her eyes.

"Hey," she sighed.

"You good? What's up?"

"I just got Scarlett Crane-ed."

"Ugh, the worst." Ada shook her head, giggling. "What'd she do this time?"

"Let's grab coffee after, and I'll fill you in."

The first time Sadie met Ada was at a new parent's group at the library. Unbeknownst to Sadie, the group was intended for "natural and holistic" parents who wanted to meet like-minded parents. They urged the children to interact and play and enjoyed preparing homemade snacks like apple-squash muffins and butternut squash cookies—squash seemed to be a favorite ingredient. Though Sadie recycled and believed in climate change, she was not necessarily the sustainable type. She just wanted to find a way to waste a morning, and this parenting group was it. Anything to suck up some hours to get her closer to dinner was a good move in Sadie's book. The days would often feel interminable alone with toddlers. Aside from going to the park, Mother Goose on the Loose at the West Falmouth Library, the Cape Cod Mall, and the coffee shop, Sadie didn't have much to do to entertain herself and the children, other than try to find other stay-at-home moms to whom she might relate.

Sitting at the long, oblong wooden table surrounded by six other mothers with kids, Sadie cradled ginger-headed, six-month-old Tina, who was still breastfeeding and too young to sit up alone on the floor. In fact, Tina really didn't need a playgroup, as she couldn't actually play—she just put things into her mouth, dribbled on a plastic bib, and made gurgling noises.

"Careful she doesn't choke on that," the administrator said as Tina mouthed a tiny wooden broom from the Melissa & Doug dollhouse. Sadie quickly removed it, wiping it off with a wet wipe before putting it back in the dollhouse.

"Do you need a cloth napkin?" the administrator asked. "I hate to see people using wipes," she chortled, followed by a strong whiff of rancid tea breath. Her hair was wiry gray and greasy, held back in a bun with what looked like chopsticks.

Sadie always felt wasteful and commercial with this group, like she was a terrible citizen who couldn't care less about the environment or sea turtles choking on plastic straws. The first day she arrived, the administrator handed her a parenting book to take home and said, "Enjoy." The book expounded upon the virtues of playing with sticks and pinecones for hours in lieu of more contemporary toys. Sadie thought about all the insidious plastic toys that littered her home playroom, including the Barbies that served as poor role models and the Shopkins, which were definite choking hazards. The book also talked about RIE Parenting, urging parents to interact with their babies as *independent human beings*. With RIE, the parent was to leave children to themselves to self-soothe and entertain. However, for a helicopter parent like Sadie, this method made no sense. She couldn't let Tina cry for a minute, let alone fifteen. This parenting group also encouraged stillness and quiet voices, so much so that it was virtually silent. The administrator would speak in a whisper, asking parents, "Did you get a chance to journal this week?" or "Can we say a prayer of thanks before snack?"

"What's that you said?" Sadie shouted.

It wasn't until the third class, and the tenth or so time that she called out, "Huh?" that Sadie looked across the table to Ada, who mouthed, "What the fuck?" She couldn't help but burst out laughing, and she knew she'd met a friend.

"What is it with that woman?" Sadie whispered at the washing sink. This was the only time she whispered. "Is it me, or is this place kind of a freak show?" She searched for the paper towels, only to find a soaked old dishcloth, very sustainable and filthy.

"It's not you. I just spent twenty minutes rolling beeswax on the table with Lilly, and I swear she was not even the slightest bit entertained," Ada said. "Not to mention, my hands feel disgusting and sticky, and I'd rather just go get a manicure." Sadie laughed and noticed the sparkling, three-carat diamond wedding ring on Ada's already-manicured ring finger. She was pretty, in a non-threatening way, and she wore Frye chunky motorcycle boots that made her look cool. *Screw these tree huggers*, she thought. *I'd rather hang with this motorcycle chick.*

Sadie and Ada returned to the classroom, and Tina started crying. It had been three hours since her last feeding, so Sadie unpacked her bottle from the cooler in her diaper bag. As she removed the cap, the group administrator decided to chime in.

"Oh no," she scowled, grabbing for the bottle. "No, you should go over to the breastfeeding area," she said, motioning with her big man hand to the corner of the room. The corner of the library classroom was a designated area for breastfeeding. *Like, what type of classroom has a corner for boobs?* Sadie wondered. There was a stuffed animal corner, a doll corner, and an art corner—but a boob corner?

"No, it's okay," Sadie said, pulling away. "I have *breast milk* here, in her bottle." Sadie emphasized that it was breast milk in the bottle, instead of, God forbid, formula or some other form of *devil's milk*. The administrator grimaced and shook her head as she wrapped red yarn around her thick paws like her fingers were a God's eye you'd make at camp, pretending to busy herself as she fumed.

"Well, we have this whole area set apart for that." The administrator motioned again. The corner was painted lemon yellow, and it had a furry white faux bearskin rug with an antique rocking chair in the center of it. It was like the mothers' breasts were on display for all to see. "You can just breastfeed her there. No one minds. Plus, it's better for the baby," she said. *Plus* . . .

"Um, well, no, I actually do sort of mind," Sadie said. "*Plus,* I think I know what's best for *my* baby."

"Well, it's only natural, sweetie."

"Don't tell me what's natural, *sweetie*," Sadie chided back loudly. "This isn't like almond butter. It's a personal choice, a mother's choice."

"Are you alright?" the administrator asked. "We don't need to raise our voices."

"*We* are not raising our voices; I am raising my voice!" Sadie said. She felt the heavy stare of the other parents on her. "And, as a matter of fact, I'm not all right! For three weeks now I have been unable to hear you while you whisper, and I wondered what the hell I am doing here making ornaments out of yarn, like a seven-year-old in camp, when I'm actually looking for a moms' group. This place is a totalitarian regime with no tolerance for personal choices!"

Sadie stood up, dangling Tina in one arm and the bottle in the other. She crouched down to reach for her diaper bag, and Tina almost spilled out of her arms, inducing her to cry. The bottle dropped to the floor, and the energy in the room was stifling.

"Shit!" Sadie whispered.

"Oh, my goodness gracious," the administrator said. She looked around to get validation from the other mothers, who avoided eye contact and continued to wrap yarn around their sticks.

"Here, let me help you," Ada said, getting up and gathering Sadie's belongings for her. "You are very indignant and rude," she said to the administrator. "I won't be coming back either." Sadie jettisoned her ornament on the table, the yarn unraveling.

Ada and Sadie hustled out of the classroom, laughing and chuckling with babies in their arms. They stood in the front parking lot, panting, amazed that they had the balls to actually do that.

"What a nightmare!" Sadie exclaimed. "Thank you. You didn't have to leave."

"Um, yeah, I did," Ada said. "You were just the excuse I was looking for. Want to go to the playground instead? Or maybe to a bar?" She chuckled. Sadie noted how pretty Ada was. She had shiny, long black hair and startling blue eyes. She was delicate, fragile looking, with a Soho chic kind of style.

"The latter sounds good right about now. It's five o'clock somewhere," Sadie said. She was trying to stop her legs from shaking.

"I knew I liked you. I'm Ada," she said, extending a two-finger hand-shake as she held the diaper bag.

"Sadie," she said. "Well, at least I got one friend out of this moms' group!" A friend. Yes, she had made a new friend.

Chapter Five

NO SAND IN HER TOES

ADA

It was three days after Power Pump class with Sadie that Ada sat at the kitchen table, holding a cold mug of coffee with *Mothers Make the Best Friends* painted in gold cursive on it. She had bought it for herself at Home Goods on clearance right after Mother's Day, when Lilly, Henry, and Ben forgot—or neglected—to buy her a present. She wasn't Ben's mother, of course, but Ada held a grudge that Ben refused to celebrate her on Mother's Day. She was, after all, the mother of his children. Perhaps this was why he was no longer sexually attracted to her. Maybe she had become too matronly, too Barbara Bush or Martha Stewart. Her attempts to seduce him in her new lacy thong and bra hadn't worked. In fact, she wasn't even able to show them to him, as he fell asleep at nine p.m. on the couch watching CNN with the volume jacked up, as she finished the dinner dishes.

Ben always did this. It was like living with a narcoleptic. Why was he perpetually asleep? It's not like he worked *that* hard . . . oh, and he always wanted to sleep with the TV on. It was so irritating. It annoyed her almost as much as his other unappealing habits. For starters, Ben didn't brush his teeth before bed, and he used her bedroom armchair as a closet. He didn't cut his toenails enough, and when he did, he sat on the toilet seat and let the shards jettison all over the bathroom floors, which later pierced her freshly showered bare feet. She wondered why these idiosyncrasies she once found endearing at the start of their relationship eventually became unnerving. Ada was also aware of what Ben didn't like about her since he blatantly pointed out his disdain for how she ate her muffins and pizza with a fork and knife, and how she couldn't make decisions without consulting at least six friends. But every time she sought his advice, he'd put his hand up in her face saying he couldn't talk about it anymore, as if she was exhaustive.

"You're going to do what you want to anyway," he'd say. Ada knew her persistent need for approval was draining, but she couldn't quell her obsession. Therapy didn't seem to help—or medication. She had tried both. A leopard doesn't change its spots, and no matter what Ada did, her spots were obsessional.

The first time Ben and Ada met was during college at Columbia. Ben was living at the Fiji house on fraternity row. He and his frat brothers would sit outside on the front stoop of the brownstone on West 115th Street smoking Camel Lights and drinking keg beer. Ada strolled by on her way to Kappa Alpha Theta, three brownstones down. She was dressed all in black, sort of emo-chic, and her long dark hair lay straight over her shoulders almost touching her belly button, which was visible in her half-tee. She glanced at Ben and smiled. There was something so cute about his one dimple and his rugged forestry look.

"Hey," he called after Ada as she walked away. She turned back.

"Hi," she said. She licked her lips. The top one was rather pouty and glistened with pink frosty lip gloss.

"Aren't you in my Lit Hum class?" he asked. That was Ben's line—to pretend he knew a girl from class. Lit Hum was short for Literature Humanities, a part of the core curriculum at Columbia that was a requirement to graduate. Almost everyone took Lit Hum their freshman year, but Ben had put it off till his senior year. This was part of his overall procrastination problem. His freshman year had been reserved for partying, and he had withdrawn from two classes, Biology and Urban Studies, and taken two other courses, Statistics and Criminology, pass/fail. He wasn't exactly a go-getter, but he was at Columbia for baseball, so he got away with a poor undergraduate GPA and an average high school report card for admissions.

"I don't think so," Ada laughed, "considering that was freshman year."

"I'm not a freshman," Ben said, taking a drag from his cigarette and running his big hands through his thick black hair.

"I know that. I remember you from my freshman year," she said. She laughed and flipped her hair over her shoulder, so it fell down her back.

"Oh really?" he smirked. "I'm Ben."

"I'm Ada," she said, walking toward him and extending her hand. She had long, thin fingers, the kind that looked good with rings on. Her biggest finger was probably a size 6.

"Nice to actually meet you for real," he said. "Can I get you a beer?"

"It's ten a.m.!" Ada gasped, despite being open to the offer.

"Never too early for a Bud Light," he shrugged, taking a swill the way frat boys do, with the back of his hand facing forward, tilting the red Solo cup.

"Well, I guess then I'll join you," she said.

"Slow your roll, Miss Ada," Ben said. "I didn't say you could join me. I just offered you a beer."

Ada laughed again, a high-pitched and somewhat coy laugh. "You're a jerk," she said, grabbing the beer. She wore blue fingernail polish and thin silver rings on her second and middle fingers.

"I'm just joking with you. Have a seat on my brownstone," Ben said.

Now washing the Mother's Day coffee mug, Ada stared intently at the square turquoise-and-white tiles on the sink's backsplash until they blurred together like she was looking into a kaleidoscope. She couldn't believe this was her life now. It certainly wasn't what she had planned. She had dreams of living in the city, working to help underserved children in Harlem. Her focus in college had been urban planning and social work, and she had interned at PS 125. If only her own children were a bit more grateful for their privileged life on Cape Cod, she thought. They didn't know how good they had it. Truth be told, they could be earning more money, which is something she often wondered about her choice to work in fundraising. It paid some of the bills, but the family was never debt-free, and the mortgage payments on their house loomed at the end of every month. Ada would check her balance nightly, making sure her direct deposit appeared on her statement.

Money and work were a real source of tension for Ada and Ben. You know that saying that you marry either for love or money? Well, she had married for love, but she thought Ben might also have some money—or at least earning potential. After all, they had graduated from Columbia together, and at the time, he spoke about working in finance at Morgan Stanley or Goldman Sachs. He was an econ major and had an internship at Cantor Fitzgerald downtown on Fridays. It's not that they had to be rich, no, Ada thought. She just wanted to see that he had some sort of motivation to succeed, that he had ambition. After graduation, Ben took his time finding a job, spending his nights with "the boys" at various sports bars, living off of an inheritance from his grandmother. When the inheritance ran dry, he told Ada they couldn't afford to live in the city anymore. It was time to move to his grandma's house on Cape Cod.

"Cape Cod!" Ada exclaimed. "But what will I do on Cape Cod? I work in urban planning and with inner-city youth. This is my passion. This is why I attended Columbia in the first place." She wasn't sure what was happening, but she knew she didn't like it. I mean, this is not what they had agreed to when they got married. They were going to live on the Upper West Side, walk their kids to school, take them to the Museum of Natural History, and enjoy all the culture and arts that the city had to offer. Collecting seashells and sea glass was not part of this vision.

"Oh, come on," Ben said, "It will be like our little adventure. We can have sand in our toes. Isn't that the saying? Sand in your—"

Ada cut him off. "I don't want sand in my toes. In fact, I hate open-toed shoes, and I prefer boots and heels," she said. But that didn't seem to matter to Ben. He was adamant about moving to the Cape. He didn't really consider her opinion, even though she tried, making lists of pros and cons, and mapping out different paths to maintaining an urban existence.

The day Ben and Ada packed up their apartment and drove in their Subaru Forester to Cape Cod was one of the worst days of her life.

"Sweetie," Ben laughed. "It's not going to be that bad."

When they pulled up to Ben's grandma's old home on Mill Road, she spotted a statue of a sea captain wearing yellow boots and smoking a pipe on the front steps, as if he held a secret. She stood in her motorcycle boots on the door mat, staring at him. If only she had known the secret he was keeping, Ada may have turned back then. But now, it was too late. She was here to stay.

Chapter Six

TOWNIES

CHARLOTTE

It was the first time Charlotte had been called a "townie," and she didn't like it one bit. A townie is a descriptor for someone who grew up on the Cape and never left, a local. It had a derogatory connotation coming from a summer person, suggesting you are regional and provincial. Yet, one could very well argue that living on the Cape was the opposite. Real estate values, for example, soared well above the millions, and it was home to the Kennedys and the Forbeses. It had fabulous beaches and boating, and Nantucket and Martha's Vineyard were the vacation stomping grounds for presidents and celebrities. However, these were second homes for most of the 1 percent, and living on the Cape year-round was quite different from being a weekender or summer resident, financially and otherwise. For summer people, their houses were vacation homes with beach rights and exclusive associations. For townies, their houses were "home," or the same house they occupied year-round, or perhaps even grew up in. This is what divided the locals/townies and the summer people: money.

Charlotte thought of the saying painted on the Woods Hole drawbridge that describes this underground tension between locals and summer people: "Summer People, Some are not." She could see it every time the drawbridge rose on the half hour to let boats pass through the channel to Eel Pond. Summer people, to locals, can be ostentatious, pretentious, rude, and entitled. They go to restaurants and order their food without salt, butter, gluten, or all of the above. When Charlotte worked as a waitress at the Fishmonger, they had a saying, "The richer you are, the more allergies you have." Those rich folks made up allergies just so they could get their food made perfectly to order, as if they had a private chef at a local seafood restaurant.

Charlotte couldn't believe she had been called a townie last night. It was at the Pier 37 Boathouse on Falmouth Harbor where she and her bombastic friend Margaret met for margaritas at the outdoor bar. A one-man band played Jimmy Buffett songs in the corner, and they joked that they felt like cougars, as most of the patrons were in their twenties, particularly as the night went on. As it grew dark, around nine o'clock, the DJ began to set up. A herd of preppy young men and their girlfriends saddled up next to them at the bar.

"Is this seat taken?" said the twenty-something named Dylan. He was wearing a pink Vineyard Vines shirt and khaki pants with New Balance running shoes, like a present-day Holden Caulfield from an elite boarding school, like Exeter or Andover.

"No, it's yours," said Charlotte, moving her crocheted purse to the hook underneath the granite countertop bar.

"What are you ladies up to tonight?" Dylan asked, clearly flirting. Charlotte noticed two of the girls next to him giving her the stink eye. They both had that generic platinum blonde hair that every girl had, with dark roots and dark eyebrows to match. She couldn't really differentiate between them as they both wore black off-the-shoulder shirts and white high-waisted jeans.

"You're looking at it," said Charlotte. "You guys here to dance?" She figured she'd continue the conversation, as it felt good to have someone as young and cute as Dylan flirting with her. Once a woman reaches a certain age—where she no longer has to show her ID to buy a drink, and where she's married and not sure if her husband, let alone any other man, finds her attractive—flirtation is welcome. It's affirmation, validation that you still have "it."

"I think we may hit the dance floor," Dylan said, smiling. He had perfect white teeth. Charlotte wondered if he had gotten his braces off in the last decade. "Can I buy you ladies a cocktail?" he continued.

"Sure can!" wailed Margaret. Margaret was big-bodied and bold, wearing a long maroon-and-black kaftan and platform sandals. Each one of her fingers had a ring on it, none of them seeming to match, and all with a big colored stone, like she was a gypsy or fortune teller. Margaret wasn't demure in any way and wasn't the best wing woman, as she kind of repelled men like Deep Woods Off repelled mosquitos. "I'll take a Silver Herradura margarita, on the rocks, and not a skinny one. That's for lightweights. Actually, make it a double and save me the trip the next time. This service takes forever, and they have a weak pour!"

"I'll take a look at the drink list," Charlotte said. She grabbed the elongated blue menu that was wet and sticky, like someone had spilled barbecue sauce or ketchup on it. Wiping her hands off one finger at a time with a wet wipe from her purse, she saw something called a twisted bikini made with melon, grapefruit, seltzer, and vodka, and another called the Boathouse mule. It was a variation of the Moscow mule, made with vodka, spicy ginger beer, elderflower, and lime juice. Charlotte liked those, particularly when they were served as they should be, in a chilled copper mug. It reminded her of the first time she and John ordered one when they were celebrating their third anniversary at the Galley bar on Nantucket. They were sitting outside on a sprawling couch with a canopy, and John held this dainty copper mug in his big hand. It looked like something out of *Gulliver's Travels*. They couldn't stop laughing and took photos of how tiny the cup was in his huge fingers.

"Know what you're getting?" Dylan asked, reaching into his pocket and pulling out a silver money clip with hundreds folded up. His initials were inscribed on the clip: DPO. What could that stand for? Dylan Preston O'Connell? Dylan Peter Ostroff? Dylan Paul O'Hare?

"Yes, I'll just have the Boathouse mule," Charlotte said. "And it's not because I'm stubborn," she joked. Dylan lightly chuckled. She wondered if this joke fell flat and made her look old. Maybe she should head home sooner than later.

"Cheers!" Margaret said, clinking her plastic rim silently against theirs. Glass wasn't allowed on the outdoor patio.

"Cheers," Dylan said. "So, what brings you ladies out here tonight?"

Charlotte hated when men called them "ladies." There was something misogynistic about it, even though he was trying to be polite.

"Who you callin' a lady?" Margaret barked, swiveling her head around violently. Dylan laughed, a real laugh this time. Charlotte wondered if he thought Margaret was gross. Then she felt guilty for feeling that way, softening toward Margaret, almost feeling bad for her. Margaret was one of those women who never had a boyfriend and never sought one. She wasn't gay; she was just sort of inert. Sexuality just didn't seem to be part of her life. Her days consisted of going to a nine to five job at a direct mailing house, with little room for career advancement, and her nights were spent either watching Netflix at home alone or going out with friends for dinner or drinks. This was the way she liked it. She was satisfied, something Charlotte rarely felt.

"We are out to celebrate," Margaret continued.

"Oh! Celebrate what?" Dylan asked.

"Your coming-of-age party!" Margaret laughed.

Dylan wasn't amused. He turned to look at Charlotte and smirked.

"She's kidding," Charlotte said, trying to pick up the pieces. "It was Margaret's birthday a few weeks ago, and we are finally getting together to celebrate. How about you? What are you up to tonight?"

"Well, my buddies and I just got down from Boston," Dylan said. There it was—the word "buddies." That was a dead giveaway that he was both young and sort of a fraternity type. Sophisticated men didn't use the word "buddies," in Charlotte's opinion. She longed for a man with sophistication, someone who knew what to order off the wine list, and how to pair meats and cheeses on a charcuterie board. Differentiating between Manchego and Brie, or a heavy Cabernet and a Pinot Noir, turned Charlotte on. This was one of the things that had first attracted her to John. He had a level of sophistication that belied his jock look. She knew this by the specificity of his asking if she was drinking a Sancerre when they first met.

"Are those your girlfriends?" Margaret asked, pointing to the blondes with dark roots who continued to give them dirty looks.

"No, they're just friends of ours," Dylan said. "We grew up together, kind of. One of them is my buddy's cousin." Charlotte looked over at Roots 1 girl, who was now texting furiously. She saw Dylan glance at his phone and then put it back in his pocket.

"She looks nice," Margaret smirked.

The volume on the music turned up, and one of the bartenders raised his hands in the air, starting to dance. A few people around the bar began moving and clapping to the beat. It was a hip-hop song, something with Jay-Z that Charlotte wasn't familiar with. Hip-hop wasn't her forte.

"Shall we dance?" Margaret asked, standing up, shaking her rump. She rested her margarita on the bar so she could join in on the clapping.

Dylan put his drink down and started moving to the beat as well. "Don't let anybody roofie this."

"Come on," Dylan said, grabbing Charlotte's hand. "Let's see those moves." Charlotte gently swayed back and forth, releasing his hand. She bit the side of her mouth, aware of all eyes on them. Margaret continued to shamelessly move about the wooden dock, shimmying her way through different groups of people, one of them being Roots 1 girl and Roots 2 girl, aka "the cousin."

"Excuse you," Roots 1 said as Margaret clumsily bumped into her while dancing, spilling a bit of her spritzer onto her shirt.

"Oops!" Margaret yelled, continuing to dance.

"You could say you're sorry," Roots 2 scoffed. "Or do us a favor and stop dancing." She chuckled a mean, bitchy laugh.

"Excuse you?" Margaret said, swiveling her head around vehemently, this time not in a joking manner.

"You heard me," Roots 2 said. "Maybe you can stop hitting on my cousin's friend, since you're like twice his age . . . and size."

Charlotte watched from afar as this ship went crashing down like the *Titanic*. Any mention of Margaret's weight and you were in for it. Roots 2 was going down. Coffin.

"Listen, you scrawny little bitch," Margaret said, getting really close to Roots 2's ski jump freckled nose. "You best be going now, before I lose my temper. You don't want to see that."

"We're not going anywhere," Roots 1 said, coming to her friend's rescue. "You don't scare us, even when you throw your weight around, literally."

"That's it!" Margaret said, lunging at Roots 1. She threw a punch in her direction, rings forward, aiming for the nose, but she missed.

"Eww, you're dis-GUS-ting," shrieked Roots 2. "I knew you were trash!"

Margaret's eyes widened, her pupils dilated, like a cat on the loose in a bus. She raised her fist into the air, ready to pounce hard on Roots 2's head, when Charlotte and Dylan intervened from across the room.

"Stop it!" Charlotte cried, grabbing Margaret's wrist. "They're not worth it!"

"Speak for yourself, townie," Roots 1 said, curling her frosted pink lip upward.

There it was . . . the T-word.

It stung. It was as if Roots 1 had lobbed it out in slow motion, with a demonic timbre. Charlotte tried to register the fact that she was in fact the townie, something she certainly never saw herself as, coming from Manhattan and a world of privilege herself. She was a summer person, after all. Or, well, she used to be.

"Excuse me? Did you just call me a townie?" Charlotte chimed in.

"I did," said Roots 1, shifting in her Jack Rogers sandals. She flipped her hair behind her shoulder as if she were readying to fight.

"Wow!" Charlotte said, aghast, eyes widening. She was stumped, silenced. *I could fight this girl, but then I'd be acting like "a townie,"* she thought. *But, if I don't defend myself, and Margaret for that matter, then I'm accepting defeat and this egregious and offensive label.* Charlotte felt a surge of aggression pulse through her wine-soaked veins.

"Cecily, back off," Dylan said, pushing her aside. "I offered to get these women a drink for kindly giving up their chair for us."

"Suit yourself," Cecily said, glaring at Charlotte. "Just be careful."

BE CAREFUL? What did that even mean, Charlotte wondered. What was there to be careful about? The only one who should be careful was Cecily, whose tires she might slash, or who she might push off the dock into the water.

Charlotte felt the blood rising and coursing throughout her body.

She wanted to remain calm and collected, but something came over her. All the rage she had about her flailing marriage and her stymied career emerged. Suddenly, she lifted her drink in the air and poured it right over Roots 2's head.

"I think you're the one who should be careful!" Charlotte yelled. Margaret began jumping up and down and clapping her hands, like she was on *The Price Is Right* and Bob Barker had called her name. Cecily lunged toward Charlotte, and Charlotte lunged back, grabbing Cecily's arms, getting scratched by a silver bracelet with a J-shaped hook. Cecily's pursed, glossed lips curled shut as she squinted and slapped at the air like a seal doing tricks for fish. Charlotte huffed and puffed, boxing with fighting fists. Everyone at the bar stood around, staring at them, some chanting loudly, "Girl fight!" in unison. Fueled by the crowd, Charlotte mounted Cecily on the wooden deck floor and put her knees on her skinny little forearms. Cecily writhed around like a Komodo dragon beneath her, moving her head from side to side and screaming for Dylan. Dylan then pounced on Charlotte, wrapping his hands around her waist and pulling her off.

"Dude, calm down!" Dylan said. "You need to chill!"

The bar manager ran from the kitchen to break up the fight. He told them the police were on their way and they'd better get out before they were written up.

Charlotte couldn't believe this was happening. She grabbed her jean jacket and purse off the stool, and Margaret steadied her as they walked quickly to the car. Charlotte got into the driver's seat, and they sped out of the dirt parking lot.

"Shit! I forgot my tequila," Margaret yelped. "Go back!"

"What the hell is wrong with you?" Charlotte screamed, gripping the steering wheel with one eye closed.

"What?!" Margaret exclaimed. "I just wanted to get my roadie."

Charlotte sped up. "WHEEEEEEE!" Margaret called out. "It feels like we're Thelma and Louise! I didn't know you had it in you, Char! This is a whole new shade of Char!"

They sped by the Friendly's and Stop and Shop down Route 28. Charlotte flipped down the sun visor to view herself in the mirror. She had eyeliner stained under her eyes, giving her the appearance of a black eye. She wiped it off using the side of her index finger and straightened out the blonde curly locks that had formed in the humidity and left a frizzy halo.

They sped by Davisville Road, and a police cruiser pulled out of the CVS parking lot, lights blazing, pulling Charlotte and Margaret over. According to the sergeant, he had received a radio alert from the station that had gotten a call from the girls Charlotte and Margaret had dubbed Roots 1 and 2 that two "over served" and aggressive women were driving recklessly away from the Pier 37 Boathouse down 28.

"I need to see your license and registration," the sergeant said. "And I need you both to step out of the car."

Margaret opened the passenger car door. Charlotte emerged from the driver's side, squinting as the sergeant held a flashlight in her eyes.

"Officer, I'm so sorry," Charlotte said. "We were only speeding to get away from those terrible women who attacked us at the bar. I was seriously afraid." She tried to appear meek, hoping the sergeant would fall for her damsel in distress act. Charlotte straightened out her outfit and began to twirl the ends of her hair. Even after a bar fight, she was still pretty, and she did all she could to work it.

The sergeant didn't fall for Charlotte's routine, instead making her walk in a straight line and balance on one foot while touching her nose. She then had to recite the alphabet forward and back, while Margaret was snorting and laughing on the side of the road the entire time. Even without drinking, Charlotte would stumble walking a straight line. She had failed miserably on the balance beam in gymnastics as a child, and she struggled in heels on the catwalk as an adult.

After refusing the breath test, Charlotte received a citation for an OUI and was told she'd have to appear in court and have her license suspended. She was also charged with aggravated assault and public intoxication for the bar fight with Roots 1 and 2. It wasn't long before the whole debacle would be reported in the police logs and word got around town: *"Charlotte Simms had been arrested for an OUI, public intoxication, and aggravated assault."*

Sitting in Coffee Obsession, Charlotte wrote in her journal. She still hadn't recovered from the bar fight, and she was sheepishly walking around, fearful that people would stare. She didn't want to live in this town anymore. She wanted to go back to the city, and Boston was the closest one. John commuted there every day anyway and slept in their Beacon Hill apartment more often than not. Why couldn't they just move there together, get a house in Newton or Brookline, and end this shenanigan to live in a seaside town during the winter? The experiment was over, as far as she was concerned. She and John had collected their data, and the hypothesis that life was better as a year-rounder on Cape Cod was incorrect. Sound the alarm. *It was time to return to real life and shut down the summerhouse,* Charlotte thought. She was over it. She decided she would go home that night and have a candid conversation with John about how she felt. They needed a fresh start, one together, and to try for a baby again. Perhaps she might reconsider and really want to have children this time around. It had never been an interest of hers—especially the getting fat and being pregnant part. John was dead set on having a junior, so for the sake of her marriage, she would try.

Charlotte and John had tried for a baby for about a year. Religiously, she would map out her fertile days on the calendar, pee on the ovulation sticks first thing in the morning, and implore John to have sex with her on days 11 to 14. In short, it was painful and like trapping a mouse, especially when she showed up at his work in a trench coat trying to seduce him. She strolled through the hallways of his office, feeling the cool air conditioning blow between her panty-less thighs as she approached John's office.

"This isn't romantic," John said, getting limp when she awkwardly straddled him on his desk chair.

"I know it isn't, but it's what we have to do," she urged. "You aren't going to be home tonight, and we need to have sex every day for the next two days. Just try a little harder," she said.

"I am trying! But I'm in my fucking office. It's bright, and I don't feel like it!" John yelled. This stung. A woman never wants to be rejected, especially by her own husband.

"I am sorry it's so awful to have sex with me," Charlotte said, starting to cry and shimmying back into her skirt. "Just forget it. We won't have kids."

"That's not what I'm saying," John replied. "I just wish we could do this more organically."

"Well, that would be nice if you were actually at home in our bed at night. But since you are not, I am taking matters into my own hands, trying for the family that you say you want so badly."

"Oh, you don't want this family?" John scoffed. "It's all just me?" He fidgeted with the belt buckle on his gray slacks.

"Yeah, maybe I don't want kids!" Charlotte screamed. "Maybe I just want to be *me*!"

"Can you keep your voice down? I have employees here," John growled. Just then, the desk phone rang. He was being paged by his assistant.

"Don't worry about it. I'm *leaving*," she said, grabbing her bag to go.

"Wait, don't go like this."

Charlotte hustled through the offices, not stopping to say hi to John's partners, and took the elevator down. She exited on Milk Street in Boston's financial district and searched for a cab. How had she gotten here? She didn't want a baby anymore, particularly with a man who didn't even want to have sex with her before the baby was born, let alone after.

Now, Charlotte reconsidered parenthood. At 46, it would require genetic testing and fertility treatments, but maybe trying for a baby was exactly what she and John needed to get back on track. She knew a baby was not a Band-Aid to a faltering marriage, but her modeling career had stalled out anyway. This would give her a sense of purpose. Maybe they could move to Wellesley. She could dress in Lululemon yoga pants and push a Bugaboo stroller with all the other stay-at-home moms. They could start a book club, go to yoga, have girls' nights.

But then she fielded a phone call from Sadie.

"Hello?"

"You, okay?"

"Ughhhhhhh. I can't even. I'm trying to forget," Charlotte replied, taking a swig of her now-tepid coffee with cinnamon afloat on top.

"Well, if you're looking for a distraction, why don't you join me and Ada at the Lobster Trap for a drink this afternoon?"

"Eh, I'm okay. I'm not in the mood to socialize. And I'm not a huge fan of Ada. I just want to go hide in a trash can."

"Oh stop," Sadie said. "It's not that bad, and Ada really wants to be friends with you. I talk about you all the time. Come on. It will be a good distraction."

Charlotte eventually agreed, packing up her things, and she resolved to talk to John about trying for a baby again that night. It would take patience with all the fertility treatments, doctors' appointments, and tests, but they'd be in it together. Maybe they'd find a surrogate. She was going to take control of her future. She repeated the mantra, "Today is going to be a great day," over and over in her head, as her therapist had recommended. Things were going to get better. She was not a townie. She was Charlotte, from Manhattan, a former elite model, a star.

Charlotte didn't really want to meet Ada at the Lobster Trap, and she certainly didn't want to be her friend. Anyone who was a close friend of Sadie's was a threat to her. Charlotte was the jealous type, worrying that she wouldn't measure up or that her friendship would be overlooked in lieu of someone "shinier" or someone wearing Frye motorcycle boots.

"I don't have time for new friends," Charlotte said when Sadie first suggested she meet Ada.

"What does that even mean?" Sadie grumbled. "So, like, that's it? You're never going to make new friends again? You've reached the saturation point?" Charlotte hated when Sadie interrogated her. She didn't want to make new friends. Friends were drama, especially with women. She was going to follow the wise advice of her mother to "circle the wagons," keep her world small to keep the toxins out.

"I'm just busy. I'm tired of trying to pretend I'm going to meet for drinks or assuring someone that I won't tell so-and-so what they told me. This town is too much drama for me. Everyone hates each other," Charlotte said.

She meant it. The last few times she had been at the gym, she couldn't help but overhear all the local gossip. Scarlett Crane was pissed at Missy Obermeier because Missy pulled her kid out of her dance camp. And Stephanie Knowlton was disappointed with Meghan Clark because Meghan didn't invite her to couples' poker night. Come to think of it, she wasn't invited to the poker night either.

"Stop being so negative," Sadie said. "I feel like you cycle in and out of your hatred for this town every time you have a bad week. Did something happen with John?"

"*Nothing* happens with John," Charlotte said. "I may as well be single. I can't remember the last time we had a conversation about something other than where his dry cleaning is."

"This is why you have girlfriends," Sadie said. "We are here for you to talk about all that other stuff. I wish you'd give Ada a chance. You have a lot in common."

Charlotte finally agreed to meet Ada that afternoon, welcoming a reprieve from her self-pity. When Ada greeted her at the hostess stand, Charlotte looked her up and down, assessing her outfit. She wore skinny dark wash Rag & Bone jeans and a thin, long-sleeved black shirt with thumb loops. Her thumbs poked out of them, making her look insecure and coy. Charlotte hated those shirts. Only skinny women who were cold all the time wore them.

"I finally get to hang out with the one and only Charlotte!" Ada exclaimed, grinning widely, extending her fragile hand.

"Yes," Charlotte replied, feigning excitement.

The women looked around the restaurant wondering if they should sit at a table or just go to the bar. The Lobster Trap was the classic old Cape Cod type of place, with dark wood, buoys hanging from the ceiling, the smell of salty air and fresh fish, and views of wetlands and water. It was the place to be on a sunny day because you could take your drinks outside to the porch or sit down by the water that had choppy currents rolling by and seagulls swooping in and out.

Charlotte opted to sit in the bar so they could people-watch. There was a young couple sitting in the corner, sipping on Trap-aritas (a spicy twist on the traditional margarita), and three men in baseball hats dressed in Carhartt lumberjack pants and hooded sweatshirts that had the names of landscaping companies stitched on them.

Charlotte, Ada, and Sadie found a four-top in the corner of the bar and ordered a bottle of Whispering Angel. They began with the simplicities and commonalities of talking about their children and then got right down to the fun and dirty conversation: sex.

"Chip wants me to put on stockings and a garter belt when we do it," Sadie said. "I can't think of anything less flattering, with my baby gut spilling over and my thighs bulging out of the thigh highs." She reached for a wonton, scooping up a lump of sushi-grade tuna and avocado. "Not to mention, it's like interrupting the mood to go put on some sort of costume! 'Oh, excuse me for a moment while I slip into something more comfortable' . . . or just downright uncomfortable, embarrassing, and libido crushing!"

"Well, Ben and I barely even have sex, so you're one up on me," Ada replied. "I wish he would want me to wear a costume. I don't even think he thinks of me that way anymore." Charlotte wondered if Ada's lingerie was also long-sleeved with thumb loops, and she imagined her holding a vibrator with the thumb loop resting on top of the speed adjuster.

"Speaking of bad sex, I feel really bad for Kim Clemson," Sadie said.

"Wait, I didn't say the sex was bad . . ." Ada replied, trailing off.

"No, I just mean poor Kim told me that she started dating this new guy after her divorce," she said, then paused. The women awaited the end of her response. "And, he has a wee-nis." The table erupted in laughter.

"Ugh, a wee-nis!" Charlotte guffawed, chewing a paper straw that looked more like a pixie stick than a straw. "What do you even do in that situation?"

"Okay, I know I'm a little bit obtuse when it comes to this stuff, but what the hell is a wee-nis?" Ada asked.

"A wee, little penis!" Charlotte yelled, holding her pinky up to demonstrate. The men in baseball hats at the bar turned their heads toward her. She lifted her glass to cheer them. "Sorry, guys. Not you," she laughed. One of them gave a raspy laugh like he'd smoked too many cigarettes and stayed out too late the night before.

"Oh my God," Ada said, covering her mouth with her hands. "That's terrible."

"Yeah, it's basically like boning a baby carrot," Charlotte said. They all burst out laughing. "So, what is Kim going to do? Is she going to stay with him?"

"I have no clue," Sadie said. "It sucks, because she really likes him, and she's had such a rough go of things after the divorce. I really wanted this for her."

Charlotte thought about what it'd be like if she got a divorce from John and wondered if she'd be the topic of discussion at the Lobster Trap, or, worse yet, dating someone with a wee-nis.

"Well, at least he has money and a huge boat," Sadie said as if that were a consolation prize.

"A big boat can't make up for a small dick," Charlotte said.

"But it can make a good summer great!" Sadie said.

"True. Maybe she should just ride out the summer, no pun intended," Charlotte said. "Even if the ride isn't much of a ride." *Friends with boats are priceless.*

Charlotte glanced at Ada, who was moving food around aimlessly on her plate. She wondered if Ada was turned off by her irreverence. Maybe she was a total prude. No wonder her hot husband wasn't interested in her. She probably was a dead fish in bed, which might even be worse than having a baby carrot for a unit. That was the problem with waif women who were too pretty. They didn't have to develop personalities to attract men or to get into bed with them, so they would just lie there and let the men do all the work, thanking their lucky stars they had such a pretty wife. Not the case. *That's why men will cheat*, Charlotte thought. They have the pretty waif for the wife, and they get a ballsy sidepiece with curves. It made her wonder: Was John getting a sidepiece? Was she bodacious with fake fingernails? She wanted to change the topic.

"So, what's the deal with the hospital gala committee, Sadie?" Charlotte asked. Sadie was chair of the Cape Cod Hospital Gala. She implored all her friends to join the committee to help her gather sponsorships and silent auction items from local businesses. She did it every year, and up until this point Charlotte had participated, even though she hated it, let alone didn't have time for it. "Is it all the same women this year?"

"Oh, that reminds me! Ada, will you join the committee too?" Sadie said, grabbing her by the wrist. "*Please?*"

"I don't know. That sounds sort of daunting. What does it entail?" Ada asked.

"It's totally just fun. A bunch of us girls get together, and we plan this big party to raise money for the hospital. We basically just sit around, drink wine, and talk about what silent auction items we can get. The commitment is fairly minimal. I mean, maybe Ben would want to sponsor with his contracting business?"

Sadie was always pushing her fundraisers and volunteer groups. It was like she couldn't help but ask everyone she came across to contribute to the gala. When they went into stores on Main Street, she could see the owners running for the back to avoid having to engage and hand over a gift certificate.

"Well, I guess I could join," Ada said. "Though I hope it's not a conflict of interest that I run my own nonprofit." There were more than two thousand nonprofits on the Cape. This wasn't going to be a conflict of interest, but Charlotte wasn't sure she wanted Ada in on it.

"Oh, that might be a conflict," Charlotte said. "I don't know. I would think it would be." She hoped Ada would take the bait.

"No, it's no problem at all!" Sadie said. "The first meeting is in two weeks on Tuesday at seven. I'll email you the information. Yay!" Sadie began to clap.

This is going to be a long fundraising season, Charlotte thought. She took another swig of her wine and peered around the bar. The landscaper in the red *Life is Good* baseball cap gave her a nod. She smiled with a head tilt and wondered if she gave off a single vibe. Would John even be remotely jealous that men flirted with her? He never seemed to notice or care. In fact, it seemed like he preferred that she dressed scantily and looked sexy when they went out, as opposed to those other husbands she heard about, who wanted their wives covered head-to-toe. It was as if he just married her to have arm candy, flaunting her for show, and then dispensed of her in private. She was a candy dispenser, like Pez.

When she and John first moved to the Cape, with visions of barbecues, boats, and a simpler life, they were all over each other. They'd tear off their work clothes at five o'clock, put on flip-flops, and head to the beach with a canister of margaritas in a cooler. They'd sit for hours watching the sunset from a blanket in the sand—an old maroon tapestry Charlotte had on her wall in college. Then they'd grill steaks in the backyard and talk under the moonlight. Time was just something that passed, not something that dictated their every move.

"Penny for your thoughts," Sadie said.

"Oh, nothing, really. The usual." Charlotte liked that she and Sadie had this internal dialogue where they didn't have to say much but they knew what each other was thinking. The exclusivity might bother Ada, but Charlotte didn't care. Sadie was *her* friend first.

The large wooden bar door opened, and fresh salty, humid air blew in. A tall man, about six foot two with blond hair and Maui Jim sunglasses, stood in the doorway. He was a head-turner.

"Who is *that?*" Charlotte asked, trying not to let her jaw drop.

"Who?" Sadie said, swiveling her head around, despite the obvious.

"Stop! You're drawing attention to us!"

"Oh. My. God," Sadie said, squinting, trying to focus. "I think that's Mack."

"Mack? As in . . . *your ex*, Mack?"

"Holy shit," Sadie said. "Yeah, he's back in town. He messaged me on Facebook to tell me he was coming back to start a resort or something."

"Wait, *whaaaat?* I can't believe you did not share this! Where? When? What the hell?" Charlotte screeched.

"Relax! I didn't say anything because it's not a big deal. I kind of forgot, even," Sadie fibbed. Charlotte knew Sadie was lying, because she smiled and would not make eye contact. This was a telltale sign. Plus, her feigned nonchalance was thrown out the window when Sadie immediately reached for her lip gloss and smoothed down the fly-away hairs.

"Fill me in," Ada said. "He's your ex-boyfriend?"

"He's the one who got away," Charlotte said, raising an eyebrow.

"Oh, stop!" Sadie chided. She had that *I'm going to barf* look about her. Charlotte knew it well.

"But he didn't get too far, if he's back at the Trap!" Charlotte whispered.

She enjoyed the discomfort. It was way more interesting than planning for the hospital gala. "Let's call him over here!" Charlotte gave Mack a wave and motioned for him to come over.

"Oh my God. Dying," Sadie said, pulling her shirt up over her mouth to beneath her nose in embarrassment.

Mack returned Charlotte's wave tentatively.

"Come over here!" Charlotte called out, laughing. Mack glanced behind him. "Yes, you!" she said. She tossed her blonde hair to the side, an expert flirtatious move.

Mack approached the bar table, smiling with his beautiful white teeth. The kind that looked like he wore Crest Whitestrips to bed.

"Hi," Mack said to Charlotte. And then he noticed Sadie. "Oh, wow! Hi!" he said, going in for the hug. Charlotte felt a pang of envy. She preferred to be the center of attention.

"Mack! You're here!" Sadie said, beaming.

"I guess I am," he said, grinning. "Got in a couple days ago."

"To start the resort?" Sadie asked. "How long will you be here? This is wonderful." She was flirting, Charlotte thought. This was going to be trouble.

"For the foreseeable future, at least," Mack said. He put his hands in his jeans pockets and leaned forward on his brown square-toed cowboy boots. Despite his obvious nerves, he was confident.

Charlotte couldn't help but notice how handsome Mack had become since she'd seen him last. He had always been handsome, but now he was downright hot. Was it terrible to be looking at him that way, since Sadie was her best friend? But what difference did it make? They'd ended things years ago, and besides, Sadie was married to Chip. Oh, and she remembered that she was married to John, too. But Mack was literally a panty-dropper.

"What brings you back to these parts? A resort, I hear?" Charlotte asked. "Wait, do you even remember who I am?" she said, reaching for him. She just wanted to touch him. His forearm was strong and tan, with bleached-out blond hairs on it. She took note of his biceps too, that bulged through the soft white T-shirt he wore underneath a navy-blue Patagonia vest.

"Of course, I do, *Charlotte*," he said, making a face. "How could I forget? When a guy gets to go skinny dipping for luminescence on Nobska beach with two beautiful women at midnight, he doesn't forget."

Charlotte's face flushed. She recalled the skinny-dipping night when she, Mack, and Sadie plunged naked into the ocean. Her leg brushed up against Mack's underwater. It was dark, so Sadie hadn't seen this happening, but it was electric, like the glow of the jellyfish.

Swimming with luminescence was something all Cape Cod kids did on summer nights. The luminescence were small comb jellyfish, harmless ones that didn't sting, and they glowed in the dark, lighting up the black night seas. Charlotte, Mack, and Sadie had been at a bonfire on Nobska beach, drinking beers and playing hide-and-go-seek in the private bathhouses that lined the exclusive part of the beach. At one point, Charlotte and Mack were alone hiding in a bathhouse, crouched down underneath a wooden bench. They had to be quiet so Sadie wouldn't find them.

"Ready or not, here I come!" Sadie yelled from the beach. They could hear Sadie's flip-flops as she opened and closed the doors to the adjacent bathhouses. Charlotte could feel Mack's breath upon her. She had the urge to kiss him but thought better of it. Suddenly, the door burst open, followed by Sadie's loud yell. "Got you!" she exclaimed.

"Let's go swimming," Charlotte said, not wanting the moment to end.

The girls ran down to the edge of the water and stripped down to their bras and underwear.

"Are you coming?" Charlotte called back to Mack, who was slowly making his way down the beach.

"Not if you're going in like that," he said. "I want to see some skin!"

"If you say so," Charlotte cooed, ripping off her underwear. She let out a shrill scream and ran into the warm, dark ocean with the sand sinking underneath her and between her toes. The jellyfish lit up like fireflies around her. As she moved her arms treading water, the jellies slipped in and out of her fingers. Mack and Sadie followed, with Sadie grabbing Mack by the hand. Charlotte tried not to look, but she couldn't help but glance at Mack's naked body. He swam out toward her, his face and strong jawline lit up by the moon overhead. Sadie swam a few feet off to do handstands when Mack's leg brushed up against Charlotte's underwater. They exchanged a look, a long moment, one just between them. Had Sadie not been there, things may have turned out differently. But Sadie paddled back and leapt onto Mack's back, trying to ride him like a dolphin. Charlotte was envious, wishing he were all hers. She wanted a boyfriend just like Mack. She made a wish on a star, hoping she'd find one.

"I'm Mack," he said, extending a hand to Ada at the Lobster Trap.

"Oh, sorry," Sadie said. "This is our friend Ada."

Ada shook Mack's hand. Charlotte noticed how weak the shake was. Her arm was going to fall off. She was so frail. *Eat a skewer.*

"Hello, nice to meet you," Ada said demurely. She looked like a lost fawn, helpless and scared. Men loved that, the damsel in distress kind of thing. They needed a rescue from the big, bad world. Charlotte rolled her eyes, hoping no one noticed.

"This is nuts!" Sadie exclaimed. "Do you want to grab a chair? Or . . . are you meeting someone?"

All three women braced themselves for an answer.

"Nope, just me," he said. "I think you guys are the only women I still know in this town."

"Let me grab the waitress," Charlotte said, again raising her hand.

"Well, I know *her* too," Mack joked.

"What are you drinking? On us! A welcome home drink!" Charlotte exclaimed.

Sadie stared at Charlotte as if to say *back the bus up* . . . Charlotte pretended she didn't feel the weight of it.

"Yes! On us," Ada said, smiling.

"Well, then, if you guys insist." Mack laughed. "I'll have a Jack and Coke."

"Old school!" Sadie said. "You always liked the dark stuff." Charlotte noticed Sadie seemed smitten. She had that glow about her.

"Well, it grows hair on your chest," Mack said.

They peered at his chest. His pecs were visible through his white T-shirt as if he'd been tree climbing or hauling bricks.

"So how is your family?" Charlotte asked, digging for answers.

"Well, I'm kind of taking a break, trying to recalibrate," he paused and took a sip. "I recently got a divorce."

All three women chimed in with "I'm sorry" and "aww" simultaneously.

"That sucks," Sadie said, even though it didn't. "Marriage can be hard, and no one really talks about it."

Sadie was definitely dropping hints. Read: my marriage is on the rocks. She peered at Mack to see how the news landed.

"I'm not far behind you," Charlotte said, finishing off her last drop of wine and motioning to the bartender for a refill.

Sadie glanced at her, as if to say, *Are you seriously announcing this right now?*

"You are?" Sadie asked, like a bad actress. *She knows damn well that John and I are basically over,* Charlotte thought. But this was like a game of chess.

"Um, *yeah*?" Charlotte retorted. "I'm, like, one step away from filing."

"I'm so sorry to hear that," Ada said.

"Meh, happens," Charlotte replied. She could hear herself sounding too nonchalant and wondered if it might be a turnoff that she was so dismissive of her husband. "I mean, no. It's horrible, but I'm trying to get through it one day at a time. What's that they say in AA? Easy, does it? One day at a time? I will not drink today!"

"Except you're drinking today," Sadie said.

"Well, is it a day that ends in 'y'? Then, yes, I'm drinking." Charlotte laughed.

"You haven't changed a bit." Mack laughed.

Charlotte liked that he recalled what she was like in the past. She wondered if he ever thought about her in that way.

"Nope. Some things never change."

But something was changing. Things were starting to look up for Charlotte and get more exciting in this town. If she were lucky, she'd get checkmate.

"Hey, I know this is kind of random, but would you guys like to join me at a party tomorrow?" I'm heading over to Chris Lawson's boathouse on Penzance Point around five for cocktails and apps. I'd love some company."

The three women made eye contact and grabbed their phones. Sadie glanced at her calendar; Ada scrolled, maniacally searching for something; and Charlotte piped in, "Sure!" After all, one would not want to miss a party on Penzance Point, as it was one of the nicest places to live in

Woods Hole. Not to mention, Chris Lawson was a reputable financier from Boston, Charlotte recalled from her conversations with John, and he surely would be a good connection to make.

"Oh, maybe I could ask Chris to sponsor the gala," Sadie said excitedly.

"Sadie!" Charlotte exclaimed.

"Sorry, that's tacky. I can't help it! I'm always working!" Sadie said.

"Great," Mack said. "I'll text you guys the info. You can meet me there."

Perfect, Charlotte thought. *Simply perfect.*

Chapter Seven

SHE'S HOOKED

SADIE

The summer Sadie dated Mack, she was twenty years old. It was one of her best memories and favorite summers on the Cape. Sadie was at Crosby's boatyard, sunbathing on the dock before her grandpa took her for a ride on his twenty-nine-foot Grady White. Mack had just tied up his boat on the end of the dock and headed toward her carrying a tackle box and a fishing rod over his shoulder. As soon as their eyes met, Mack tripped over his floppy white Topsider sole and accidentally cast the hook on the pole right into her Calypso straw beach bag.

"I got one!" Mack yelled, trying to make light of the fact that the rusty hook was slowly unraveling her overpriced straw bag.

"You can get me another one!" Sadie shouted back. "Another bag to replace this one," she said.

"Aw, man. Sorry," Mack sighed, shaking his sandy blond hair, bleached from the sun, like he had squeezed lemons in it. "Is that expensive? I'm such a goof." His candor and innocence were disarming.

"Well, maybe you can make it up to me by taking me fishing sometime," Sadie said, surprised by her bravado. What the hell. It was summer! It was called "freckles dating" for a reason. All singles were on the prowl in the summer, and what happened over the bridge stayed over the bridge. Thinking about a relationship beyond August was just foolish.

Well, until Mack and Sadie fell in love.

On the day of their first date, Sadie was restless all morning. She was scheduled to meet Mack at his boat in Woods Hole's Eel Pond at noon so they could make the twelve-thirty p.m. bridge. The bridge schedule was tight in Woods Hole. The drawbridge rose every half hour for the waiting watercraft, and a boat couldn't get into the harbor without first passing through the bridge. Two longs and one short. You needed to do two long bursts with your boat horn and one short burst to notify the bridge tender that you wanted it to go up. Either that or you could radio in.

Sadie wasn't sure what to wear on a fishing date. She didn't want to be overdressed, but she also didn't want to look frumpy. So, she opted for jeans and an aqua-blue tank top. She wrapped a hooded sweatshirt around her waist in case it got cold, particularly around the bluffs off Martha's Vineyard. She knew about the colder air by the bluffs from the many excursions on her grandfather's boat, cruising around Vineyard Sound. As soon as they approached the turn to go to Oak Bluffs, the water grew choppier with whipping winds.

Sadie watched the clock all morning, applying and reapplying her makeup. By the time she was ready to go, she had tweezed almost all her eyebrows off and burnt her hair to a crisp with the straightening iron. She drove her car down to Woods Hole and parked in the Woods Hole Oceanographic Institution's parking lot, despite the fact that she didn't have a parking permit. She figured she'd most likely be late and would risk a tow versus ten parking tickets at the meters.

Before going to the dock, Sadie stopped at Woods Hole Market to grab a bottled water, a Gatorade, and some breath mints in case they had their first kiss. She looked around, wondering if she might run into

Mack. She didn't want him to see her getting breath mints, after all. That would look presumptuous.

As she walked down the dock of Woods Hole Marine, she saw Mack bending down on his boat moving his tackle box around and tidying up. She knew boat owners tended to be maniacal about keeping their boats clean. Not only must you remove your shoes and not wear black soles, but you must also tuck any bags and belongings underneath the boat or in compartments, so they didn't roll all over the floor when you hit a wave. A woman showing up in heels to go boating was a rookie move—so JV—like not wearing whites on a tennis date at the club. Mack's boat was a twenty-eight-foot Boston Whaler with wooden trim. It was old school and classic, and it had the name *Gone Fishin'* on the back with two 300-horsepower Honda engines.

"Nice boat," Sadie said, taking off her Dr. Scholl's sandals and handing them to Mack. He extended a hand to help her aboard.

"Thanks. It gets the job done," he said. Mack was always humble, despite his clearly opulent existence. He wore a sun visor, wraparound Ray Ban sunglasses, khaki shorts, and a pink collared shirt. Sadie liked a man who wasn't afraid to wear pink.

"Do you need me to get anything? Sandwiches, beers?" Sadie asked. She noticed she was going into *wife mode*. She often did this on dates early on in relationships. Part of it was habit, and part of it was her inherent mating instinct. It was like she wanted men to see her as wife material, making sandwiches and doing their laundry. She was maternal, and nurturing, perhaps to a fault. She was the beta, and the guys were the alpha. She didn't mind rolling over or taking one for the team.

"I grabbed a few things; we're good," Mack said, opening his boat cooler, filled to the brim with ice, a chilled bottle of Sauvignon blanc, a six-pack of Coors Light, and two sodas. Prepared. She liked it.

"Great!" she said, thinking this date was already looking up.

Mack turned on his twin engines, which rumbled with exhaust and created bubbles in the water. He sounded his boat horn. One long, two short. Even though she knew it was coming, Sadie jumped, startled, and grabbed ahold of Mack's arm.

"Sorry," she said, letting go.

"No, I like it," he said. "Put it back." He smiled. She re-engaged her arm, her tummy tingling.

They puttered through the channel underneath the drawbridge. Sadie looked up and waved at the young children on their bicycles peering down at her from the street. They waved back. She also saw two girls she knew who worked at Shuckers Raw Bar and flashed them a smile and a wave, feeling proud to be on the boat with Mack. She wondered if they were envious. She was almost envious of herself; she was so happy.

The boat picked up speed, the engine roared, and Sadie turned around to watch the boat's wake bubble up white and frothy behind them. It was a beautiful summer day, seventy-five degrees and sunny, not a cloud in the sky. Her straight-ironed hair blew crazily in the wind, sticking to her lip gloss, and she tied it back into a loose bun.

"Want to grab me a beer?" Mack yelled over the sounds of the engine.

"Sure," Sadie said, holding on to the side rails to balance and trying to gracefully open the cooler that was nailed down to the surface of the boat. She cracked open two Coors Lights, one for him and one for her. The can was freezing cold to the touch. "I think I need a Koozie," she said, laughing. "My hands are freezing!"

"We think alike. Grab one in the side panel, there," Mack said, motioning to the narrow wooden cabinet door flapping in the wind. In it were two foam green Koozies with the golf club's emblem on them. She wondered how many other women had used these Koozies. It seemed too perfect that there were two. But, then again, everything about Mack and this date seemed perfect, almost too good to be true.

"Do you like to go fast?" he asked.

"Hell, yeah!" Sadie said.

Mack pushed the gear all the way forward and sped up to 50 mph, the boat cruising at what felt like light's speed through the glassy waters. Like a washing machine with heavy towels, the boat gently bumped up and down until they almost reached the Vineyard. Mack pulled up closer to a sandy area called Lambert's Cove. Other fishing boats, swimmers, and beachgoers surrounded them.

"I figured we could drift here a bit and throw a line in," he said. Mack slowed the boat to a halt and grabbed his fishing rod from the stern of the boat. He threaded a fake eel lure onto it and cast it in. "I think the albies will be out today," he said.

"Albies?" Sadie asked.

"False albacore," Mack replied. "They're the most fun to fish for. They put up the biggest fight."

She wondered if this was a metaphor for how he liked to date. All men seemed to like the chase. *We chase that which retreats*, she once heard.

"Want to throw a line in?" he asked.

Sadie really wasn't a fan of fishing. She felt terrible every time one got hooked, begging for it to be thrown back to sea. But she would go along with it this time.

"Of course," Sadie said, grabbing the rod. "I might need a little help casting." Mack came up behind her and grabbed under her elbow to show her how to move her arm back and forth, in and out, like a swinging door. She felt the heat of his body against hers and melted into it. She gazed at the horizon and took a long whiff of the salty air. There wasn't any place else she'd rather be. She didn't want this day to end.

"There! You see that?" Mack said, pointing out a flock of seagulls hovering above the water. "It's fish! Cast your line in! You got this!"

Sadie moved forward, cast the line, and waited for a hook. She was hooked on Mack.

Sadie had great hopes for her and Mack. However, as the temperature outside dropped, the temperature of their relationship also cooled. She had met his parents on Labor Day at the Taylor barbecue, and then Mack slowly grew distant. She barely saw him after the holidays, and he never initiated weekend visits with Sadie in Boston. She grew to distrust him and questioned his commitment. This backfired, hard. Instead of pulling Mack closer, it repelled him, all the way into Missy Mark's bedroom. That was the end of Mack and Sadie—then.

Now, twenty years and one divorce—his—later, he was back in town, and she felt that same spark. She couldn't believe it. It was as if the universe was giving her another chance.

"What's for lunch?" her husband Chip asked.

Sadie didn't answer. She was too busy thinking about rekindling with Mack.

"Hellooooo?" Chip said, pretending to talk into a walkie-talkie. "Calling my wife, Sadie! Earth to Sadie! 10-4?"

Sadie snapped out of it. Chip's improvisational humor was not funny, not today at least.

"Huh?" Sadie asked.

"Lunch? We having it?" Chip asked. "I'm on a break. Do you want to go out, or should we make something here?"

"Let's just make something here. I'm tired from going out last night," Sadie said.

"Oh, sounds like a rager . . . Tell me more about it," Chip said, opening the fridge and perusing the options. "Was Charlotte hammered?" He grabbed the smoked turkey and Swiss cheese.

"Of course," Sadie said. She took the deli meats from him and laid the slices of bread out with Boar's Head Dijon mustard, Hellmann's mayonnaise, hot peppers, and slices of tomato next to them.

"Who else was there?" Chip asked.

Sadie immediately thought of Mack but wasn't sure if she should mention him. But, then again, if she didn't mention him, wasn't that more obvious? Like, what if Chip found out later he was in town and wondered why Sadie failed to bring it up?

"Oh, it was kind of crazy," Sadie said, using her terrible actress voice. "You know who showed up?"

"Who?" mumbled Chip with a mouthful of cheese Doritos.

"Mack Taylor!" Sadie shrilled.

"Mack? As in . . . your Mack?"

"Yes! Isn't that nuts?" Sadie blurted out, her face getting flushed. "I guess he got a divorce or something."

Or something.

"Huh, that's too bad," Chip said. He was so oblivious. Couldn't he see that Sadie was literally amped?

"Yeah. Well, I hope he finds some happiness here," Sadie said. "I think he's going to stay awhile."

"Did you talk to him?" Chip asked.

"A little," Sadie lied. "I mean, for like *a second*. Charlotte was all over him."

"Was she really?" Chip smirked. "That Charlotte, got to hand it to her."

"What?" Sadie asked.

"She's just a piece of work," Chip said. "Was Mack into it?"

"Into *her?*" Sadie asked. She felt her blood temperature rising.

"Well, yeah. You said she was flirting with him. What's up? You jealous?"

Sadie could hardly stand Chip right now. "No! That was, like, a hundred years ago! Plus, I'm married to *you!*" she said, pitching the plastic jar of mayonnaise clear across the counter at him. It landed with a thud on the kitchen tile and cracked, mayo oozing onto the floor and splattering all over Chip's calf.

"What the hell?" he said, grabbing a towel.

"I'm not jealous!" Sadie shouted. "Maybe, though, *you*, for once in your life, could be a little jealous!" Sadie was a master of turning the tables and deflection.

"What's that supposed to mean?" Chip asked. He looked gross with mayonnaise on his legs.

"Just what I said! It's like you're so apathetic and couldn't care less if I ran off tomorrow with someone else."

"Hold on. We are talking about you here. Don't Jedi mind trick me into thinking I have some sort of problem just because you have bunched panties over your ex-boyfriend. And I put the emphasis on *ex*," Chip said.

This made Sadie even angrier. He didn't know squat about her relationship with Mack. In fact, if he actually did, he would be *extremely* jealous, as that passion dwarfed any kind of passion she'd ever had with Chip. If you could even call it that anymore. Those days were long gone since having their second baby. Nowadays it was television in separate rooms and dinner with the nightly news on in the background. Slippers and sweatpants.

"Like you would even know what my vagina really looks like anymore." Sadie seethed.

"Well, maybe if you weren't bundled up like an Eskimo every time we got into bed, I might."

"First of all, we don't go to bed at the same time," Sadie said. "You're fast asleep on the couch, snoring, at nine. And, secondly, when you are in the bed, your hands are resting on the remote control, far from my vagina."

"Well, maybe I got tired of having to initiate every time."

"Are you serious right now?" Sadie retorted. "Since when do you initiate anything? You're like the definition of vanilla and complacent. Not to mention, I can't remember the last time you worked out, made any kind of plans for us, or even stepped up as a father! You are just okay with being okay! I am just bored with how boring you are!"

This landed hard. Sadie knew she'd hit below the belt. Telling a man he was a crappy lover, provider, father, and husband all at once was totally unfair. She started to feel bad, but it was too late.

"Go F yourself, Sadie," Chip scowled, grabbing the keys.

"Where are you going?" she called after him into the mudroom.

"Out," Chip said, and he slammed the garage door, got into the car, and peeled out of the driveway.

Sadie looked down at the mayonnaise all over the floor. She began to pace back and forth, wondering how to respond. On the one hand, she felt terrible. Poor Chip was just making conversation about the night, trying to eat some lunch, and she had raged on him at the mere thought of Mack and Charlotte being together. But then what about the fact that Chip was utterly lame in the romance department? Couldn't she be pissed at him for that? Like, he was the reason she was in this headspace in the first place. He'd bought her a wet vacuum for Christmas! I mean, that said it all right there. He literally sucked the romance out of their lives.

Sadie began to spray the kitchen floor with Lysol and wipe up the mess. She got down on her knees and started crying. How could she be in this spot right now? She felt like she had so much promise in her twenties.

Now, not so much. She sobbed and heaved, wiping the mayonnaise in circles, its grease spreading further.

When she finally finished cleaning, she decided to call Chip and apologize. He was her best friend, after all. She felt bad for him, really. He had no clue what she was thinking, and she had totally turned the tables on him. She just got so infuriated when he talked about Mack. What had come over her? Was Mack's return to Cape Cod this powerful and going to ruin everything she had built here? She could not risk this. They had children together, assets, and a life. They were so intertwined.

She grabbed her phone to call Chip but paused and let her stubborn nature take over. *No*, she thought. *That is not enough. I need more out of this life. You only live once, and I am here for the ride. You will not read "Good mom and wife" on my gravestone! I am a mover and a shaker, not some shrinking violet. I need more.*

So instead of calling Chip, Sadie texted Mack:

Looking forward to seeing you at the party. Xx

Chapter Eight

SWEET CHARITY

ADA

Ada arrived at the Penzance Point party first. She was always on time, and this was one instance where it didn't serve her well, or at least she thought. She drove slowly past the long line of cars parked alongside the road's edge outside of Chris Lawson's house. Mercedes, Audi, BMW, Porsche, Range Rover, Mercedes, Volvo, Audi, Range Rover, Jeep . . . What a display of opulence. A tightly packed row of tall green pine trees shot straight up to the sky, fourteen feet high from the lawn's edge, so no part of the Lawsons' house was visible from the road. The place was like a fortress of shrubs. As Ada continued to drive, she didn't see Charlotte and Sadie anywhere, so she picked up her phone.

The phone rang and no one answered. *Shit,* she thought. Now she would have to go into the party alone, knowing no one except Mack, whom she had just met. Well, maybe that wasn't such a bad thing. Maybe he would notice her new strappy silver sandals and her long legs. After all, she had been sitting on the bar stool at the Lobster Trap. He couldn't have known how tall she was or that her legs were long and thin. Maybe he'd imagine those legs around his neck, her ankles at his ears. *Stop!* Ada thought. How disgusting of her. What a hoe bag. But Mack certainly elicited salacious thoughts. He was like Robert Redford in *The Way We Were* combined with Robert Redford in *The Natural*—ruddy and weathered, but salty and sweet. Come to think of it, salt and sweet were her favorite flavors, like chocolate-covered pretzels from Ghelfi's on Main Street.

Ada decided to park and check herself out in the rearview mirror. She used gobs of concealer on her undereye circles, but she still looked tired. Working late into the evening, rushing home to make dinner for the family, and waking every night at three a.m. in a panic was not helping her looks. She straightened out her crocheted tank top, pulling it down over her flat tummy. Her abs were at least tight after all those early-morning sit-ups. She tried to keep up, to stay attractive. She wondered if Ben even noticed. Maybe she would send herself flowers. Maybe that would rattle him. Perhaps he'd get jealous and wonder if they were from Mack. Actually, how amazing would it be if they were in fact from Mack? How exciting it would be to start over with a new romance. Those first couple of months—dopamine flowing, hearts fluttering—those were the best. She decided it might behoove her to get to the party first then, to have Mack all to herself.

Ada emerged from her car and walked up the long driveway with trepidation, feeling the crushed bits of white clamshells that paved the driveway crackling beneath her heels. The lawn was a manicured, vibrant Kelly green, plush and expansive with rolling hills. It was a far cry from the crab grass and moss covering her lawn at home. She'd been meaning to call a landscaper but was holding out hope that Ben would do it himself during those off days that he wasn't working on a job site. He seemed to take care of everyone else's landscaping and leave theirs to rot.

Ada spied a rose garden to the left, shaded by a white trellis and fenced in to keep the rabbits out. The pale pink roses were perfectly in bloom, the color of cotton candy. Manicured hedges in front of the large house had new apricot-colored shingles. Ada walked up to the two front doors and rang the doorbell. A small woman in a maid's uniform sporting a tight black bun opened the door.

"Are you here for the party?" she asked. She held a tray of champagne flutes filled with bubbly.

"I am, thank you."

"Please, help yourself," she said, leading Ada inside the marble foyer. "The guests are out back," she said. "Follow me."

Ada followed the tiny woman down a set of stairs into a great room decorated in all white with dark wood and windows lining the wall with a view of another extravagant lawn, a pool, and the ocean. She felt like she was in a dream and anxious all at the same time as she scanned the room to see if she knew or even recognized anyone besides Mack. In the far corner, she saw Patricia Avon, a socialite who was one of her donors at work, and then there was Fred Gibson, another donor, chatting it up and making Dad jokes with some women in pearls who feigned amusement.

Ada stepped onto the back patio and approached the buffet table. A rowboat raw bar was perched next to the table, filled with ice and freshly shucked clams, jumbo shrimp, and oysters. She picked up one of the shrimp tails between her two fingers, dipped it into the cocktail sauce, and took a bite. Just then, Ada felt someone grab her elbow. She turned around quickly.

"You made it!" Mack said.

"Oh my God. You scared me!" Ada said, laughing. "I don't know anyone here! I feel like a wedding crasher."

"You know me!" he said, extending his beefy arms. His teeth were perfect and bright white, like the color of the tablecloth on the buffet table.

"Well, kinda?" Ada said. "We did just meet . . ."

"So, get to know me," he said. "Come on. Let me show you around

73

and introduce you to Chris." Mack led Ada to the other end of the patio with his hand on the small of her back as if they were a couple. It felt warm there, against her sheer, flowing top. She wore a beige pencil skirt and a silk tank top under her shirt. She wanted to look appropriate among what she assumed would be a conservative crowd.

"Chris, this is my new friend Ada," Mack said. Ada extended her hand and gave Chris a warm handshake. He was about five foot eight with curly blond hair and dressed in a plaid blazer and white pants. His oxford shirt under his blazer was unbuttoned just a smidge too low, and she could see his curly chest hairs peering out at her like lawn weeds.

"So nice to meet you, and thank you for having me," she said. "Your house is breathtaking."

"Well, that's generous of you. Thanks," Chris said. "Did you get a chance to try the raw bar?"

"Yes, I did!" Ada said, holding up a shrimp tail. She wondered if part of the shrimp was stuck in between her teeth and hoped to find a toothpick.

"This is my wife Cammy," Chris said.

"Hi," Cammy said. "So nice to meet you, Ada. Any friend of Mack's is a friend of ours." Ada couldn't help but notice the six-and-a-half-carat diamond ring weighing down Cammy's ring finger. It was stunning and sparkled like a freshly cleaned ice rink. Ada quickly hid the shrimp tail in a napkin.

"Well, we actually just met," Ada began, but then Mack interrupted her and scooted her down to the lawn.

"She's being coy," Mack said. "Let's go down to the finger dock, Ada."

Ada wondered if she'd put her foot in her mouth and immediately regretted being too honest with Chris about having just met Mack. Was Mack embarrassed now? She had to make up for it. She felt herself reeling.

"I'm sorry. Did I say something wrong?" Ada said.

"Nah, no worries," Mack said. "I just wanted to get you to myself and show you this awesome dock."

They walked down the lawn to a long finger pier that extended into the harbor. Two boats were tied up to it.

"Are those his boats?" Ada asked.

"One of them is his," Mack said. "And one is his dad's dinghy that he uses to get to the bigger boat, out there." He pointed to a large sailboat on a private mooring set to the right of the dock. The sailboat stood tall and regal, about forty-five feet long, with navy-blue mast covers on it. It had the name *Sweet Charity* scrawled on the back in cursive with *Woods Hole* underneath that.

"Wow, that's some boat. Are they philanthropic? Is that what the 'charity' name stands for?"

"I mean, they are. Everyone hits them up for cash, but it's really because Chris's mom's name is Charity. She's an old Southern belle from Charleston."

"Got it," Ada said. She wondered if she had recently sent Charity an appeal letter for her nonprofit. She made a mental note to mention the boat and Chris in the next letter to personalize it.

Mack held Ada's hand like she was walking on a tightrope, wobbling in her heels on the grass.

"Let me take these off," she said, grabbing at her heels. "Ah . . . I love the feel of bare feet in the summer," Ada said, "and cold grass in between my toes."

"How about sand?" Mack said. "Isn't that one of those corny Cape sayings, 'Sand in my toes'?" He laughed.

"Oh yeah, it's like on all those signs they sell at Christmas Tree Shop and Home Goods," she said. "I think I may have a few myself." Of course, she knew that saying "Sand in Your Toes." That was what Ben said when he first mentioned moving to the Cape from the city. She told him she didn't like open-toed shoes, and she still didn't.

"I'm coming over," Mack said, laughing. "So where do you live anyway? And tell me about your family." Mack was looking out over the harbor, squinting, and then he pulled his Ray Bans down over his icy blue eyes and looked at her.

"Well, I'm married and have two kids," Ada said. "A girl named Lilly, who is 12, and a boy named Henry, who is 10."

"Nice," Mack said. "I figured a woman like you would definitely be taken."

Ada was chagrined and flattered. Had Mack really thought of her like that? She hadn't been hit on in years, and, admittedly, it felt invigorating.

"Well, who wouldn't want to lock this down?" Ada said, gesturing up and down, laughing. She wasn't very good at taking compliments.

"I tell ya!" Mack said. "Cheers." He lifted his glass. "To my new friend, Ada. Thanks for coming. I'm definitely impressed you showed up here by yourself, not knowing anyone."

"Well, I have to do it for work all the time, so I'm kind of used to it," Ada said.

"I bet you're awesome at what you do," Mack said. "You mentioned it was some kind of nonprofit work? Fundraising?

"Yep, good memory!" Ada replied, again flattered that he remembered. He was listening.

"People skills are huge," Mack said. "Especially in sales and resorts, which is what I do. But enough of the small talk. Let's get to the good stuff. How about a spin around the harbor? The sunset is amazing." Indeed, the sunset was bursting with vibrant shades of pink, orange, and yellow. It was a perfect summer evening.

"Now? Is that okay with Chris?" Ada asked.

"Sure, we've been friends forever. I know where he keeps his key!" he said, jumping onto the boat and turning the key that was left in the ignition. "Good security system out here!"

Ada laughed, searched behind her for her friends, and not seeing them, hopped onto the boat. She felt so free! No kids, no husband, no friends. Just her, the ocean, this boat, and this new guy. Where had he come from anyway, this Mack? And how had she ended up on this boat in the harbor? The day had taken an amazing turn. A turn she could never have anticipated. If only she knew the maze ahead . . . there was no turning back now. She was going for it.

Chapter Nine

REVERSING THE F*CK UP

CHARLOTTE

Charlotte stood in front of her closet, naked, shuffling through her clothes, moving hangers left and right, trying to find the perfect outfit for the Penzance party. Would the white, sheer, spaghetti-strap dress she wore in St. Thomas be appropriate or too sexy? Or, how about that Talbots skirt and Lilly Pulitzer tank top, something more conservative? No, that was too neutered soccer mom, and she definitely didn't want to give Mack that vibe.

She felt slightly guilty she was dressing to impress Mack, but actually, not at all. No, in fact, Charlotte liked the idea of getting attention from another man, since John certainly didn't give her any at home. He'd been staying late at work and taking the old boys' club financiers out for steaks and whiskey at Capital Grille and Abe & Louie's in Boston for the last few weeks. Perhaps a little dalliance would make John jealous. Maybe he'd realize he'd taken Charlotte for granted. Maybe she wouldn't be that old ball and chain he left behind on the Cape at home, and she could compete with some of the young Boston College or Harvard girls interning in his office. They were all out on summer break now, and she was sure to hear stories from John of so-and-so breaking up his marriage because of some floozy intern weighing in at 115 pounds who resembled tits on a stick.

Charlotte pulled out the dress she was going to wear and held it against her in front of the mirror. It hugged her cleavage and was low cut, like the bathing suit she wore in *Sports Illustrated*. She remembered when John used to grab her C cups. He said they were perfect, like ripe melons. He would spoon her with her breast cupped in his hand every night when they went to bed. It helped him to sleep, he said. She missed those nights, snuggling up, especially when it was a cold, dark winter on the Cape, the wind whipping about outside, the front wooden door banging because the latch hook was broken.

Charlotte reflected on the first time the latch broke. She and John had been lying in bed when the door slammed.

"What was that?" she yelled.

John shot up in bed, his eyes huge in the dark.

"Shh," John said, reaching for the aluminum baseball bat he kept under the bed.

"What the hell is that?" Charlotte said.

John got out of bed and crept across the floor, one foot in front of the other, like a trapdoor spider, holding a bat over his head.

"I'm scared," she said.

"It's going to be fine. Wait here." He opened the door and crept out. Charlotte's heart pounded as she sat alone in the bedroom. What was going on? What was taking so long? Then John emerged, bat down.

"I hit him," he said.

"What?" Charlotte exclaimed.

"Just kidding. It was nothing, just the door." He started laughing and lunged back into the bed.

"You suck!" she exclaimed, slapping his naked skin on the back so it made a smacking sound.

"Oh really? What would you have done without me?" John asked. He meant without him there with the bat, in case there was a burglar, but Charlotte took it the other way. What would she have done had she not met him, she wondered?

"I don't know," she said. "I am just glad I don't have to find out."

Charlotte turned from the mirror and tossed the dress on the chair. She instead chose her silk beige camisole and a cream-colored skirt that fit like a glove. She looked sexy/professional, nothing soccer mom about her. She painted her lips a bright matte red and elongated her lashes with mascara. Her long blonde hair was blown out and flat-ironed, not a hair out of place, with party curls. She smoothed it out with some Lancôme serum and Bobbi Brown finishing paste, knowing the humidity in the air on the Penzance property surrounded by water would wreak havoc on her locks. Charlotte peered at the clock. She was running behind, and Sadie would be in her driveway momentarily. Her phone beeped, most likely a text from Sadie that she was on her way. Charlotte swiped onto the message. It was from . . . Mack!

Where are you? The raw bar is calling!

Oh my God, she thought. *Is this really happening?* She imagined Mack feeding her an oyster with mignonette sauce, or spooning her a bite of caviar, the warm air blowing through her hair, and Mack's sun-kissed skin close to hers.

Honk! Honk! Sadie's Range Rover pulled into the driveway.

"Coming!" Charlotte yelled.

She grabbed her heels, purse, keys, and phone, then dashed out the door.

"Sorry," Charlotte said, getting into the car. Earthy honeysuckle scent filled the air. "Yum. You smell good!"

"Thanks! It's that new Tom Ford body oil I got," Sadie said.

"Oh, pulling out the good stuff, are we?"

"Shut up." Sadie laughed and blushed. "Though I must admit, I'm actually kind of nervous!"

"Are you?" Charlotte asked, even though she too had butterflies, but she dared not share. "Have you heard from him since we saw him?" Charlotte hoped Mack had only texted her, that she had the upper hand. She was gauging his interest.

"No," Sadie said, "I'm sure he's crazed being back in town and running into everyone."

"Yeah, totally," Charlotte said, holding her secret close and thinking about Mack's text and the oysters. "Well, I'm sure you'll get to catch up with him there."

"I hope so!"

Charlotte observed Sadie's plump lips glossed in a shade of frosty pink. She looked pretty. "I feel sort of bad," Sadie said.

"Why?"

"I lost my shit on Chip and threw mayonnaise at him. It splattered all over his leg, and he stormed out."

Charlotte laughed. "Wait, *mayonnaise*? Why?"

"Well, we were making lunch, and he started ribbing me about Mack and insinuating that I was jealous he was flirting with you!"

"Oh my God! That's nuts! Wait, were you? *Are you?*" Charlotte asked. She hadn't really thought about that angle, her friend being annoyed. It was against girl code to date someone's ex, but Charlotte figured once you're married, a boyfriend from summers past was fair game. It's not like Sadie and Mack were ever going to get married. And what about the night swimming? Mack had clearly been flirting with her back then, rubbing up against her in the warm water.

"No!" Sadie asserted. "I am *so* not jealous. I mean, I don't know. It's just weird, the whole thing." She picked up her phone and put it back down like she was checking to make sure she didn't miss a text.

"What's weird? Mack being back?" Charlotte asked.

"Yeah. I don't know. Maybe it was the wine and us being together again, the three of us. It felt like nothing had ever happened, like time hadn't gotten away from us. It was like we were young again—no husbands, no kids. It was . . . liberating. It felt good. You know?"

"I know," Charlotte said. Boy did she know. She fidgeted with the automatic seat adjuster, sliding it forward and back. There was a long pause. "Sometimes I wonder if we fucked up," Charlotte said.

"Oh, we definitely fucked up." They cracked up, harder than the comment warranted.

Def Leppard's "Pour Some Sugar on Me" played on the radio, and Sadie turned the volume all the way up and rolled down the windows. The smell of beach roses floated in the temperate summer air.

"My hair!" Charlotte yelled over the wind, holding down her pristine glossy party curls like a helmet. They drove down Sippewissett, past the old Cape Codder hotel and toward Woods Hole along the bike route. Cyclists in tight biking shorts and colorful spandex wind shirts turned their heads as Sadie and Charlotte flew by. They passed the Woods Hole Golf Club, blasting by a golf cart with two old men in sun visors and collared pink shirts. The golfers frowned and motioned for the women to slow down as they blew by the crosswalk.

"Sorry!" Charlotte yelled, waving her hand in the air, looking behind her.

The car wound down Millfield Street, past the bell tower that chimed at seven a.m. and six p.m. daily. Charlotte felt a wave of anxiety and anticipation as they approached the gate to Penzance Point. They stopped to talk to the guard at the gate.

"Where are you headed?" the seventy-eight-year-old gray-haired man asked, holding a clipboard, dressed in a blue uniform. He didn't look too daunting for a security guard.

"We're going to the Lawsons' party?" Sadie said as if she were unsure. Charlotte wondered if Sadie also dreamt of Mack feeding her oysters at the raw bar. Would Mack say hi to her first or Sadie first? And what about Ada?

This is going to be an interesting night, she thought. Maybe it was another chance for all of them.

A chance to reverse "the fuck up."

Chapter Ten

THE SHAME SPIRAL

SADIE

When the party ended, Sadie stayed behind, cherishing a moment alone with Mack. She didn't feel like going home so Charlotte got a ride with Ada. Sadie and Mack decided to walk into town to grab a drink at Shuckers Raw Bar for old times' sake. Holding their tequilas with lime, they shuffled down the floating dock of Woods Hole Marine, right in front of Shuckers. It wobbled over the ripple of Eel Pond as they made their way to the end. Sadie took a seat on the dock, careful not to get a splinter. The three-quarter moon gleamed brightly above her, illuminating the sailboats on the dozens of moorings with stadium-like light.

"Should we take off our shoes and dip our feet in?" Mack asked, rolling up his pants. He submerged his feet in the dark water. For a moment, Sadie worried about a shark or some kind of creepy electric eel.

"Is it cold?" Sadie asked. She took off her sandals.

"No, it feels good. Hope a fish doesn't come and chomp my toe!"

"Or an eel," Sadie replied. "I think the striped bass are here for the summer. There's a story that they swim up to Eel Pond from the South every summer. Apparently, they remember that the scientists dump out their squid in the pond by the marine fisheries building post-experimentation at the MBL. They herd around the building, waiting in schools to be fed."

"Really?" Mack asked, enthralled. Sadie liked that she had these sorts of stories to tell Mack, that she was a local in the know and sounded intelligent. She remembered back when they were dating in college, and she visited him at school for the weekend. He had to study for a chemistry exam and needed her help. She was happy to oblige and quizzed him with flash cards while they drank Rolling Rock beers in his dorm room.

"I miss college," Sadie said, chuckling.

"What made you think of that?"

"Remember when we'd have sex on the top bunk in your dorm room, and I'd put my legs up so my feet touched the ceiling?" Sadie was a perpetual line-stepper.

"That was a good angle!" Mack said. "Stop it! You're giving me a semi!" He gave her a soft punch on the upper arm. Sadie loved that she could still arouse him and that he used words like "semi" to refer to his half-erection.

"It really was a good angle," she said, staring off into the pond. "I like that—*Forever Summer.*"

"What's forever summer?" Mack asked.

"The name of that boat," Sadie said, pointing to a thirty-four-foot sleeper boat clear across the pond.

"I wish it was forever summer," Mack said. "Being back on the Cape, it feels like it is." He took a sip of his drink.

"And being back with you," Sadie whispered. "You remind me of summer." She turned to him.

"Is that right?" Mack asked, smiling back at her with half of his mouth turned upward, a devilish smile.

"What do you think it'd be like if we had gotten married?" Sadie asked.

She knew that she was going down a dangerous path, but she couldn't help herself. She had always dreamed of running into Mack again and having a second chance to make things work. Maybe it had just been bad timing before; maybe it was supposed to happen this way.

"Marriage isn't for me," Mack said. "Or maybe I'm just burned from my divorce." He looked momentarily downtrodden, and Sadie realized bringing up marriage wasn't the best move. Not to mention, she noticed she felt sort of hurt that he said marriage wasn't for him, as if she had no shot at becoming his wife. His second wife.

"It's not for me either," she said.

"But you're married!"

"Well, maybe not forever." She paused. "Is that bad to say?" she asked. "Don't tell anyone."

The tequila had gotten to her head. She was seeking some sort of indication that he was still interested in her. She wanted desperately to see that she could have him again.

"No, not bad at all," he said. "Cheers to that." Mack lifted his glass.

"I can't believe this is happening. I'm here cheering to a divorce with you, of all people."

"Strange things happen," Mack said. "But sometimes you have to listen to the universe when it knocks." He leaned closer toward her, and she shimmied next to him. Mack placed his drink down on the dock and gently guided Sadie's face toward his.

"This okay?" he whispered. She nodded and closed her eyes. Their lips touched ever so slightly.

Then a pause.

Mack slid his tongue softly between her lips, and Sadie opened her mouth, her tongue meeting his. She felt the warmth of his breath as she exhaled. Their tongues twisted together, dancing to an old familiar song.

They embraced under the moonlight, lost in a moment as if there was no such thing as time.

The universe knocks, Mack had said.

Was this a knock, she wondered?

Sadie jolted up in bed at three a.m. with a pounding headache, like she always did after a night of drinking. What was it about waking at three, she wondered. It was four hours after going to bed, mid-sleep cycle, that you must wake as the alcohol exits your system. So, what were those four hours then? No sleep? She stumbled across her bedroom heading for the bathroom, her bare feet shuffling along the cold, dark wood, arms extended in the dark so as not to bump into anything.

"Shit!" Sadie said, stubbing her bubble-gum-pink polished toe on the corner of the scale next to her bathroom toilet. She felt a shooting pain. Why hadn't she moved it? She hit that scale every time she went to the bathroom, the same scale she weighed in on at the Weight Watchers meeting each week. She knew she'd have to face the music this week, after eating all those apps at Chris Lawson's party, and then the drinks at Shuckers.

Shuckers, she thought.

Fuck! The kiss. There was a kiss! Sadie sat on the toilet in the dark, her feet pointed at the glass shower wall. Panicked, she reached up and opened the window with one hand to get some fresh air. The whir of the white noise machine sounded in the background.

What had she been thinking? She felt light-headed and met with a cold sweat. How could she be such a terrible wife and person? She was a mother of two, after all. A happy mother to boot! Wait, was she happy? *That might be a stretch,* she thought. Okay, so she was sort of happy.

Maybe like a B- or a C+, if she were to give it a grade. She just felt lost, and like she wanted a redo. She still dreamed of getting her career back on track, and maybe even publishing a book, but she didn't have time now between kids, Chip, the dog, volunteering, sports, chauffeuring everyone, and being a general slave to her family's wants and needs. And now this? This was going to complicate everything even more! And she was a cheater! She'd kissed Mack! What was happening?

Sadie got up from the toilet, holding her hand on her forehead, trying to erase the memory of last night's events. It was hot. She was sweaty. She had massive self-loathing as she swallowed two Advil and headed back to bed. Chip was snoring ever so slightly. It was kind of cute and innocent, the little gurgle noise he made. He had no idea that his troll of a wife lying next to him had been throwing herself at her ex-boyfriend all night while he stayed home with the kids. She was unable to fall back asleep, her thoughts racing. Sadie pulled the covers over her head, and before she knew it, she woke up to the dog in her face, squeaking to go out.

"Hi there," Chip said, opening his eyes. They were small, like newborn kitten eyes. Sadie was jealous that he looked so rested. She had slept about three hours.

"Hey," Sadie said.

"You look like ass. What time did you get in? I crashed hard."

"Maybe around midnight?" Sadie lied, recalling her wet toes dangling off the dock in Eel Pond, Mack toasting to them.

"Was it fun?" Chip said.

"It was okay," Sadie said. "I missed you, though." She hadn't really missed him, but she felt bad: first, because of the mayonnaise incident, and second, because she'd barely thought of him the entire night and had thrown their marriage under the bus.

Chip didn't respond, but she scooched up close to him, placing her hand on his back. His body was hot, like the coils on a radiator. He was sweaty and smelled of sleep.

The dog barked from the floor. "I better go let him out," Sadie said. As she stood at the slider, she felt pangs of excitement about Mack but also fear. She couldn't wait to see him again. She reached for her phone on the kitchen counter and found a text from Mack.

Thanks for getting wet with me. ;)

Sadie reread the text over and over again. She desperately wanted to text back but thought better of it. Should she reply? What would she say? Of course, she wanted to write, "Let's do it again!" But wasn't that too forward? And, um, yes, there was her husband. What the hell was she doing? She would keep this as her little secret.

Chapter Eleven

A NEW FRIEND

ADA

It took everything Ada had to concentrate at work the Monday after Chris Lawson's party. First off, it was a sunny summer day, and working during the summer on Cape Cod is like a prison with a view. A bumper sticker many locals plastered on their cars read: *I am not on Your Vacation. How true,* Ada thought. She lamented hearing about all the beach fun, hikes, and bike rides that she missed out on while sitting in a quiet, chilly office. At least she had a window and could see the honeysuckles and the orange tiger lilies shooting up to the sky that lined the driveway in front of her office building. Concentrating was also especially hard for Ada on this particular Monday after the party. All she could think about was the boat ride with Mack and how amazing it felt. She was desperate to see him again, but there wasn't any plan. Was he as attractive as she had remembered? She decided to google him to find out.

Ada landed first on Mack's LinkedIn profile page, after carefully managing the privacy settings on her account so he couldn't see that she had viewed him. She looked over his credentials, which were impressive: Exeter, then Yale, and then an extensive marketing and hospitality background. The only issue was it seemed he hadn't worked in the last decade or so. What had he been doing all these years? Maybe being a Mr. Mom? *Is that why he got divorced?* she wondered. Ada then clicked on Mack's Facebook page, which was private. However, she was able to peek at some photos he had posted to his profile and cover page over the years, and a few that he had been tagged in, none of which were very revelatory—except one, the one with his ex-wife and family. Ada zoomed in on his ex, staring intently at her. She wasn't *that* pretty, which gave her a sense of relief. She was cute and fit, like a gymnast, with ashy hair and a delicate nose. Maybe she was extremely intelligent or funny? What if Mack didn't think she was either of those?

Ada ended her sleuthing and checked her phone to see if she had any text messages. There was just one from Ben, writing that he was going to play pickup basketball with some of his buddies. Must be nice to have leisure time, Ada thought, while she slaved away at her computer on a beautiful day. Ben's contract work hit a halt this time of year because summer residents were on vacation and didn't want to be bothered with a work crew and bulldozers on their properties. Ben was mostly busy in the off-season, which left him ample free time to play, something that always made Ada envious. When the children were little, it was great, because Ben was available to take them to swimming lessons or tennis at the Cataumet Club. Now that they were older, they wanted truly little to do with their father during the day. Lilly had a part-time job as a Mother's Helper and the rest of the time she was off with her friends. Henry left early on his bike for the beach and returned home later to play video games or hang out with his friends. Ben could do as he pleased. Ada really couldn't complain since he had made a good salary this past year, charging nearly $60,000 per job.

Ada pulled the big black scissors from her desk and started to trim her split ends, one at a time. She couldn't remember the last time she got a haircut or manicure. These were luxuries she didn't indulge in, both for lack of time and money. It was a treat to get her nails done by someone else, reserved for weddings or special occasions. She imagined Mack asking her out on a date. For that, she might splurge on a new outfit and a blowout. The next party up was the Falmouth Art Center Gala, but she couldn't decide if she was going to go. Charlotte had mentioned it, and maybe Sadie was going. She couldn't remember. Speaking of which, she wondered if Sadie had spent time with Mack after Chris Lawson's party. She decided to text Sadie.

ADA: *Hey. How was the rest of your night Saturday?*

SADIE: *Great! Until I got hammered and decided it was a good idea to stay at Shuckers till closing.*

ADA: *Oh really? So fun! Who did you go with?*

SADIE: *Just me and Mack. Everyone else bailed.*

ADA: *Oooh . . . how was that?* ☺

SADIE: *Fun! Just good friends is all. Like old times.*

ADA: *Gotcha. Was a good night!*

SADIE: *Yes! Let's do it again soon!*

ADA: *Def. Text me soon. Back to work. xo*

Ada set down her phone, seething with jealousy. Alone with Mack? How did Chip feel about that? Did Mack have feelings for Sadie? They used to date, so perhaps he had some residual feelings. *Whatever,* Ada thought. She didn't really care. After all, she was married to Ben, all was . . . well, sort of fine, and she had no business crushing out on some salesman who was back in town for God only knew how long. In fact, the entire crush was ludicrous and needed to end straightaway. That was it. She was done. Moving on. No more private investigating, no more boat rides. She would go home and be the good wife and mother she always wanted to be.

But then she got a text. From Mack.

How's my new friend today?

And her resolve was gone. So much for being a good wife and mother.

Chapter Twelve

CHARLOTTE'S WEB

CHARLOTTE

Charlotte sat on the deck of the club peering at the view of the harbor beyond the rolling green hills. A few white-haired, blue-blood men in visors and collared shirts were finishing off their golf game in the distance. She unrolled the crisp white dinner napkin on the table and put it on her lap, removing the cutlery. She glanced around the room, unsure of herself, and then at her reflection in the shiny, polished silver knife on the table. *I need eye cream*, she thought. More eye cream, or fillers.

"Hey! Sorry I'm a bit late," Ada said, grabbing the back of Charlotte's shoulder. Her head shot up.

"Hey! No worries," Charlotte said. She felt a bit strange meeting Ada alone without Sadie, kind of like a first date. The two had never made plans alone before, but Ada had texted asking to meet for drinks, so she figured why not.

"Did you have fun at the party the other night?" Ada asked while settling into her chair, like a dog looking for a good spot to sleep. She grabbed the cocktail list, perusing it. Charlotte couldn't help but notice how perfect Ada looked. She had freshly applied lip gloss, blown-out black silky hair, and bright turquoise pom-pom earrings that lit up against the dark backdrop of her hair, like a prop on a dark stage. Her eyes were steely and intense, as if she was keeping a secret.

"I did!" Charlotte said. "That's such an amazing spot, right?"

"So nice. I'd never been to a party on Penzance Point before. It was stunning."

"So, I have to ask," Charlotte cooed. "I saw you and Mack head out on the boat. And you were both gone for a while." She smiled like the Cheshire Cat, both disarming and eerie. Ada giggled, covering her thin face with her hands. Her diamond wedding ring refracted the sunlight, sparkling. This annoyed Charlotte, and she wasn't sure why.

"It was nothing, really. I mean, it was nice; he's nice. We went for a ride around the harbor, just chatted."

"For an hour?" Charlotte asked, raising an eyebrow. "Hadley Harbor takes less than a minute to circle by boat." Charlotte was good when she went into lawyer mode. She may have been a model, but she was no dummy. She had a sharp tongue and wit.

"Were we gone that long?" Ada asked. "It didn't seem like that."

"Um, yeah, that would be yes!" Charlotte replied.

"I don't know, he's fun," Ada said, smiling. "What can I say?" She fidgeted with her spoon, tapping it up and down on the white linen tablecloth like a toddler. "He was just asking me about my life, where I'm from, pretty harmless."

"I just wonder what his agenda is," Charlotte hinted. She knew where she was going with this. Truthfully, she did wonder about Mack's agenda, as he was flirting with both her and Sadie also. But she too had an agenda, bringing this up to Ada. She wanted Ada to doubt Mack, and to doubt herself. She wanted to bring down that high she was riding on and smack that glossy smile right off her little face.

"What do you mean?" Ada asked.

Charlotte considered that this was all part of a naive act. How had Ada gotten by this long being a deer in headlights? Didn't she run a nonprofit? Perhaps this was her game; this is why Mack liked her—guys always liked those helpless damsels in distress. Surely, she noticed Mack was whisking her off into the sunset and paying oodles of attention to her at the party.

The club's general manager approached the table dressed in a green cashmere vest from the Pro Shop with the golf club's signature logo on it.

"How are we doing today, Mrs. Simms?" he asked.

Charlotte's temperament changed immediately when she gave a big hello. "Great! How are you?"

"Terrific," he chimed back. "Lovely day to sit on the porch."

"It is!" Ada said, sipping her wine. The GM gave her a slight smile and strolled off to the next guests, hands behind his back.

After the pleasantries ended, Charlotte got back on topic.

"I don't know," Charlotte said. "He spent an awful lot of time with you, and then that whole late-night thing with Sadie was really shady at Shuckers."

"Oh, I know!" Ada said. "What's up with that? Did anything happen between them?"

"She claims not," Charlotte said. "But I can't imagine there wasn't some massive flirtation going on. I just wonder how Chip feels, you know?"

"Yeah, I mean, do you think he even knows?"

"I don't know. Personally, and *please keep this between you and me*," Charlotte whispered, "but I think Sadie would ditch Chip in a hot minute if Mack wanted her back."

"I don't know. You think?" Ada replied.

"Totally! They have been fighting a lot this summer. Did she tell you about throwing the mayonnaise at him the other day?"

"No! Wait, *what?*" Ada asked. "Mayonnaise?" Charlotte got a little high off the gossip.

"Yeah! She threw a jar of mayo at him, because Chip insinuated that Mack was into *me!* Can you *imagine?*" Charlotte feigned disbelief.

"Wait, stop it. That's horrible!" Ada said. She frowned, and her eyes darted back and forth, like she was watching a tennis match. "Do you think he's into you?"

Charlotte sighed and looked off into the harbor. "I don't know. I mean, whatever. The point is, Sadie should really watch her step. This is a small town and people will start talking. They already have, actually."

"What are they saying?" Ada asked.

"Well, I ran into Scarlett Crane this morning on the bike path jogging, and she said she heard that Sadie was out late with Mack the other night and inquired about her and Chip's marriage."

"Oh my God. What did you tell her?" Ada asked.

"I mean, I was being a good friend," Charlotte said, tooting her own horn, "and I told her she and Chip were just fine. I squashed the rumor then and there! I'm saying this between you and me . . ."

"Right," Ada said. "That was good of you." She fell silent for a moment. "It is pretty shady, though."

"What is?"

"Just how she's been flirting with Mack. I mean, clearly, she's not over him," Ada said. "I feel like if I were Chip, I'd be pretty bummed out my wife was throwing it out there with her ex-boyfriend in front of everyone else. It's not a good look."

"Agreed. Do you think I should tell her? Like that people are talking about her?"

"I don't know," Ada said. "Maybe we should stay in our own lane."

"Wouldn't you want to know if people were going around saying that about you?" Charlotte asked.

"I guess so, yeah. But, I mean, maybe she will just think we're jealous. Which, honestly, could not be further from the truth."

Charlotte doubted that. *Quite the overt cover-up*, she thought.

"Yeah, I hear you," she said. "All I'm saying is she better pull it back and take it down a notch, because she looks slutty."

They both cackled at the word *slutty*.

"Wait, this is so high school!" Ada said.

"I know!" Charlotte laughed. "It's so fun having drinks with you. We never spend time by ourselves, you know?"

"Yes! And I'm sorry if you felt like I was coming between you and Sadie before."

"Not at all!" Charlotte lied. "But thank you for saying that. I'm sorry if I seemed like a curt bitch!"

"You kind of did!" Ada chortled. "But I like a good bitch!"

"Well, cheers to our friendship," Charlotte said, raising her glass of Sancerre covered in wet droplets of condensation.

"To our friendship," Ada replied, clinking her glass.

The next day, Charlotte sat on a couch at the coffee shop writing in her journal. She loved the smell of the freshly ground beans, the acoustic music, and the comfy vintage chairs and couches strewn about the old wooden barn. She felt particularly edgy this morning and needed to write down her feelings. Mostly, she felt alone. Under normal circumstances, she would talk to Sadie about her problems. But this time, Sadie *was* her problem. Charlotte took a sip of her vanilla chai latte and scanned the room. The barista sporting a man bun joked with a young scientist while filling his reusable mug. Off to the side, a couple of crunchy-looking moms in frocks drank their coffees, while simultaneously rocking their strollers back and forth and playing Scrabble.

But then Mack walked in, closing the door with the overhead chimes sounding. She glanced at him and gave an undecided, faint wave. He waved back, grinning.

"Well, well, well," he chuckled, coming closer. "Look who we have here. If it isn't Charlotte's Web."

"Am I the pig or the spider in this scenario?" Charlotte asked. She twirled her long blonde hair, looping it in and out of her index and middle finger.

"Obviously, the pig!" They both chuckled. "You good? I'm going to grab a coffee . . . and then maybe join you?"

He was stunning and charming as usual, wearing an orange sailcloth bathing suit with a Maui Jim's T-shirt on top and sunglasses hanging around his neck. He looked like he was going surfing. How could Charlotte say no? She shut her leather journal in a grand gesture, resting her hand over it, and slid the chair across from her forward with her foot.

"Please do," she said. "That is, if you don't mind sitting with a pig."

"You know me, I love a good pig!" Mack said.

"Yeah, I've heard," Charlotte said, rolling her eyes. Truth be told, Mack did have a reputation for slaying the ladies, and even the "pigs." He didn't have much discretion back in the day when it came to his choice of women.

Mack walked up to the counter and ordered a witch's brew from the barista. Charlotte watched Mack as he poured his creamer into his coffee. He had a tight little butt, one that she'd like to cup in her hand. *Stop it!* she thought. She was going to try to work on things with John. The baby? Remember? How quickly she forgot.

He sat down across from her, grinning.

"So, here we are," he said.

"Here we are!" she beamed.

"Hey, I have kind of a weird question for you."

"What's that?" Charlotte asked. "Nothing is too weird for me, as you know . . . "

"Any chance you want to go to the Falmouth Art Center Gala with me tonight?" Charlotte's eyes widened as she peered over her coffee, taking a gulp. "I mean, like as a friend thing," he continued. "For old times' sake. I have an extra ticket, and I need to mingle with some of the heavy-hitter investors in my resort."

"Of course, as friends," she emphasized, fully not thinking it'd be as friends. How could they be friends when she wanted to have sex with him? "Um, yeah, sure, I think I can make it. Let me just check."

She whisked out her phone and pretended to scroll through her calendar on her phone, racking her brain to think about what John would say. Well, he couldn't really say anything, actually. First off, Mack was a longtime friend. Granted, they hadn't kept in touch in ages, but he still constituted an old friend, right? Second, John was never home, and he probably wouldn't be home tonight, so what was the difference? Why should she sit home and watch *Bachelor in Paradise* while texting him in Boston to talk about trying for a baby? Third, and she guessed most important, she didn't *have* to tell him. She could just say she ran into him there, if anyone asked. Yes, that was her plan. She would go on the date with Mack. *I mean, not a date . . . the friend—thing—with Mack!*

As Charlotte emerged from her taxi in front of the Falmouth Art Center later that night, she lifted the hem of her long blue dress to ensure she didn't face-plant before all the other gala guests in the parking lot. She felt self-conscious arriving by taxi alone. Other couples walked arm-in-arm into the glass doors, decked out and dressed to the nines. This was one occasion in Falmouth where all the guests dressed up and looked forward to it. As opposed to the other three hundred-some-odd days where they looked like a J.McLaughlin or Vineyard Vines catalog in their gingham and Nantucket red-whale print pants. Charlotte had rented her dress from Rent the Runway, something she'd never tried before. It was a pale blue, to match her eyes, with spaghetti straps and a thin belt that went around her petite waist. It was tight. Very tight.

As Charlotte wobbled across the parking lot in her silver strappy sandals, she noticed Mack across the way. She gave him an inconspicuous wave, lifting her hand up a bit, but she was careful that others didn't see. She wanted it to look like an accident that they ran into each other there. Mack was a tall drink of water in the desert. He had that unshaven look that made him sultry-sexy, like he was a bad boy underneath his WASPy charm. *Maybe he'd pull my hair or spank me,* she thought. *That might be fun . . .*

"Hey, there. Fancy meeting you here," he called out too loudly. He was in on this little charade. It was like fantasy role-play. "Can I give you a hand in those heels?"

Charlotte pulled off the piece of blonde hair that had glommed onto her Chanel lip gloss and flashed her best smile. Maybe this could make up for looking like a Weeble Wobble walking on stilts.

"Oh my God. The struggle is real in these things!" she said. "Sure, thanks for the arm." She hooked her gangly, long arm into his and could feel the linen from his navy-blue suit tickling her. She felt like a million bucks having Mack as arm candy. And she had him all to herself tonight.

"Hey there, Charlotte," sang Scarlett Crane, looking her up and down.

"Gorgeous dress." Scarlett extended her hand to Mack. "I'm Scarlett Crane. You must be Mack. I've heard *a lot* about you since you've been back in town."

Mack shook her hand. "Hi, Scarlett. And, yes, I'm Mack. I'm not sure if I should say yes or no, depending on what you've heard." He chuckled.

"Well, I guess you'll have to find out. Dance with me later?" Scarlett winked at him. Charlotte wanted to rip one of those big false lashes off Scarlett's meddling face.

"That would be nice," Mack said. "Well, that is, if my date here doesn't mind." He ribbed Charlotte.

"Stop! I am *not* your date! We are just *friends*!" Charlotte chimed back emphatically, making sure Scarlett heard the word "friends." She didn't need this on the Scarlett telephone chain in the morning.

"What's John up to tonight? Working?" Scarlett asked. She had her *Dateline* Keith Morrison investigative reporter cap on. Everyone knew John always worked, but they would politely ask anyway.

"Yep," Charlotte said. "Where's Scott?" Scott was Scarlett's husband, who was also often missing, as he managed a large golf course and worked nights and weekends. It didn't seem to bother Scarlett one bit. She was always flitting about, gathering gossip, like an old-time bitty.

"John's up in Boston. He has a client dinner, so he's staying in the apartment for the weekend," Charlotte said. She knew saying "the apartment" sounded horrendously ostentatious as if she had an opulent lifestyle and a pied-a-terre in Boston. However, the apartment was a 700-square feet, one bedroom apartment on Phillips Street in Beacon Hill and nothing to write home about. But it was John's second home—sometimes it seemed more like his first. Charlotte hoped he was the only one sleeping there, but she had her suspicions. Maybe it was the faux fingernail she once found sticking to the bedspread. He claimed it was from one of his buddies' girlfriends who also used the apartment as a crash pad when they didn't feel like driving home to Natick.

Mack and Charlotte walked through the art center entrance, and she could feel the weight of everyone's eyes on them. It might not look so good to be there together, but she didn't care. She was never one to follow the rules. Charlotte slowly inhaled the smell of Mack's Old Spice deodorant and wondered if he could smell her faint Tom Ford body oil. They headed straight for the bar, a respite from the crowd.

"What can I get you?" Mack asked.

"Oh no, drinks on me!" Charlotte joked, referring to the open bar. You couldn't go to a gala with a ticket price of $225 and not have an open bar. She wondered if Mack knew that.

"Ha! Right. Makes sense," Mack said, laughing. Charlotte could tell he was nervous. He licked his lips a lot and was unusually quiet. She pondered what it would be like to kiss those lips and imagined them enraptured in pleasure in a hotel room. She loved hot, sultry hotel sex.

Charlotte sipped at her Kim Crawford Sauvignon blanc and admired the pastels lining the art center's walls. They were mostly of scenes on the Cape: dunes at Sandy Neck, sunsets at Chapoquoit Beach, and trails in Beebe Woods. She was giddy, amped. Her pink-powdered cheeks felt rubbery from smiling. She never realized Mack was so funny before. She wondered if they'd have another chance to talk at length and alone.

Crooked Coast, her favorite local band, began to play. She slid carefully toward the dance floor, trying not to wobble in her heels. These would have to come off, she thought, relieved she still had a pedicure and had brought some flip-flops in her purse.

"You like these guys?" Mack asked, reappearing by her side.

"They're so good!" Charlotte said. "Have you seen them play at Landfall? They have a huge following, and they just released a new music video."

Charlotte had always been into music. During her modeling days in New York, she spent many nights going to music halls like the Slipper Room, the Bitter End, and Bowery Ballroom.

"I think I once waited to see them, but they didn't start till eleven and I fell asleep," Mack said, rolling his eyes. "Maybe I've aged out."

"Well, lucky for you, they're starting early tonight. But I can't promise you'll be home in bed by eleven." She looked up at him, batting her lashes, and sipped wine. *Hells no*, she thought. They were not going home early.

"Is that so?" Mack chuckled. "Shall we dance?"

Charlotte set her wineglass down on a high top by the dance floor, next to a brilliant centerpiece of blue hydrangeas in a vase filled with seashells and sand. She and Mack joined hands, and she put her left hand on his shoulder while holding his right, a typical waltz formation. He spun her around and she snickered, trying not to stumble in her heels.

"I'm going to teach you my signature move," she said, grabbing his arms and twisting them over their heads, landing on their shoulders. "The pretzel!"

They did the pretzel a few times and spun around, laughing and smiling. Charlotte felt dizzy, not only from spinning but also from the endorphins and undeniable chemistry. The song ended and they decided to grab another drink at the bar. A short woman with tortoiseshell glasses, wearing a red dress with a big bow on her shoulder, approached asking if they'd like to buy raffle tickets to the silent auction. Mack pulled out a $100 bill, and she thanked him profusely for his generosity.

"Whoa, big spender," Charlotte said. "You going to put your name in for a spa treatment at Chatham Bars Inn, or would you prefer a night at the Sea Crest Hotel?"

"Hmm . . . I think I'd prefer a night with you," he said. Charlotte blushed.

"Well, isn't that what this is?" she slurred. Her eyes felt heavy with the buzz.

"It's whatever we want it to be," Mack replied. He grabbed Charlotte by the hand, and they walked about the art center looking at different pieces. They stopped at one of a nude woman, lying on the beach.

"I think I remember you looking kind of like this night swimming at Nobska," he chuckled.

"Shut up!" she said, giving him a slap on the shoulder. "That was a fun night. Do you remember we, like, touched legs underwater? I was kind of into you!" She was putting out the feelers.

"Um, yeah? How could I forget?" Mack said.

"But you were dating Sadie." She was going close to the fire, the danger zone, and she liked it.

"I always had eyes for you, Charlotte," he said. "You know that." He took a sip of bourbon and led her by the small of her back to the stairwell. "What's downstairs?"

Was this an invitation? she wondered.

"I think the clay studios? I'm not sure," Charlotte said. Then, against her better judgment, like a moth to a flame, she asked, "Do you want to check it out?" She knew she was crazy to suggest this, but she didn't care.

"Sure," he said with an inviting smile. Those dimples, that hair. This was not going to be good . . . but maybe it would be amazing.

When Mack and Charlotte got downstairs, they looked around for lights, but only one was on at the end of the hall. It was a broom closet. From what she could discern, the first classroom was a knitting room. There were four wooden looms with foot pedals and baskets of yarn with various fabrics littered the tables.

"Well, I don't think there's another bar down here," Charlotte said. She giggled to hide her discomfort.

"I never thought there was a bar down here," Mack said, moving toward her. They stood face-to-face, close, in the dark hallway. She wondered if he could smell her breath, and she wanted to taste his. She wanted to touch him, to rest her long arms on his wide shoulder blades.

"Well?" Charlotte said. "Want to play with some clay and pretend we are Demi Moore and Patrick Swayze in *Ghost*? I think the kiln is down there."

"Maybe," he said. "But I like just looking at you."

"Can you see me?"

"I see you," he said. "More than you know." Mack leaned in and kissed her gently on the mouth. Charlotte didn't know how to respond at first, but she couldn't help moving closer, kissing him over and over again, getting faster and more passionate. Their tongues twisted lightly, mouths opening and closing. She was still holding her wineglass, which encumbered her ability to embrace him.

"Let me put this down. Here, let's go in here," Charlotte said, grabbing his hand and leading him into the clay studio. Her heels made a sharp clicking noise as each one hit the floor. She leaned on her front toes, trying not to make a sound. She worried someone would hear them. Now they could be alone, away from the crowds. The thud of the music from above reverberated on the ceiling, along with people dancing and talking. But all Charlotte could hear was the sounds of passion she and Mack made as they pushed each other from wall to wall, his knee rubbing up against her. It was as if they had wanted to do this all along. She could feel him get hard. She wanted him.

"What should we do?" she asked, pulling away. His eyes were dilated in the dark, a deep brown, like a leopard pursuing its prey.

"I like this," he said, pulling her back into him for another kiss. "I've wanted to do this for a long time."

"You did? I always thought you were into Sadie, not me," she said.

"Sadie was a teenage crush. You, Charlotte, are the one I've thought about over the years, even when I was married. I never forgot you, the feel of our legs rubbing up against each other, your smile." Mack was close to her, tucking her hair gently behind her right ear. She inhaled his musky scent and nuzzled her nose into his chest.

"I've wanted this too," she said. "I guess I didn't think it'd ever happen."

"It's happening," Mack said, and he knelt to lift her dress, hiding underneath. Charlotte gasped and held her breath momentarily, resting her palms on either side of the cold wall as she felt his tongue part her underwear and his fingers enter her. She closed her eyes and tried to imagine them on a beach somewhere, somewhere far away from the gala and far away from their real lives She exhaled deeply taking it all in. Of Mack. Of this moment.

She never wanted it to end.

Chapter Thirteen

PT-NO

SADIE

The school auditorium was broiling hot. It had poor ventilation, with only a few windows, and it was July on the Cape and humid. Sadie was running late to a summer PTO meeting. She tried to hide the sweat under her armpits as Principal Gray welcomed her at the front door.

"So great to see you, Sadie," he said. "How are the kiddos enjoying summer? We miss them!" Sadie didn't have time for small talk, so she assured him they were fine, blabbed on about golf, swimming, and tennis camps, and then ran across the yellow linoleum tile toward the end of the hallway. She was so tired of running. That was all she did: run from home to the grocery store, to baseball practices, to sleepovers, and to barbecues with Chip. She knew she shouldn't complain, as she wasn't working, but it was exhausting.

"So glad you could join us," Emily Coleridge said, opening her Lilly Pulitzer spiraled notebook. She sat in a tiny chair, like Goldilocks, at the kids' table in the library. Sadie wasn't sure if she was being facetious or sincere, but she chose to see the good in Emily.

"Thanks, sorry I'm late," Sadie sighed, grabbing a tiny chair for herself.

Sadie looked about the room and silently waved to several of the other women at the table. She was no longer interested in working on the

PTO, but she felt guilted into it by Caroline Wall. This particular group was very spirited with bake sales, raffles, book sales, and spirit days. She simply didn't have the time for it anymore. As Emily droned on about the new Falmouth Clippers shirts that she'd ordered with a V-neck, Sadie wondered if it would be rude to read her emails surreptitiously. No, she should make eye contact with Principal Gray and nod and smile like the other PTO moms, holding sign-up sheets for the book fair and Halloween party. Sadie looked over at Pam hiding in back who also arrived late. Pam waved and improvised sipping a glass of wine and pointed to Sadie. This was an invitation; one she was desperate for. *Yes, please*, Sadie thought and nodded aggressively. Sadie had once considered joining the PTO as treasurer—the only open seat on the committee—but it required daily trips to the bank, which is why no one else wanted to do it either. It was the "hot potato" position on the PTO. Instead, she just attended some of the meetings and went out to the Beach Bar afterward with the girls.

Sadie pulled out her phone and saw a text from Chip. He was wrapping up dinner with the kids and thinking of taking them to the band shell on Scranton Avenue to listen to music. Every Thursday at five, a different band would play, and kids would run around visiting the food trucks and lemonade stands along the harbor. Sadie readjusted in her tiny, uncomfortable seat and pulled her skirt out from sticking to the backs of her sweaty thighs. *I'm disgusting*, she thought. *Must go to the gym, train, stop eating cheese, and forgo carbs. Okay, well after tonight.* It was always "after tonight."

"Sadie, you have to do book fair again for us! Puh-lease?" Emily urged.

"Okay, put me down," Sadie agreed. "But not for the day shifts. I'll do an after-school one. I have too much going on right now," she said.

"Ooh, must discuss later!" Emily replied, raising and lowering her eyebrows like a Marx brother. "Let's put a pin in that one!" Emily's work jargon was embarrassing.

When the meeting ended, Sadie walked down the halls adorned with children's artwork. She reached into her purse and grabbed her phone to let Chip know she and Pam were heading out for a drink. She hoped to find a text from Mack—she'd only checked about fifty times that day. But there wasn't one. After the night at Shuckers, kissing on the dock, she was sure she'd hear from him more often, but the communication had kind of fizzled. She wondered if she should reach out, maybe text something like, "*How's it going?*" Or find something pertinent she needed to ask him. But every time she drafted a text, she ended up erasing it, knowing deep down that he'd reach out if he wanted to. Guys were not that complicated. If they wanted to find you, they would. *Mack didn't want to find her,* she thought. Why had she let herself go down this rabbit hole? What the hell was she thinking? She wasn't thinking, is the point. Life had thrown her a curveball, and if she wasn't careful, she'd be down for the count.

Chapter Fourteen

GOSSIP

ADA

Ada folded the laundry in the basement and wondered where all the missing socks went. Why were there so many socks without matches? She recently got into the habit of buying the same kinds of socks every time so there would always be a match, at least for Ben. He liked the white Adidas high-rise athletic socks. They fit nicely and didn't bunch in his work boots. Lilly, however, was more fashion-conscious and demanded a variety of socks with cutesy emojis on them. They were about $5.99 at TJ Maxx for a pair of four, and they inevitably shrunk a size smaller every time she put them in the dryer. By the end of two months, none of them were left.

Ada stared off into the distance as she folded Ben's undershirts and boxer shorts just the way he liked them, into a small square with three fold-overs, not four. She daydreamed about her time on the boat with Mack at the Lawsons' party. She wondered if she'd see him again and hated to admit they'd been sending some flirtatious texts back and forth. She'd called him her "Salty Captain" in one, and he referred to her as his "Spicy First Mate." They chuckled back and forth by text, using the LOL emoji with the crying face, saying they should start a band called Salt and Spice. She knew what she was doing was dangerous, but she couldn't help it. It felt so good! Ada thought about Mack's thick tan fingers on the controls of the boat and what they would feel like touching her bare skin ever so slightly, a tickle, a wisp, like a butterfly fluttering around after its wings were wet.

Her cell phone dinged. She woke from her daydream to find a text from Ben. He told her he was going to the gym after work, something she wished she had the time to do. The idea of even taking an hour to get a manicure was absurd, especially since the paint chipped off after one round of dinner dishes and vacuuming the crap out of the back seat of her car filled with gummy bears, Slime, McDonald's ketchup packets, pretzels, hair bands, sand, and unidentified goop. *Well, that must be nice for Ben*, she thought. *Wish I could go to the gym after slaving all day at work!* Then, she stopped herself for a moment of panic. Was Ben's new fascination with working out a sign he might be having an affair? Wasn't that one of the signs she'd read somewhere, that when you first meet someone you're attracted to, you start to work out and get new underwear? Maybe Ben had met someone at the gym, or a stay-at-home mom on one of his contracting jobs, like on that show *Desperate Housewives*. Maybe she wasn't the only one toying with the idea of an extramarital affair. Or maybe she was just transferring her own pathology onto him?

Ada didn't have time for this bullshit. She needed to finish the laundry and get dinner started. The kids would be home from ballet and the beach any minute. Sadie was dropping them off. She thanked her lucky stars for Sadie. During the school year, the kids got a half-day and were dismissed at 12:40 due to "teacher development" in-service day. On these days, Ada was desperate for childcare. She didn't want to send her kids to the YMCA after-care since they'd recently switched over to using untrained sixteen-year-olds to supervise the kids. So, she was grateful for moms like

Sadie, who picked up her kids for her, fed them lunch, and entertained them till five o'clock. Ada would then repay the favor on Saturdays, taking Sadie's kids to soccer and dropping them off so she had time to get a blowout or just have some peace for a few hours.

Sadie pulled into the driveway backward. This was a habit of hers. She'd pull her car just a wee past the entrance of the driveway and then back it in, making it easier for her to get out. The drop-off always included at least one drink. Ada made sure to thank Sadie for her help with a chilled glass of Sauvignon blanc waiting for her on the kitchen island when she arrived.

"Thank Christ," Sadie said, wrapping her hand around the stem of the wineglass like an ill-trained child holds a fork. "You have no idea how much I need this right now." She took a gigantic gulp and made a smacking sound with her lips. The wineglass had a cartoon image of a woman painted on it that read "Wine Time!"

"What's going on?" Ada said.

"Let's see. Where should I start? Hmm. Maybe that my marriage is falling apart, my best friend is losing her shit, or my children want nothing but rides and money from me." She took another swill.

"Jesus, that's a lot," Ada said. "Wait, *who* is losing her shit? Charlotte?" Ada had heard some rumblings about Charlotte in town, getting into a drunken bar fight at the Boathouse, but she wasn't sure if it was true or not. The kids entered the kitchen, and she paused to let them grab some Pringles and candy from the snack drawer by the fridge.

"She's out of her mind," Sadie said. "Ever since Mack got back into town, I feel like our world is spinning out of control."

Mack. What did Mack have to do with it? She was immediately jealous and needed to know more.

"What do you mean?" Ada asked. "What does Mack have to do with it?"

"Well, first I made out with him at Shuckers, and then Charlotte went to the Art Center Gala with him. Now Chip is pissed at me, and who knows if John even gives a shit about Charlotte and Mack. Not that there's anything to really give a shit about. Mack probably felt bad for her for acting like an asshole at the Boathouse and gave her a sympathy invite."

"Wait, hold on. When did they go to the Art Center Gala?" Ada asked. She could feel the warmth of her blood rising, but she tried to remain nonchalant so as not to alarm Sadie.

"Saturday night. It's all over Facebook and Instagram," Sadie said. "*Did you deactivate again?*" she asked, scrunching her face up. Ada was in the habit of deactivating all her social media accounts when she saw something that made her feel: (a) bad about herself, (b) angry she wasn't included or invited to something, or (c) irritated by a political rant.

"No, I guess I've been off it. I don't know," Ada replied. She felt dizzy and took a sip of wine, hoping it would help to relax her. She looked behind her to see if the kids were around to hear.

"Well, anyway, I don't think he's into her. Like I said, I think he just felt bad for her," Sadie said. *Was this envy Ada sensed? What was going on here,* she wondered. *Had Mack told Sadie that, or did she tell herself that to make herself feel better?*

"Really? Did he say that?" Ada asked.

"Say what?" Sadie asked, looking down and scrolling through her phone messages.

"That he invited Charlotte to the gala because he felt bad for her." It drove her nuts when Sadie stared at her phone when they talked.

"Um," Sadie said, still scrolling, moving her thumb up the iPhone screen. "Da, da. Dee, dee," she mumbled while scrolling. "Whatever." She lay her phone screen side down on the kitchen island. "I don't know. I can't think."

"I feel like you're hiding something, but okay." Ada smirked. She could tell Sadie was done talking about Mack, even though she was itching for more information and wanted to see the photos on social media of Charlotte all dressed up and hanging on Mack. Why hadn't he asked *her* to go, Ada wondered. Oh, right, because she's *married* . . . happily married? Which reminded her Ben was off to the gym.

"Ben is at the gym. "Do you guys want to stay for dinner?" Ada asked out of obligation. She desperately wanted Sadie to go home so she could investigate and scour the internet for photos.

"Sure, what are you cooking?" Sadie asked.

"That's a dumb question. You know I don't cook," Ada said.

"Oh, right," she said and paused. "What are we ordering in then?"

They both laughed and took a gulp of wine.

"I know we are at least ordering another bottle of wine!" Ada said.

She excused herself to go the bathroom and shut the door behind her. This was all too much. She didn't like how she felt, but she couldn't stop herself. Her resentment of Charlotte was palpable. She stared at herself in the mirror, backing up, farther and farther, until she edged her back onto the glass shower door. She heard it rumble as she backed into it. She slowly slid down the glass onto the black-and-white tile floor. She felt paralyzed.

Chapter Fifteen

MATCH POINT

CHARLOTTE

> MACK: *I want to see you.*

> CHARLOTTE: *Me too*

> MACK: *When?*

> CHARLOTTE: *Now?*

> MACK: *Great. Meet in the high school parking lot. I'm down the street.*

> CHARLOTTE: *See you in a bit. xx*

Finally! She was going to see Mack! Charlotte leapt up the stairs to her bedroom to shower and change. She had been gardening and hadn't shaved in a few days. Her suntanned legs were dry, like an alligator's skin. There was too much to do in too little time: armpit hair, legs, panty line, big toe. After applying gobs of body lotion and finding a matching pair of lacy white underwear and bra, she was ready to go.

Mack sat in the driver's seat with a baseball hat in the lower lot of the high school. The kids in the summer camp were outside on the playground.

Charlotte feared someone like Scarlett Crane would arrive to pick up her kid. She pulled her Audi up next to Mack.

"Hi, stranger," she said, rolling down her window.

"Hey. My car or yours?"

"Yours is fine," Charlotte replied. She quickly checked for pepper in her teeth and eye crusts in the rearview mirror before getting out of the car. She wore a long white sheer cotton dress that was a cross between a nightgown and a beach cover-up. She looked ethereal and whimsical, just how Mack made her feel.

Mack's car was sweltering hot. The digital thermometer on the dashboard read eighty-five degrees. He had all the windows down and no air conditioning. He looked disheveled and unkempt.

"I can't take this," Mack said. His vulnerability was a turn-on. He put his hand in between Charlotte's thighs and leaned forward over the center console. She moved closer to his face, feeling the warmth of his breath, and they kissed, deeply.

"I think about you," Mack whispered in her ear. "I know I shouldn't, but I can't help it."

"I do too," Charlotte whispered. She closed her eyes to take in the moment.

"What are we going to do?" Mack asked.

"This," she said. She took his hand and put it on her breast inside her dress. "Just this." With that, they proceeded to kiss more passionately and moved into the back seat. Charlotte pushed aside Mack's fishing tackle box and golf clubs and lay down on her back. She thrust into Mack. He thrust back. With two fingers, he pushed her lacy white underwear aside and rubbed her clit slowly in circles. She was wet with anticipation. Charlotte pumped her hips up and down, breathing heavily as their tongues whirled. Mack fumbled with his belt, the buckle making a clinking sound. He unzipped his pants and slid inside her. They moved together in sync, a slow dance.

Time passed, and Charlotte eventually moved to the front seat, straightening out her dress and smoothing down her matted hair, while Mack zipped up his pants.

"Shit!" he exhaled. "That was nice." His eyes widened, looking at her in disbelief. "This is nuts."

"Yes," she said, laughing. It was the first time Charlotte had laughed in days. *I'm going to hell,* she thought. Karma was a bitch, but she was willing to gamble.

The next day, Charlotte had tennis lessons with Coach Sean at the golf club. Sadie, Ada, and Charlotte were getting dressed in the locker room. Ada sat on a bench tying her Adidas, and Sadie sprayed her underarms with the Sure deodorant provided for members only on the freshly cleaned sink. That was one of the great things about the club: the bathroom perks, like the mouthwash, tampons, and hairspray. It was like a free trip to CVS. Well, with the hefty initiation fee and annual dues thereafter, it wasn't exactly free. But it felt nice, and smelled lovely too, with freshly picked lavender and hyacinths in square glass vases along the marble countertops. In the sitting area, crushed rose potpourri sat next to the plush cream-colored armchairs. Charlotte recalled her small studio apartment on the Upper East Side of Manhattan. She thought it would have been a lot nicer to just live in the club's locker room for $1,200/month.

"Who is our fourth today?" Ada asked, since it was always rotating. Sometimes Scarlett Crane joined in, and other times it was Mitzy Pierce.

"Caroline Wall," said Sadie, widening her eyes.

Caroline Wall, in short, was perfect. She had the perfect house, perfect husband, perfect children, perfect job, and perfect body. Her life was just perfect. Well, at least from the outside. Every woman in Falmouth wanted to be Caroline Wall. On some level, she was annoying because she was able to have a successful full-time career as an architect while simultaneously raising three young, well-behaved children. Plus, she found time to work out and go on date nights with her hot husband—featured on Instagram with lots of heart emojis and #blessed. But on another level, one couldn't hate Caroline Wall because she was also kind, generous, and thoughtful.

"Caroline Wall is coming?" Charlotte asked. "When did that happen?" She was annoyed. She didn't feel like putting on a front. And she didn't want to pose for selfies that would go on Caroline's page with something like "Good times, Good friends!" next to them.

"Scarlett texted me last night that she had a 'thing,' so she got Caroline to sub. Why?" Sadie asked.

"No reason. I guess I just don't want to feel like a fat shit when I see her," Charlotte said. "But, whatever. I'll deal. Who wants an Arnold Palmer? I'm going up to the bar."

"Me!" chimed Ada.

"I feel like I need something stiffer," Sadie said. "Grab me a Sauvignon blanc. I'm going to dump it in my Yeti."

"That's, like, intervention-worthy," Charlotte said, laughing.

"Um, you're the last person who should be talking about an intervention," Sadie said. "Miss Rough and Tumble at the Boathouse. You're lucky no one buys the *Enterprise* anymore and didn't see you in the police logs." Sadie smoothed her hands over the front of her top knot.

"Suck a bag of dicks," Charlotte laughed. "And people do read the police logs!" she called back, closing the heavy bathroom door behind her.

"We are going to get kicked out of here," Ada said.

"Whatever. No one is here," Sadie said. "Let's go out to the courts so we're not late. I told Caroline we'd meet her there."

The women headed outside onto the U-shaped driveway paved in bleached, crushed clamshells overlooking the Vineyard Sound. It was a bright, sunny day, and the warmth from the sun made the hairs on Sadie's arms stand up after having been in the cold air conditioning of the club.

Caroline emerged from her black Range Rover wearing a visor, a navy-blue tennis skirt, and a stretchy tank top. Caroline was petite. A size 4 and some change, but at five foot seven, she wasn't short. Her long, tanned legs and toned arms perfectly complemented her highlighted blonde hair and big brown eyes, like saucers. She waved using her tennis racket. Sadie waved back. Charlotte walked down the hill to join, holding two paper coffee cups.

"This one is yours," Charlotte said to Sadie.

"Oooh. Is that coffee? I definitely need one," Caroline said. Her lips were painted a shade of coral pink.

"Yes," Sadie fibbed. "So tired. You want us to get you one inside?"

"Nah, that's okay," Caroline said. "I probably shouldn't have another cup anyway. I brought my coconut water."

"How are you guys doing?" Caroline asked, smiling. "I haven't seen you in a while! The pics of the kids are so adorable!"

"Thanks," Ada said. "Yours too. Is DJ playing rec soccer now or is he traveling?"

"Oh my gosh, I can't even," Caroline said. "He does travel soccer, but he also does travel hockey, so Dave and I live out of the car driving him around to games and practices in the evening."

"I told Henry he can't play hockey," Ada said. "I just can't deal with the expense of the equipment and all those games. It would kill me. I don't know how you do it."

Charlotte suspected that Ada said this to be nice, even though she knew for a fact how Caroline did it. She had two nannies: one for the twin girls to take them to Tumble Time for gymnastics, and one for DJ to drive him to and from youth soccer and hockey games. The nannies were retired women in their sixties living in Falmouth who worked for the Walls five days a week.

"I have two nannies!" Caroline said, calling out the elephant in the room. The Walls lived in a $3.2 million waterfront home in Saconesset Hills, West Falmouth, a gated community during the summer months with private beach rights. She graduated from Amherst College, where she met her husband of ten years, David Wall, and they had twin girls, Alexa and Ariel, and a boy, David Jr., who they called DJ.

"True." Ada laughed. "I need to get a nanny."

"No, you don't," Charlotte said, rolling her eyes and taking a sip of her Arnold Palmer. Charlotte picked up her racket and headed down to the tennis courts, where Coach Sean stood with a clipboard.

"I guess we should go down," Ada said.

Coach Sean was a notorious flirt. It was rumored he had affairs with several of the women at the club, whom he coached privately, but somehow, he was able to keep his job. He was like Patrick Swayze in *Dirty Dancing*, minus the black soft dance shoes and chino pants. He had longish brown hair that sprung out on the sides of his tennis visor, and a deep tan from being outside all day.

"Well, well, well," Coach Sean said. "Look who we have here today: the Witches of Eastwick."

"You wish," Sadie said, giggling.

"So, what are we working on today?" Sean asked. "Round robin? Backhands? Serves?"

"Let's do doubles," Charlotte said, walking to the other side of the court, her blonde ponytail swinging back and forth like a pendulum.

"Sounds good to me," Caroline said.

Charlotte and Caroline paired up on one side with Ada and Sadie on the other. They began to volley.

"Argh!" Charlotte wailed, slapping the ball across the court with her racket like in Wimbledon. She had the awful habit of grunting loudly when she hit the ball. It sounded like half orgasm, half torture.

"Nice, Char!" Sean yelled from the sideline. "Ada, watch your backhand!"

Ada leapt to get the ball, doing a backhand, and fell to the ground, laughing.

"I suck!" she yelled.

"And that's a bad thing?" Sean joked.

"Oh my God!" Sadie said, smiling. "Sean, you're disgusting!"

Caroline hit the ball with precision and grace, running up to it like a fawn doing a springtime dance.

"Way to go, Caroline," Sean said. "You should join us more often!"

Caroline gave him a nod of acknowledgment. "Hope to!"

The doubles match went on for about an hour, and then it was time to go. Coach Sean gave some individual pointers to each of the women and did a few practice exercises where he'd hit the ball from one side of the court, and the women had to circulate and hit it from the other.

"You guys want to grab lunch here?" Sadie asked.

"Sure," Charlotte said.

"I'm dying for the bog salad," Ada said.

"Oh, I wish I could, guys," Caroline frowned, "but I made lunch plans."

"Oh, who are you going to lunch with?" Sadie asked. "She can join."

"Oh, um, it's just this client of mine. He's new in town and looking to buy a house."

Charlotte heard the words "new in town" and "he" and couldn't help but wonder if it was Mack.

"Oh, really? What's his deal?" Charlotte asked.

"I don't know," Caroline said. "I think he's recently divorced and maybe spent summers here? He is looking to build somewhere out by the Cape Codder Hotel on Sippewissett," she said. "He called me and wanted to go over some architectural plans."

Charlotte recalled Mack talking about plans of building near the Sippewissett marsh and Wood Neck Beach. She thought of mentioning his name but didn't want to sound any alarm bells or encourage a line of questioning, especially since she was trying to keep her feelings for Mack on the down low.

"Where are you going to lunch?" Sadie asked.

"Probably Pickle Jar," Caroline said. "They have the most amazing fresh edamame crispy tofu salad!" Caroline looked at her phone. "Ooh, I gotta run, ladies," she said. "So good to see you! Are you guys doing the house tour?"

"When is that again?" Charlotte asked.

"Next month," Caroline replied. "I somehow got sucked into having my house in it again this year."

"Well hopefully we will see you before then!" Sadie said.

"With my schedule, doubtful," Caroline said. "Plus, Dave and I are going to Turks and Caicos for our anniversary in a couple weeks."

"Oh, happy anniversary!" Ada said. "Which one is it?"

"Ten years," Caroline said. "I can't believe it."

"I remember that anniversary," said Sadie. "I think we had dinner at the 99 or something."

"Yeah, no Turks and Caicos for me," Ada said.

"Oh, stop," Caroline said. "You both look amazing. I have to run. But let's try to get drinks sometime soon!" She hopped into her Range Rover, texting on her phone. Charlotte wondered if she was texting Mack and thought to send him a text herself. They were supposed to meet up for a drink or lunch this week. Maybe she'd drop Caroline's name to see how he reacted.

Chapter Sixteen

FORBIDDEN FRUIT

ADA

Ada sat at her desk and swiveled from one side to the other in her chair. She couldn't concentrate, wondering if anything had happened between Mack and Charlotte at the Art Center Gala. She wished Sadie hadn't told her about it. This was why she was off social media. This kind of social crap sent her reeling. Charlotte, of course, was so urbane and funny, so why wouldn't Mack be interested in her? *How could I compete?* she thought.

The phone rang, startling her. It was Ben.

"Hey, hon," Ben said. "I'm going to hit a bucket of balls with the guys and then grab a chowder." Ada started to grind her teeth.

"Sounds good," she replied. "I guess I'll just have dinner with the kids or maybe get takeout from Quick's Hole or something."

"Are you mad? I don't have to go," Ben said.

This was a trap. If Ada said that she was in fact mad that he was going, then she would seem like a nag who didn't want her husband to enjoy his life. She was left with no choice but to lie and pretend she didn't care.

"No, go have fun," she said. "I'll see you when you get home."

She hung up the phone and shook her head. Was he actually going to hit a bucket of balls with the guys? Should she snoop around and ask some of the wives if they knew about this plan, or was that being crazy? Why did she think he was cheating? Well, maybe, because she was cheating.

Then Ada had an idea. She would send Mack one of the boudoir photos she had taken a few months back to reignite her sex life with Ben. She'd read about doing this in one of her women's magazines and hired a local photographer who specialized in boudoir photography to come to her house one evening when Ben and the kids were out. Ada scrolled through her phone and found a suggestive, sultry one of her in black fishnets and a corset, lying on her back on the bed with her breasts spilling over. Yes, this was the one she was going to send to Mack.

After hitting "send," she immediately felt impending dread and embarrassment. If she didn't hear back from him in one minute—okay five—then she would have to leave work and go for a run or something to get the butterflies in her stomach to stop fluttering about. She looked down at her phone, waiting, and she saw the bubbles. He was texting!

Wow. Beautiful. I'm speechless.

Ada wasn't sure how to respond, so she just sent an emoji of the abashed smiley face. Her efforts to woo Mack paid off because he quickly responded that he wanted to see her and asked if they could meet on the beach for a walk later that evening. She'd have to figure out a way to get out of the house without Ben knowing, so she scurried to find a sitter to agree to come by for a few hours at sunset.

Ada knew what she was doing was wrong, but she liked the feeling of it. Forbidden fruit always tasted the best. When she got to the beach, Mack was waiting on the jetty, looking over the sunset. She walked toward him and grabbed his shoulders.

"Boo!" she said. He shrieked.

"Shit! You scared me!" Mack stood up and gave her a kiss on the lips.

He tasted like salt water and beer. They embraced for a moment, and he put his hand on the small of her back, then moved his fingers about, rubbing her spine up and down. She melted into his hands.

"Mmmmm, that feels so good," Ada said.

"I can do other things to make you feel good."

"Oh yeah? Like what?" Ada asked. The chemistry was undeniable and charged.

"Like this," he said, sliding his hand down the front of her white jeans.

Ada and Mack lay on a towel on the beach, side by side, looking up at the sky. It was early evening, and the air had cooled. Her underwear was wet from when he had touched her on the jetty, and she wanted more.

"So, what are we doing?" Mack said.

"Having a drink?" Ada said.

"I mean, are you into this, or me, or?" Mack asked. It was interesting how someone so confident could suddenly seem insecure and need affirmation.

"Obviously, or I wouldn't be here," said Ada. "I mean, I don't know. What do you think is going on?"

"I think I love being with you," Mack said, grabbing her thigh and rubbing it. A seagull flew overhead and dipped down close to them, searching for food.

"I love being with you too," Ada laughed. She put her hands over her mouth, holding the edges of her sweater in the finger loops. He made her feel like she was in high school, young and foolish. "I don't know! I mean, I like you! But I shouldn't!"

"It's okay. I didn't mean to put you on the spot," Mack said. He leaned in to kiss her. He smelled of pine and aftershave. She wanted to devour him.

"No, I know this must be confusing for you," she said. "I'm sorry."

"Don't be sorry," he said. He turned on his side, gazed at her, and pushed a strand of her long black hair over her shoulder, gently. "I just like being with you. I'm enjoying you. Us."

"Are we an *us*?" Ada asked, turning toward him, her head on her arm in the sand.

"Maybe," Mack said. "If you want us to be an us."

Of course, she wanted to be an us! Ada wanted to yell "yes" and dance around in the sand! But she was married. And what if Ben found out? Would everyone think she was a terrible mother and wife? Would she have to move? Would Sadie be pissed? She knew Sadie had some residual feelings for him and that they'd made out that night after the Lawsons' party. But Mack assured Ada it was just a drunken kiss for old times' sake.

"I do want that," she said. Ada dipped her fingers into the back of his jeans, feeling where his back ended and his ass began.

The sun began to set. The sky burst with shades of yellow, orange, and pink, like a gallon of sherbet ice cream. The white sand was cold in between her toes. Lady's slipper shells lined the edge of the shore with clumps of dark brown seaweed, frayed and course, like crazy hair. She turned onto her back, looking up at the sky, holding hands with Mack. *They were an "us,"* she thought. Perhaps this was the happily ever after she was hoping for.

Chapter Seventeen

IT ISN'T FAIR

SADIE

Sadie pulled her minivan into the dirt parking lot off Route 151 for the Barnstable County Fair. The fair came around once a year for two weekends at the end of July. It was a tradition for Sadie and Chip to take the kids. They all looked forward to it with great anticipation when the children were little. Inevitably, Sadie always felt remorse once she was inside, as it was hot, dirty, expensive, and one of the children consistently had a sugar meltdown.

"Why are you parking here?" Chip asked. "We can park for free and walk if you turn down Currier Road."

"I don't want to walk," Charlie chimed in from the back seat. "I have a blister from running in my new Crocs."

"It's only ten dollars, Chip," Sadie said curtly. "I'll give you the money, okay? It's boiling hot out."

"It's not about the money," Chip sighed.

"What's it about then?" Sadie barked, staring at the gray stubble growing on Chip's face that she loathed. She didn't know which she loathed more: his stubble or his face.

"It's about the fact that you are just a spendthrift."

"So, it *is* about money?" Sadie said, parking the car where the man flashing yellow traffic control signals stood. "And I'd hardly call me a spendthrift. You're just *cheap*." She threw the keys in her large Louis Vuitton tote bag.

"Oh, so eight bucks for a chai skim nonfat-whatever latte each day is not wasteful? And you used to do your own hair and nails. Now you spend two hundred bucks every three weeks on foils and forty a week on nails." Sadie gave him a death stare. "It adds up, is all I'm saying." Chip shrugged.

"Wow. Just wow," Sadie replied, opening her door. "Kids, put your phones down. No phones at the fair."

"But I told Lilly I'd meet up with her! How will I find her?" Tina whined.

"Fine, bring your phone," Sadie said. She didn't have the energy for discipline. In fact, she rarely did. She was too tired to fight with both the kids and Chip. She wondered if this was why they didn't seem to respect her. Chip walked ahead with Charlie who was overdramatically limping from his blister. They stopped at the bottleneck and entrance to the fair with about twenty families in front of them. Country music blared from the Monster Truck show, and a dolphin trainer from Sea World yelled into a megaphone for someone to toss a piece of fish into the pool.

Once they reached the entrance, Chip paid the exorbitant entry fee of $15 per person—on top of the $10 parking fee—just to enter the park, which didn't include tickets for rides and games. They walked through looking up at all the moving rides and lights. There were the usual suspects: the Zipper, the Gravitron, the pirate ship, the Scrambler, the Ferris wheel, and the Yo-Yo.

"Should we get wrist bracelets?" Sadie asked.

"Spendthrift?" Chip joked. "Let's just buy individual tickets. I won't go on the rides."

"Oh my God," Sadie said, shaking her head. She got in line for tickets.

"Mom, can I play balloon darts?" Tina asked. "I want to get that giant stuffed hamster."

"You don't get the hamster unless you play like ten times and keep upgrading your prize." Sadie was proud of the fact that she knew the ins and outs of the system and couldn't be duped.

"Puh-leeeze?" Tina begged, pulling at her wrist to veer off to the games section of the park.

"Fine. Here's five bucks." She handed her a crumpled five-dollar bill from the back pocket of her dark blue Citizens jeans. It was change from the latte at Starbucks earlier in the day.

"Why does she get to play?" Charlie balked. "I want to play too!"

"No one said you can't," Sadie said, handing him a five also. A trip to the beer tent was in order.

"How many games are we going to play?" Chip asked.

"We just got here!"

"I'm just wondering because I might go grab some fried dough. Jeez," Chip huffed.

Sadie was so tired of the bickering, but she couldn't stop herself.

"Do you really need it right now? Can't it wait?"

"I guess so," Chip said, pouting and walking away to look at the pop-a-shot basketball game. *What a baby*, Sadie thought. He was so emotional and extra. Like, who cared about fried dough, especially when he was looking pretty doughy himself. Sadie's thoughts trailed off to Mack and his tight abs. He had a solid six-pack, amazing for a man in his late forties. She recalled wrapping her hands around his firm waist as they kissed on the dock. She wanted to be remorseful, but she wasn't. That's what Chip got for taking her for granted. *Spendthrift.* What a joke.

"Look, Mom! I got a Pokémon stuffy!" Charlie shouted, limping toward her holding the yellow stuffed animal in the air.

"That's awesome, Char!" Sadie said, giving him a hug. She looked over at Tina, who appeared forlorn holding a small, limp furry snake stuffy.

"No hamster?" Sadie asked.

"Shut it," Tina said, staring down at her phone.

"Is Lilly here?"

"Dunno. Haven't heard from her yet," Tina mumbled. She put the phone in her back pocket and tucked her long, silky blonde hair behind her right ear. She was getting so grown up. All legs in those jean cutoff shorts and cute little A-cups on her petite upper body. Sadie remembered when she wore tap shoes and striped leggings in first grade. How time flew.

Sadie, Chip, Tina, and Charlie got in the back of the line to the Polar Express, one of the most popular rides at the fair. The line stretched past five game booths: balloon darts, kiddie magnet fishing, horse racing, and water shooting. Music blasted and riders screamed and screeched as a man with a greasy ponytail, a red face, and crooked teeth stood by its side, jiggering the lever up and down, adjusting the speed. It circled around five or six times, then came to a slow stop before circling again backward at rapid speed.

"I smell roasted peanuts and cotton candy," Tina said. "Can we get some?"

"Your dad wants to get fried dough first," Sadie said, looking over at Chip. He was on his phone, scrolling through his emails.

As they got on the ride, Sadie got in first, as this was the seat for the "larger passenger." She thought back to high school, when she and Charlotte went to the fair and argued over who was the larger person and who should be able to sit on the outside of the ride. Charlotte won. She was the smaller rider. Sadie wondered how Charlotte was doing and if she had spoken to Mack since the Gala. She was still kind of irked about the gossip and that Charlotte wouldn't tell her the entire story. She thought they were best friends, and now this guy was getting in the middle of it . . . her guy, her old boyfriend. So much for girl code. *Did girl code exist when you're married though,* she wondered. Yet, Charlotte was married too! Well, sort of, if you counted John as a person. He was more of a shadow.

The Polar Express started up. Faster and faster, round and round it went. "EEEEEEEEEE!" Sadie screamed over the Taylor Swift music blaring from the speakers. "WHAAAAHHHH!" She held on to the metal bar in front of her with all her might so as not to crush Tina. "Holy SHIIIIIIT!"

The ride came to a slow stop. When it was over, Chip looked back at Sadie from the seat in front of hers. His hair was standing on end, and he was smiling wide. He looked happy for a change.

"You sure had fun!" he said. "I haven't heard you scream like that since we went camping in the Adirondacks and found that black bear in our tent!"

Sadie's first instinct was to be angry that Chip suggested she was no longer fun or that they didn't have sex. In fact, she had been the last one to initiate, as far as she remembered. But she was trying to change that instinct. Her therapist told her in order to work on their marriage, she had to come from a place of forgiveness and friendship, as opposed to resentment and acrimony. Sadie recalled the trip to the Adirondacks and was sad that they didn't do stuff like camping anymore. Everything had become so regimented and routine. And she couldn't even recall the last time Chip got her to scream in bed. Weekends were about getting the kids to sports, watching football, cleaning, and having dinner with friends. They had lost the "we" in their marriage. They had lost the friendship.

She suddenly missed him.

"Now can we get fried dough?" Chip asked.

And then she didn't. Tina grabbed at her mom's wrist and started to sway back and forth like she was going to faint. Suddenly, she jerked her head to the side and threw up all over Sadie's shirt.

"OH MY GOD!" Sadie screeched, jumping backward. "Are you okay?"

Tina's eyes watered and she started to vomit on the dirt.

"I'm so nauseous from that ride! We need to go home. This is super embarrassing," she cried.

Sadie ran to the lemonade stand and grabbed some napkins, wiping the pink and red vomit from her shirt. She spotted a young boy off to the left, clutching a bag with goldfish in it. He'd just won them in a game. The bag appeared to have a hole in the bottom of it and was leaking water. The boy lifted the bag to eye level to see how he could repair the hole, and it suddenly burst open, gushing water, with the fish falling to the ground. The fish flopped over to Sadie's Gucci sneaker.

"Need a hand with that?" a male voice said.

Sadie peered up, wiping the throw up off her shirt as the fish bounced around on her sneaker.

Yes, she did need a hand. In fact, she needed more than that.

She was a fish out of water, gasping for air.

She couldn't breathe.

Chapter Eighteen

SEX AND BLUE LOBSTERS

CHARLOTTE

When the Barnstable Fair ends and the rides are packed away, Cape Codders know the summer is half over. The best months of the year are seeping away, and time is of the essence. Charlotte hoped to spend as much time as she could with Mack. She was more than excited when he invited her to see his nana's cottage in Hospital Cove, one of the more affluent sections of Cataumet. It was set on a cove off Bassetts Island, with a long "finger" dock running from the bottom of a bluff out into the cove. The cottage was traditional gray shingles and shutters painted captain's blue with white trim. Hydrangeas and pink roses on a trellis added pops of color about the lawn as Charlotte and Mack walked up the stone path to the front door.

"This is lovely," Charlotte said.

"Thank you," Mack replied. "It's been in the family for nearly a century. I come here every now and then to clear my head, find some solitude. I only share it with special people." He squeezed her hand.

Charlotte blushed and gave him a slight kiss on the cheek. John was out of town, so she and Mack made a last-minute plan to get together, and he had suggested the cottage.

Mack unpacked the canvas tote on the kitchen island countertop: grape tomatoes, Manchego cheese, artichoke hearts, olives, salami, prosciutto, and a bottle of Sancerre. They stopped at the North Falmouth Cheese Shop on the way there, when Charlotte explained to Mack that the sign out front was supposed to be upside down. It was painted that way by accident, but the owners liked it, and it was their signature signage on Route 28. Mack riffled through the cabinets looking for a cutting board.

"Need help?" Charlotte asked. Not that she knew where Nana kept her cutting boards, or anything for that matter. She slowly walked around the cottage barefoot, peering at old photos and the spines of vintage books that lined the shelves on the wall: Plato, Freud, Camus, and Socrates.

"Was your nana into philosophy?"

"Philosophy?" Mack asked, still crouched on the floor looking through pots and pans.

"Her books. She has a lot of philosophers."

"Oh," Mack laughed. "Yeah, I guess you could say Nana was philosophical. She loved a good debate. She was a real spitfire. I think, in some ways, that's why I like you. You remind me of her," he said, now standing and opening the cheeses.

"Really?" Charlotte asked, smiling. "Well, I guess that's a huge compliment."

"It is," Mack said. "Few women compare to my nana. She taught me to swim and play tennis. She is—I mean, *was*, an amazing athlete. See? I can't even get it in my head that she's gone . . ."

"Oh, Mack, I'm so sorry," Charlotte said, going in for a hug. She liked being able to nurture him, to mother him, especially since she didn't have any kids of her own.

"Thanks," Mack said, his eyes welling up. "Can I get you a drink?"

"I'll have some Sancerre."

Mack reached in the cabinet for a petite wineglass. He grabbed a cloth by the sink to wipe the dust from it. "Can't have my girl drinking from a dusty stem," he said.

Charlotte warmed to *his girl*. "Aw, chivalry isn't dead," she replied.

They walked to the couch, decorated with bursting pink peonies and green leaves, and sunk into it next to each other with a giggle. Mack put his arm over her shoulder and reached in for a long, slow kiss. His plump lips were like soft pillows. She loved kissing him. Charlotte couldn't remember the last time she had a real make-out session with John. Sure, they'd kiss on the lips goodnight or hello, but not like a real kiss, a French kiss.

"This is nice," Charlotte said.

"It is," Mack said, pushing her hair away from her face. "I love this tiny freckle on the end of your nose." He touched it gently.

Charlotte hated that freckle. She thought it looked like she had a spot of dirt on the tip of it and worked hard to conceal it, an imperfection on her otherwise porcelain skin. She recalled her modeling days when the makeup artists would make every effort to conceal that same freckle for the photo shoots.

"Well, that makes one of us," she said.

"No, stop. You're beautiful. You must know that."

"I don't know," Charlotte mumbled. She was not good at accepting compliments. "So should we go swimming?" she asked, changing the subject.

"You just want to get me naked," he said, poking her in the ribs. She laughed.

"Well, that too. But I'm hot!"

"Well, we can't have that! Let's go!" Mack rose from the couch while taking off his Menemsha Blues T-shirt. His back was smooth and in the perfect shape of a V, and he looked as if he'd played football. He turned to her. "Need help taking that off?" he asked.

"I think I got it," Charlotte said, raising her arms over her head to remove her floral sundress. "I brought a bathing suit just in case." She walked to her bag in a Cosabella white thong and lace bra, which she'd made sure to match. Charlotte had ordered that special lingerie from La Perla. So what if it cost more than $200 for the set; she knew he'd probably seen a lot of expensive lingerie, most of it ending up on the floor.

Charlotte wondered if Mack was a player. Was she hoodwinked with all this sweet talk and good looks? Why had he gotten a divorce if he was so perfect? She couldn't imagine anyone leaving him. What was the story? She wanted to get to the bottom of it, but she refrained from asking too early on. Maybe she could get bits and pieces of information as the night wore on.

"I don't think you should put on your bikini," he said.

"Oh, no?" she chortled.

"I'm feeling sort of tired. How about we jump in the shower instead to cool off and maybe lie down for a nap?"

"A shower? Well, I guess that's sort of swimming."

"It's in the water?" He shrugged.

They scampered to the bedroom and pushed open the white wooden door that had one of those old black latches that you push down on with your thumb to open. The room smelled of cedar, and the queen-sized bed looked tiny with a thin white crocheted blanket covering it. It was like a doll's bed. Charlotte guessed Nana wasn't a big fan of down duvets and pillows in her summer cottage. And there was no air conditioner in sight, just a small fan resting on the bedside table next to a box of tissues and an oil lamp. On the other side of the room was a white wicker rocking chair with an antique doll sitting in it. Charlotte wondered if this was the guest room, a child's room, or perhaps Nana's room. She remembered when her grandmother was lonely after her grandfather died and sewed herself a doll made of stockings to keep her company. Maybe this had been Nana's companion doll.

Mack walked into the narrow bathroom to turn on the shower. It was an antique claw-foot tub with a big showerhead hanging from a tall pipe. And the toilet had one of those hanging metal strings to flush it. She felt like she was in another century. She pulled the string.

"What are you doing?" Mack laughed.

"Sorry, I had to test it. That's so crazy, the string!"

"Get in here," Mack said, reaching for her to join him in the shower.

The water spilled over his head, making an awkward part in his hair that was pasted down over his face. He looked completely different with flat hair in a middle part. His eyes were closed, and he spit water out as it rushed down his face. She stood in front of him with drops of water splashing onto her.

"Your turn," he said, scooching around her, holding her hips.

Charlotte was conscious of the fact that he was staring at her naked body under the shower head. She sucked in her stomach and tried to look skinny as the water rushed over her. She imagined a shower scene in a movie and tried to play the part. Mack reached for the Oil of Olay bar of soap. It smelled floral, like roses, and he glided it over her stomach and arms.

When they got out of the shower, they toweled off and jumped on the bed. The mattress was old and rubbery without any support. She imagined she'd have a terrible backache after sleeping there.

"Whoa, this is like a carnival ride," she said, sinking back onto the stiff blanket.

"Let's get in," he said, turning down the sheets. She maneuvered herself under the blanket and sheets. They smelled untouched and musty and felt rough on her skin.

"When's the last time you were here?" she asked.

"In this bed?" Mack asked.

"No! The cottage," she said.

"God, not for a long time. Seems like it's been ages." He rolled over on his side and reached for her. They kissed again. It was quiet, with only the sound of the bees outside the window and the cicadas stirring in the summer heat. The sun was high, the grass dry. It was Cape Cod in July, not a care in the world.

As Charlotte pulled into her driveway, she went from the feeling of elation to pure dread. She spotted John's silver Audi and knew he was home from his trip. It occurred to her she'd have to cover her bases as to where she had been last night, since she hadn't bothered to text him back. But she was so used to his indifference that she didn't even try to find an alibi.

"Hey," Charlotte said, closing the front door behind her. Seated on a bar stool at the kitchen island, John looked up from the *Wall Street Journal* he was reading. He wore the navy-blue Armani suit they'd bought together at Nieman Marcus.

"Hi," he said, biting into a pistachio. He had a bowl of them by his side.

"Did you just get home?" she asked.

"About an hour ago." He jettisoned the pistachio shell across the counter, and it fell on the floor next to a few others.

"How was it?" she called out, on her way to the mud room with her bag. She glanced at herself in the mirror to see if she had that "freshly fucked" look.

"Great," he said.

"Good." She walked back into the kitchen, picked up the pistachio shell, and stared at John who was now back reading the paper. He reached for his tumbler of bourbon, took a sip, and set it on the marble countertop. John didn't bother to ask Charlotte how her day was or elaborate on his own travels, but she didn't feel like trying anymore. She left the room even though she hadn't seen him in four days.

Charlotte shuffled up the carpeted steps to her bedroom. It had essentially become her own bedroom, as John often slept on the couch or out. He kept a separate room in the house for his clothes and had his own bathroom for privacy. John and Charlotte never spoke about bathroom habits. Any mention of uncouth business was offensive. "Women shouldn't speak like that," he said. John grew up in a patriarchal home with a strong matriarch. His mother didn't curse, she was intentionally affable, and she played servant to her boys and her husband, always coiffed and in lipstick. Her mother-in-law didn't have any daughters, so Charlotte was her "first," even though it was by law. "She's my first daughter!" she'd say introducing Charlotte to her friends at the Brookline Country Club. This was the oldest country club in Boston, and John's parents had been members there for about fifteen years. The wait list was long, despite the egregious membership dues. Charlotte hadn't been impressed, but John liked to wear garments with their emblem and take his clients there as a shoo-in deal.

Charlotte lay her Vera Bradley overnight bag on the bed. She began to unpack her clothes when a whiff of Nana's house filled the air. She was going to throw her T-shirt in the wash but instead held it close to her nose. She carefully folded the shirt in half, and then three quarters, and put it in the bottom of her dresser drawer under her workout pants.

"What's for dinner?" John called up.

"I hadn't thought about it."

"Do you want to go out?" John asked.

She didn't want to go out. She wanted to ride the high of her night with Mack, not sit in awkward silence with her husband.

"Sure," she said, scrunching her face and rolling her eyes. Charlotte walked over to her closet and moved the hangers one by one to the right, selecting a shirt. Even though she and John were rarely intimate, she still wanted him to find her attractive. She settled on a black silk tank top and sprayed some of her Gucci perfume on her wrist and hair.

Sitting at the sushi bar, John and Charlotte decided to share an order of fried dumplings, followed by spicy tuna rolls, crab rangoon, and yellowtail sashimi. They sat right in front of the sushi chef, who was busy unwrapping raw fish from Saran wrap. The overhead lighting was severe and bright, lacking ambiance, and she and John were the only two on this side of the bar.

"We haven't been here in forever," John said.

"I know. Why don't we come here more often?"

"Well, I've been out of town a lot lately, I guess."

"Oh really? I didn't notice," Charlotte balked.

"Ha-ha," he said.

The air was heavy. Charlotte looked off to her right at the pristine ten-gallon fish tank filled with brightly colored angelfish in yellow and royal blue hues. There were a few clown fish and a tiny blue lobster creeping along the pebbles on the tank's floor. This was a crawfish, she recalled. She tried to buy one as a pet at Petco and was warned that they were super aggressive and could potentially eat all the other fish in the tank. John reminded her of a crawfish.

"You're lucky, you know," Charlotte said, clawing for a fight, like the blue lobster.

"Oh yeah? Why's that?"

"Because I don't ever put any kind of leash on you; you have free reign to do whatever you want, no questions asked." She was looking for a sense of gratitude and appreciation. Her love tank was empty.

"That's the way it should be," John said. The vein in his temple started to protrude and turn blue. "And if it weren't, I wouldn't be with you."

This stung. *So, he was only with me because he didn't have to be with me?*

"Wow, noted," Charlotte said, holding back tears.

"Don't shit-stir, Charlotte. I'm not in the mood. I'm tired, and I'll walk out right now."

Charlotte wanted to tell him off, but she thought better of it, especially since she had been having sex with Mack just hours earlier. Part of her strategy embarking on this conversation was to get a sense if there was anything left between them. She was looking for a sign, any sign that he was the one, and it didn't happen. Instead, John was the crawfish.

"Fine," she said. "Sorry . . ." She took a gulp of her drink and stared off into the distance. There wasn't much left to say, other than that she wanted a divorce. She was done with being treated this way. He didn't appreciate her, and this was especially clear when she was with Mack. He doted on her and made her feel special and sexy. John never tried to hold her hand or caress her back. He made her feel invisible. She was his paperweight. Or maybe it was the other way around.

Chapter Nineteen

EVERY ROSE HAS ITS THORNS

SADIE

"Your turn," Sadie said. She reached for new Scrabble letters from the maroon felt drawstring pouch.

"Xi? That is not a word!" Mack chuckled.

"Sure, it is! Look it up."

"Where do you come up with these? This is not Words with Friends; it's old-school Scrabble, and you're making my nana turn over in her grave right now using her board for crappy nouveau made-up words!"

Mack and Sadie sat in Nana's cottage at the kitchen table. There was a bottle of wine between them, and their legs intertwined under the white wicker table. They'd arrived just hours earlier when a huge rainstorm passed over Hospital Cove and thwarted their plans to kayak across the way to Bassetts Island for a picnic.

"I can't believe your nana died. She seemed so healthy and active! The last time I saw her, she was playing tennis at the club. She came over to say hi, as always, and she looked amazing."

"It is really unbelievable," Mack said, shaking his head. "I mean, it was sudden, you know? I actually can't really talk about it." Mack fumbled with his letters. Sadie squeezed his hand.

"Oh, I got you with this one: inverted. Triple word score and triple letter score on the V!" Mack stood up from his chair doing a victory dance like an NFL player in the end zone.

"You suck!"

"No, *you suck*." Mack laughed, pulling her face toward his jock.

"I did!"

"True, and I can't stop thinking about it. I want more."

"Well, you don't have to ask," she said.

"Should we abandon Scrabble for now? I can think of a four-letter word . . ."

They dashed toward the bedroom, jumping in the sheets that had just been washed from when Charlotte stayed over. They laughed and rolled around like ferrets, or puppies at play, and ripped at each other's clothes. Sadie reached down and fiddled around awkwardly for Mack's belt buckle. It was so much more exciting than things at home with Chip, when she'd just get into the bed already naked, or they'd discuss whether or not they should have sex. She reached down his boxer shorts and grabbed hold. It was hard and thick. Then she slowly made her way down his chest with tiny kisses, gently, until she put her mouth on him. She slowly moved her head up and down and made a sucking noise, the way he liked it. Just as he was about to cum, and the head of his dick swelled, she brought herself forward and sat on top of him, moving back and forth. Sadie tried not to look down at her flabby stomach, so she instead closed her eyes and lay forward on his chest. She could only imagine the beautiful bodies of the younger, childless women that he'd been with since his divorce, but now was not the time. She had to stay focused and think sexy. After the climax, Sadie rolled over and laid on her back, sweat beads gathering between her breasts that now fell to either side of her, almost under her armpits. She pulled the sheet over her, just below her chin.

"I can't believe this is happening," Sadie said, gazing at the wooden beams on the ceiling. "I feel like it was yesterday that we were fooling around in Nana's shed, hiding from your mom with a couple Rolling Rocks and a pack of Parliament Lights."

"Yeah, it's kind of nuts," Mack said, drifting off. He seemed distracted.

"What's up? Are you okay?"

"No, I just . . . I don't know," Mack said. "I just wonder how this will end. I mean, you're married. With kids. And I don't want to break that up." He stared out the window.

"You're not breaking it up," Sadie reassured him. "And why are we talking about how it will end when 'it,' whatever it is, just began! And you didn't break up my marriage, Mack. It's *broken*. I wouldn't be here if it weren't."

"I don't know," Mack said, sitting up. Sadie caressed his back. His skin was smooth and tanned, no freckles or spots. She wondered if he waxed it.

"You don't know—what?" Sadie said. She started to feel a sense of panic, or maybe it was more like history repeating itself. Wasn't this how he started the breakup way back when, when she was living in Boston after the summer they dated? She was having déjà vu.

"I just don't know if this is something I can continue to do, without feelings getting in the way." He now turned toward her, looking like Bambi when he found out his mother had been shot.

"And what's so bad about feelings?" Sadie asked. She wasn't sure if this was a game.

"It's complicated. I'm just getting over my ex and the divorce is all."

"Well, I don't want anything from you. I just want you to be here with me, right here, right now. Just be present. Hold me," she said. Sadie knew she sounded desperate, but she was. She didn't want this to end, and she would take anything, even a small morsel of love and acknowledgment, even at the sacrifice of her own better judgment and self-respect.

"Okay, I just want to be clear is all," Mack said. "So, you're not, like, disappointed."

"Not disappointed at all!" Sadie lied. "Now get back in here and fuck me!" She tried to act like a temptress and push her own feelings aside to make him feel better. This is what she always did—put herself second.

Mack lay back down and slid into Sadie. It felt so good to feel so bad. It was like strolling down memory lane—his body, his rhythm. The rain splashed against the old windows and onto the roof. It was getting darker out, near sunset. Mack rolled over when he was finished and turned on the oil lamp next to the bed. A dusty framed photo of his grandfather shone in the light.

"Is that your grandfather?" Sadie asked.

"Yeah, he was a good man, solid."

"What happened to him? When did he die?"

"He had a heart attack about three years before Nana passed. She was so lonely when he was gone. I think she died that day with him." Mack got up and put on his boxer shorts.

"That's so sad," Sadie said.

"Is it? They lived a wonderful life together. She was ready. She wanted to join him."

"Do you believe all that stuff?" she asked. "Like, life after death? Heaven?"

"Sure, don't you?"

"I don't know." Sadie glanced across the room and noticed the wooden cross hanging on the wall. If heaven and hell were a real thing, she was heading in the wrong direction. She gathered her things next to the bed and followed Mack out to the living room. The rain had stopped, and he was pouring bourbon.

"Should we go for a walk?" she asked.

"Let me just grab my shoes."

Mack went into the other room to get his sneakers. Sadie putzed around the kitchen, looking through the drawers and picking up the Waterford crystal wineglasses. In one drawer were several old dish towels in a yellow-checkered pattern folded nicely into fours along with an empty cake dish. Suddenly, she felt something cold and sort of sharp under her feet. She looked down on the black-and-white tiled floor and noticed something more interesting than the cake dish, something distinctly newer than the dish towels. It was a necklace with a broken chain.

But it wasn't just any necklace.

Sadie had seen this necklace thousands of times.

She'd shared secrets with this necklace, vacations with this necklace, friendship with this necklace.

This was the necklace of her best friend. *This was Charlotte's.*

It was the vintage rose necklace she had inherited from her mother. It was distinctly hers. Sadie's stomach dropped. She looked around the room quickly for any signs of Mack and stuffed the necklace into her pocket. Her mind felt like scrambled eggs, her head light.

"Ready!" Mack said, emerging from the bedroom, suited up for a walk.

"I'm so sorry. You're going to kill me, but I just got a text from Charlie. He needs me to pick him up from his friend's house, and Chip is out for the night with his friends."

"Oh, that's a bummer," Mack said. "But I totally understand." He went in for a hug, and she dodged him to reach for the door. "You okay?"

"Sure, I'm fine!" Sadie shrieked, smiling, gripping the tiny pewter doorknob to the wooden screen door behind her.

"Okay, just checking." Mack smiled. He gave her a kiss on the lips. "That was fun."

"Yes," she said, hurrying out. "I will, um . . . I don't know. Call you later."

Sadie rushed to her car, down Nana's long driveway, muttering to herself. *What an asshole. What an idiot!* She wasn't sure whom to hate more: Mack, her old lover, or Charlotte, her so-called best friend. Either way, she felt betrayed. *All the more reason I should never have gone down this road in the first place,* she thought. The anger began to turn to shame and embarrassment. She felt like a fool. He had played her all day, perhaps mere hours after Charlotte left! No, wait. Maybe it was nothing at all, she hoped. Maybe Charlotte was in the area and stopped in to say hello and it was all a big mix-up.

Sadie sped out of the driveway down Scraggy Neck Road. It was almost dark as she drove down the windy road toward 28. She pulled over at the Parrot restaurant to catch her breath. A group of twenty-somethings stood in the parking lot having a smoke. She didn't know how she'd gotten here. She was a married woman with two kids and a husband, and she was having sex with her summer boyfriend from decades ago. Was this a midlife crisis? A lapse in judgment? She was paralyzed. Then she felt a vibration coming from her purse. She reached inside to pull out her phone. It was Charlotte.

"Hi."

"Hey! Whatcha doing?" Charlotte chirped.

"Nothing, how about you?" Sadie said. She stared at a young man in a knit cap with pierced ears and tattoos, blowing smoke rings.

"Not much. Just wondered if you wanted to grab a drink. Ada and I were thinking of having a boozy evening to quell the rainy-day blues," she said.

"Sure," Sadie said. Perhaps she could get some answers.

"Great! Meet us around 5 at The Flying Bridge."

"See you then," Sadie said.

"You okay? You sound funny," Charlotte asked.

"No, I'm good. I'll see you then." Sadie hung up the phone and reached into her pocket. Her fingers grasped the rose on the necklace, and she turned it around and around between her fingers. A rose was a perennial that is often armed with sharp prickles. Sadie felt pricked. The person she was closest to had stabbed her in the back. She drove off seeing red. The red of a rose.

Chapter Twenty

THREE'S A CROWD

ADA

Ada was ready for a night out with the girls. By the time she got to The Flying Bridge, she'd spent half the day working on the summer fundraising appeal letter at work, and the other half taking the kids to *Angry Birds 2* at the Cinema Pub. Sailing and tennis camps had been canceled due to the rain, and this had royally screwed up her day. When it rains in July, the Cinema Pub is packed to the gills with loud children chomping on popcorn and Skittles and slurping cokes. It smells of cheeseburgers and nachos, and it's difficult to find a seat. Ada had been planning to send the appeal out by the end of the week, but at this rate, it wouldn't mail for another week. She'd have to answer to her boss as to why the donations were rolling in so late.

"Hiiiii," Ada said, plopping into the green captain's chair at The Flying Bridge.

Charlotte was dressed in a red tank dress with red lipstick to match. Sadie was wearing a straw cowboy hat and a white linen shirt with a jean skirt.

"What'd I miss?" Ada said. "You guys look serious."

"Nothing." Sadie shrugged. "We were just getting caught up." Sadie's mouth was turned down slightly as she spoke, which was not a good sign. Charlotte just smiled an awkward half-smile.

"Oh . . . good. Well, fill me in," Ada said. She took a sip of water from the mason jar. "I can't bear to talk about myself. My life is so boring." Ada knew this to be a fib, but she certainly didn't want to delve into her beach date with Mack. She wanted to keep that to herself, a tiny present under the tree for her eyes only. "And don't even talk about my hair. It's so frizzy from the rain. Why don't you guys look heinous like me?"

"I was inside all day," Sadie mumbled.

"I, um, I don't even know what I was doing," Charlotte replied. She peeled at her beer label, rolling the tiny wet pieces into balls between her fingers.

"I was just telling Charlotte about how I boated to Bassetts Island recently, and swam in Hospital Cove, near Mack's grandma's house. We used to party there all the time."

"Hospital Cove? I don't know it," Ada said. "Oh, wait, is that like off of Scraggy Neck Road in Cataumet?"

Sadie nodded.

"Those were fun times," Charlotte said.

"So, you said you haven't been out there in a while?" Sadie asked.

"Where? Bassetts?"

"Yeah, or Scraggy Neck, that area in Hospital Cove, before the guard gate." She was very specific.

"Um . . . not really, no," Charlotte said. She continued to peel the Devil's Purse amber ale label. It was now just sticky goo on the outside of the cold brown bottle. Ada noticed it ruining her manicure.

"Not really, or you have?" Sadie asked.

Ada wondered what the hell was going on. Why was Sadie being so aggressive and interrogating Charlotte?

"Oh, wait. I have," Charlotte said. "Sorry. I forgot!" she said, shaking her head. "I stopped by and saw Mack there one day. Oh, and his nana died. It's really sad. Do you remember her, Sadie? She used to wear these flowered pants all the time with pearls. And she drove that old Mercedes? With the poodle in the back seat?"

Mack? She saw Mack? Ada's ears perked up. *And wait, his grandmother passed?*

"Yeah, I *know*," Sadie said. "I actually knew Nana."

"Oh, sorry, you said she lives there, so . . ."

"So have you been, like, hanging out with Mack?"

"Honestly, Sadie, I didn't even go inside the house. I was in the neighborhood, and I saw him out in the driveway by the clay courts, so I stopped. We chatted for a bit, and that's when he told me about his grandma."

"Hmm," Sadie said.

"Is everything okay here, guys? What's going on?" Ada inquired.

"Ask Charlotte," Sadie said.

"What is that supposed to mean?" Charlotte retorted.

"It *means*, obviously you have been lying about your relationship with Mack since the entire Art Center Gala night and that you have been seeing him behind my back without telling me!"

"Fine, I've seen him! What does it matter to you? He is your ex-boyfriend from like a hundred years ago, Sadie. It's hardly behind your back. And frankly, it's none of your business!"

"Well, it does matter, *Charlotte*, and it *is* my business because I just kissed him a few weeks ago . . . and I slept with him at his nana's cottage *today!*"

Charlotte grew crimson.

Hold on, Ada thought. *Sadie just slept with him? And Charlotte's been doing what?* "Wait. I just kissed him too. I mean, more than kissed!" Ada chimed in.

"What?" Sadie shrieked, her head turning swiftly toward Ada with a demonic look in her eyes. "You've been with him too? You're married!"

"So are you," Ada retorted. "And you!" She pointed to Charlotte.

"Barely, and I'm getting a divorce!" Charlotte replied.

"Since when? *Who even are you?*" Sadie screamed.

"Who even are *you*? Not like I would know since you've been MIA for the past year!" Charlotte said.

"So that's what this is about? You're revenge fucking Mack to get back at me because I actually have a life and a family, not some loser husband who's off roaming with God only knows who in Boston? Miss faux fingernails?"

"How can you bring that up? That's low."

"I think low is not following basic girl code and sleeping with her best friend's boyfriend."

"Do you hear yourself, Sadie? He's not your boyfriend! You're married. He's been married. He's free game!"

"So, he's a game to you? No, Charlotte, he's *a person*. A person who is wounded, and you're taking advantage of him to feel better about yourself since your modeling career is over, and you're getting old like the rest of us. Face it. You're in your forties. You're not twenty anymore."

"Speak for yourself. You should know!" Charlotte yelled.

"Oh, I'm good with myself, believe you me. And so is Mack. When I was riding on him about six hours ago, he didn't seem to mind the extra weight."

"You're embarrassing yourself."

The bartender stared at them, and a man in a baseball cap with pink flamingos on it turned to look.

"Oh yeah? Well, you're a huge liar. Oh, and here's your necklace, I found it on the floor in the kitchen." Sadie flung the vintage rose necklace across the table, and it fell onto the floor.

"I've been looking for that! My mom's necklace!" Charlotte reached down to the floor and scooped it up, dusting it off. "So, you knew?" Charlotte asked.

"Put it this way: I was hoping that there was some sort of explanation, that you were not the shitty friend you have panned out to be. I was giving you a chance to redeem yourself and explain, but you fell right into my trap."

As the girls continued to fight, Ada began to get increasingly agitated.

"HELLO? Does anyone care that I've been sleeping with Mack too?" Ada interjected. "Yeah, me! I'm here!" She had her fingers in her thumb loops.

"No one cares about you, Ada!" Charlotte said.

"Oh, so here it is. I thought we had made progress," Ada said. "I can't believe I actually thought you were my friend!"

"I was being *nice*. I was being kind to Miss Piggy over here since you apparently struck up some ridiculous friendship over lactating. I can't even remember it was so boring."

"Wow, you really are something," Ada said.

"Well, I wish I could say the same about you," Charlotte replied. "But you're kind of a snoozer."

"And you're a hot mess!" Ada said.

"Honestly? Can't hear you talking. You're nothing to me."

"Are you in eighth grade?" Ada asked.

"She wishes," Sadie said.

"Enough," Charlotte replied. "Don't you ever talk to me again."

"Oh, you need not worry about that," Sadie said. "All set here."

Sadie threw her napkin in her lap and rose from the table.

"Where are you going?"

Ada just wanted to go home. How had she gotten herself involved in this in the first place? What a pathological liar Mack was. And dirty. She grabbed her purse and headed out to her car. She would fix things. She would work on her life with Ben, and she would be a good mother. This was all just some sort of midlife crisis. This was her wake-up call. Yes, that's it. She should be grateful for it. She could reclaim her life and move forward with self-respect. As for Charlotte and Sadie, they were a chapter in her life, and that chapter was over.

Chapter Twenty-One

RETAIL THERAPY

SADIE

Sadie stood at the kitchen counter observing the chicken defrosting. She couldn't recall what she'd intended to cook for dinner. Her mind was spinning after the argument. She felt duped, disgusted. Not only had she fallen for Mack, who'd apparently fallen for all three of them, but she had also been blindsided by her friends.

"What's for dinner?" Chip asked. He emerged from the basement wearing New England Patriots sweatpants and a Red Sox baseball cap. He looked like he worked at Gillette Stadium in a fan stand.

"I can't remember," Sadie replied. "Hot dogs, pretzels, and cheap beer?"

"You hate this outfit," he said. "Well, it's comfortable. And I'm a fan. Is that so bad?"

Sadie did not reply and instead started to feverishly search through the kitchen cabinets for something that could accompany lemon pepper chicken. There were three boxes of rice pilaf, one box of roasted red pepper and garlic quinoa, and two boxes of Prince spaghetti.

"Do you want to just order out?" Chip appeared meek, like a cricket trapped in a tarantula cage.

"What's that supposed to mean?" Sadie barked.

"Nothing. Jeez! Do you hear your tone?" he replied.

She hated that word: *tone*. Chip seemed to use it a lot, especially in couples therapy.

Sadie stopped and took a breath, trying to be mindful. She looked over at Chip in his dumb sweatpants and began to cry. "I'm sorry," she said. "I had a bad day."

"Do you want to talk about it?" Chip asked.

For a moment, Sadie saw him as her best friend again. She thought about the laughter they'd had over the years and how she used to call him "kitty" because he was always sleepy, like a kitten. She did want to talk about it, but not to repair what she had done to their marriage. Instead, she wanted to launch into a defamatory tirade about Ada and Charlotte and what sluts they'd been. She started to open her mouth to vent when Charlie walked in.

"Mom, did you remember to order me the snorkel from Amazon? It's in your cart," Charlie asked.

"I think so?"

"You *think* so, or you *know* so?"

"I am not sure, Charlie," Sadie chided. "Why don't you check on my phone and see if there's a confirmation email?"

"Why can't you just remember to do it in the first place?" Charlie asked.

"Maybe because I have more important things to worry about than your snorkel, *Charlie*. Did that ever occur to you? I do not exist to serve you. You need to help out around here sometimes and stop asking for things! Jesus!"

"Sadie, give him a break," Chip interrupted. "You don't need to take your aggression out on Charlie too."

"Give him a break? Are you serious right now?" Sadie slammed the box of rice pilaf down on the countertop. "You know what? I think takeout is a good idea. Go ahead and order Peking Palace. I'm going out!"

Sadie grabbed her Louis Vuitton bag and headed for the door, leaving Charlie and Chip in the kitchen confused. Moments later, she tripped over Charlie's lacrosse stick and screamed, falling to the floor.

"God damn it!" she cursed. "And clean the mudroom while you're at it. This isn't a hotel!"

When Sadie got into the car, she folded over. She didn't know where to go. In fact, she had nowhere to go. She couldn't be at home, because she felt like a fraud in the room with Chip, and she couldn't call her friends, because she didn't have any left. She decided to go to TJ Maxx.

Driving down Route 28, she heard the song "Perfect" by Ed Sheeran.

"UGH!" Sadie yelled, punching the radio button violently to change the station. "I hate that song!" She passed the exit for Brick Kiln Road, Charlotte's exit, and lifted her middle finger into the air like an acerbic high schooler, flicking off the exit.

"Go F off, Charlotte. And you too, Ada!" she yelled, whizzing by. She rolled down the driver's side window and blared U2 on the radio. She could feel the tepid summer air on her face. The highway was extremely dark, like all Cape roads at night. She spotted a coyote, with his eyes aglow, off to the side of the road, looking for prey.

Then she thought of Mack.

Who was Mack texting now? she wondered. Was she his prey? Who would be the winner of his little threesome? Hell, why didn't he just take them all together to Nana's cottage and bang it out all at once? He could have saved everyone some time!

It seemed Mack's ears were ringing, or his nose was itching, because he texted right at that moment.

"How's my girl?"

Sadie froze. *Your girl? Which one?* She was tempted to write that but wasn't prepared to get into another fight. She needed peace—and TJ Maxx, retail therapy. She tossed the phone onto the passenger seat. Another text pinged. This time, it was from Charlotte. She peered over at the phone to read.

"Can we please talk?"

Sadie let out a labored sigh. No, no talking to Charlotte. Sadie was done with her. She had shown her true colors.

Chapter Twenty-Two

SHE SAW A GHOST

CHARLOTTE

Charlotte couldn't stand the fact that she and Sadie were fighting. Honestly, she did feel a little guilty about Mack since she knew Sadie had feelings for him. But Sadie was married. It's not like she could cock block or claim a guy when she had a ring on her finger. Charlotte pushed her grocery cart through Windfall Market. Windfall was the choice supermarket over Stop & Shop if you wanted to get prepared foods like rosemary rotisserie chicken or calzones. They also had an avalanche of fine cheeses and specialty homemade dips, like spinach and artichoke or red roasted pepper hummus. She strolled down the cereal aisle, grabbing some Kashi cereal, even though it made her feel bloated, and she turned right into the candy aisle. Maybe she needed a Kind bar to cheer her up or some gum for her oral fixation.

As Charlotte approached the frozen foods aisle, she stopped suddenly. She wasn't sure if what she was seeing, or rather *who* she was seeing, was real or a figment of her imagination. She rolled her cart a bit closer to focus and reached into her purse to put on her glasses that she only wore for driving at night. *Holy shit*, she thought. *No, it couldn't be.* She had to be imagining it because she was so upset . . . The person standing in front of the frozen peas was in fact Nana—Mack's nana.

Wasn't she dead? After all, Charlotte was having sex in her cottage mere days ago, listening to Mack recount what a wonderful woman she was, as in *past tense*, not present.

Charlotte pushed her cart at minimal speed, baby steps, following Nana down the aisle. She pretended to look at the Lean Cuisines and the Boca burgers, grabbing for a Hot Pocket and an Annie's burrito. She then slowly approached Nana with her cart, pretending to reach for the edamame in the freezer. She intentionally bumped arms with her.

"Oh, excuse me," Charlotte said.

"No problem, dear," Nana replied. She was smaller than Charlotte remembered and frailer than she was in the photos of her in the cottage living room.

"Hey, can I ask you something?" Charlotte said. She knew she was stirring the pot and potentially stepping into the lion's den, but she didn't care.

"What's that?" Nana replied, smiling. She wore hot pink lipstick, the kind that old ladies wear, and she smelled of Aqua Net hairspray that held her blonde bun tightly at the nape of her wrinkled neck.

"Are you by any chance Mack Taylor's nana?" Charlotte asked.

"Oh, my Mackey! Why, yes! You know Mack?" Nana replied, looking at Charlotte more intensely now and down at her finger to see if she was wearing a wedding ring, which she never did, nor did her husband John. Nana's hands were soft and wrinkled, and the blue veins protruded over her age spots. She was attractive for a woman in her eighties and carried herself well.

"I do!" Charlotte replied. "In fact, I think you and I met long ago at your cottage on Scraggy Neck. I was a teenager and swimming off your finger pier with Mack and my best fr—with Mack and Sadie."

Nana's eyes seemed glazed over like she had no idea what Charlotte was talking about, but she politely nodded.

"Those were wonderful times," Nana said. "I miss those days." She put her hand to her face. Her fingernails were painted the same color hot pink as her lipstick.

"But Mackey comes and visits me often now that he's back in town. I will tell him you said hello! What's your name, dear?"

Charlotte paused. She couldn't tell Nana her real name, because if Nana told Mack that she ran into "Charlotte," then Mack would know she was onto his lies and deceit. Here she was in the flesh, hardly a distant memory! *But maybe that would be the best way to let him know,* she thought. Maybe he *should* be caught by surprise, just as she, Ada, and Sadie had been blindsided by his disingenuousness. Then she thought better of it.

"Pam," Charlotte said. "My name is Pam."

Nana looked down, trying to jar her memory. "Pam. I don't recall a Pam." Charlotte felt bad making this elderly woman believe her memory was fading. "Oh wait, is your father the owner of the Shed Place?"

"No, sorry. He's not. Just tell him Pammy said hi. He liked to call me Pammy for fun."

"Oh, how sweet! Pammy!" Nana said, smiling. Her teeth were perfect, like Mack's. Charlotte wondered if they were real or dentures. "I'll be sure to tell him when I see him tomorrow!" She strolled away slowly, pushing her cart toward the butter and eggs. *You do that, Nana,* Charlotte thought. *You go ahead and tell that* scumbag *that Pammy said hello.*

When Charlotte arrived home, John was sitting on the couch watching CNN with his feet up.

"Hey, hon," John said. "You go grocery shopping? We have no food." This was his passive-aggressive way of saying she was a shitty housewife.

"Yes. Got a rotisserie chicken from Windfall," Charlotte said.

"Cool. I'll be right in."

Charlotte began unpacking the grocery bags. It would be nice of him to offer to get the rest of the groceries from the car, she thought, but it was just easier to do it herself. John would often tell her "Don't poke the bear," and she'd learned the hard way that bugging him when he was tired and hungry did not end well. John was never physically abusive to Charlotte; however, his name-calling and stonewalling, some might argue, was emotional abuse. He'd tell her she was crazy and that she was making things up, whenever she questioned the motive behind his impromptu overnights in the city.

"So how was Boston?" Charlotte asked.

"Good. It was a late dinner. Took the clients to Capital Grille and then passed out in the apartment."

"Hmm," Charlotte said, not really listening and putting the food in the fridge. She just wasn't interested anymore. In the past, she used to ask who the client was that John took to dinner, how the meal was, or what was next on his agenda at work. Now she was resigned to the fact that they had grown apart and had little in common. Plus, he never reciprocated by asking her how her day was. It was like she was a houseplant—a cactus that didn't need water from him.

"I've been thinking maybe we should go away," John said. "You know, do something fun together." He started tapping his black and gold fancy pen on the granite countertop. *Tap, tap, tap.* It annoyed her.

"You're going to scratch the counter," Charlotte said, pointing to the pen. John stopped.

"So, what do you think of that? A vacation?"

"Sounds good," Charlotte said. She rummaged through the drawers looking for salad tongs. She had too many extra spatulas, spoons, ketchup packs, and chopsticks. The kitchen needed a deep cleaning and reorganization—something to get to later.

"You're not even listening, Char," John said. He hadn't called her Char in a long time.

"I am listening! I just don't know. Okay?" she said, pointing a spatula at him.

"You don't know what?" John asked.

"I don't know. I just don't know what I'm doing anymore, what we are doing," she said. She wondered if she should open the can of worms. But she was aggravated after seeing Nana, fighting with the girls, and Mack. She couldn't take it anymore. So why not just blow up the entire situation? Seemed like a good idea to her at the time. Rip off the Band-Aid and walk into the fire.

John put his hands on the kitchen island and leaned toward her. She could smell his aftershave. He hadn't been close in some time. "What are you talking about? Do you want to leave me?" he asked.

"Honestly, I don't know," Charlotte said.

"Charlotte, no," John said. He looked as if he actually cared for a moment. Something she hadn't seen in his eyes in maybe forever. He seemed small and deflated.

"What's the difference? I'm basically single anyway," she said. "It's not like your life would really change."

"That's not true," John said. He walked closer to her. "I love you." This came out flat like he was doing a cold read from a script.

"Well, you might want to think about showing it," she said. She handed him a plate with chicken on it. "I think I have some rice I can cook. I also made a salad."

"I'm not in the mood to eat," John said, putting the plate down. "Can we talk? Go to therapy? What can I do?"

"Are you serious right now?" Charlotte asked. This was just irritating. Wasn't it like men to always show up a little late for the game. You beg and plead for years for them to improve, to talk, to go to therapy, and it's not until you're completely dead inside and ready to move on that they somehow wake up.

"Of course, I'm serious," John said. "Look, I know I haven't been a great husband . . ."

"Yep." Charlotte stared dead cold at him.

"And I haven't been good about showing you I care," he continued. She remained silent.

"And I think . . . I don't know. I guess that's why I wanted to go away together, to sort of reconnect. I miss you."

Charlotte started laughing, an overemphatic loud guffaw. "Well, that's rich!" she said.

"Jesus, Charlotte. Can you cut me a little slack here?"

"Um, I think I've cut you a lot of slack here for the past five years. Sorry that I'm not falling to my knees overjoyed that for one second you seem to be taking an interest in me and not being a complete asshole."

"Wow, I can see you're really angry," he said, starting to walk to the other room.

"Oh, so now you're just going to walk away? Like you usually do?" She wanted to throw a dart at his back and watch him topple over. She hated him in this very moment.

"It doesn't seem like you want to talk," John said.

"No, I don't want to *talk*. I want to scream and yell and punch you in the gut. I want to tell you how much I hate you for ruining our marriage, for sucking up the last ten years of my life for nothing. For flat-out ignoring me and making me feel like a piece of worthless shit!"

John stared at her. "What has gotten into you?" he asked.

"I had sex with someone else, okay?" Charlotte said.

"What? You cheated on me?"

172

"Oh. My. God. You may as well come clean yourself now. I know you've been cheating on me for years. I figured I'd just tell you about this as an entree for you—to make things easier and assuage your guilt."

"I don't need to feel any guilt. I haven't done anything. You, on the other hand . . ."

"Oh, spare me, John. I'm not as naive as I used to be. Give me a little bit of credit here. Just a little."

"You know what? I don't care. I want to move past all this and work on things with you. That's what I was trying to say when I wanted to go on vacation!"

"So, you don't care that I slept with someone else?"

"I mean, no! I don't. I don't want to know the details. Unless it's, like, you care about this guy? It is a guy, I assume?"

"No, John. I decided I like to eat box suddenly . . ."

They both started to laugh.

"Don't make me laugh. This isn't funny," Charlotte said.

But then, like when you're in church and can't stop laughing, they busted out into cackles, so much so that Charlotte fell to the floor. "Holy shit, you're killing me!" she said.

John lay on top of her and began to kiss her. It actually felt good, really good. Charlotte obliged, putting her glass down, and grabbing his ass. It felt familiar, like an old robe, something she had discovered in the back of the closet that she hadn't worn in a long time. Her hands moved around front to unbuckle his belt, but she couldn't figure out the clasp. She fiddled around awkwardly, like a teenager.

"Let me help you," John said, undoing the belt and pulling down his pants. They were breathing heavily while kissing. His tongue slid into her mouth and out and then he moved to her neck and lightly kissed it, slowly moving down to the buttons of her shirt. He undid them one by one, following with a kiss on her belly and farther down. He unbuttoned her pants and Charlotte started to lean in.

"Do you want me?" John asked.

"Yes," Charlotte said. "Please."

"Tell me you want me. I want to hear it, for you to beg me."

"I want you," she said, continuing to rock her hips up and down. "Please . . . fuck me."

"Then you can have me," he said. "I'm all yours."

He slid inside her, and they made love there on the kitchen floor, real love. Like the kind they had not made in a very long time.

Chapter Twenty-Three
A DISCOVERY

ADA

Ada muttered to herself as she filled out the cells on the Excel spreadsheet. She glanced at the photos of her family and Ben on her desk framed by the shelves in her office. Her Columbia degree hung framed on the wall, next to her Certified Fundraising Professional certificate, and two yellowing Christmas cacti sat potted in the window. She couldn't focus since learning that Mack had also been sleeping with her two best friends. She felt so betrayed. After all, it was only a few weeks ago that they had walked on the beach and labeled themselves an "us." False promises. She grabbed her phone to look through the text messages from Mack. She hadn't responded to his last two texts, but it wasn't because she didn't miss him. In fact, she missed him terribly. For a month, he'd been checking in on her every day, asking her how her meeting went, how Lilly's dance recital was, and encouraging her to talk about her feelings. That was all gone now, taken from her in a moment without her consent. Scrolling through their text history, Ada felt closer to Mack just by reading back over the course of their "relationship," if she could even call it that.

Ada moved her index finger down the phone's screen and landed on a dirty sext exchange. She covered her mouth, blushing, recalling the phone sex that happened right there in her office. She remembered laughing to herself. In the middle of reworking a financial spreadsheet and donning a puffer jacket to go grab lunch, she sexted, *"Feel me sliding down your wet shaft and riding you up and down?"* She started to wonder if she made this entire relationship up in her head. *I mean, he'd taken part, but not really.* Like, what really happened anyway? He'd never told her he loved her, had he? Maybe she was just driving that train the entire time, desperately trying to create meaning out of something that was no more than sex. That's all it was. A tryst. An affair.

She felt exploited and stupid, and then something worse: guilt. Guilt that she had been lying to Ben and her children. Guilt that she had put herself first for months. This was not in her nature. What a shitty mother she'd been. From arranging for the kids to get picked up from ballet and hockey by their friends' parents to sending them on sleepovers, all so she could sneak out in time to see Mack. And the lies to Ben! Telling him she was staying late at work or going out with the girls when she was sneaking off to meet Mack for a beer at the Trowbridge Tavern or to mess around in his car. She thought back to the last time they met up in secret.

It was in the parking lot of the Stop & Shop in Mashpee. Seemed like a safe, clandestine spot to meet, as none of her friends from Falmouth would grocery shop in there. It was far down Route 151, and people didn't venture too far from their homes on the Cape. It was like some unwritten rule that you didn't go more than ten miles for groceries, gas, to see friends, or go out at night.

It was raining that day, and Mack had hunkered down in the front seat of Ada's minivan, sopping wet in a bright yellow fisherman's raincoat. He was so ruggedly handsome with wet hair and facial stubble. He smelled like he'd been fishing. He was the kind of guy who didn't care to shower before meeting her. He was confident, smelling of squid bait and all. It was hot. His apathy made Ada want him even more. She'd leaned over and put her lips on his and felt water droplets on his nose. His lips were soft, like velvet.

"I think I really like you," she confessed, pulling back from his face. The rain splattered down on the windshield. Their breath was fogging up the windows.

"Ha! You're crazy," he said, giving her a push. Then he pulled her back into him, giving her soft, supple kisses.

Recalling that now, Ada thought, *Yes, I am crazy. I was crazy. Here I was telling him how I felt about him, and he didn't say it back; he didn't say anything other than that I was crazy.* She started to feel dizzy and put her phone down. Maybe it was time to leave work for the day. She could make up an excuse that Lilly was sick or that she had a migraine, anything to get out of there.

When Ada got home, Ben and the kids were sitting around the kitchen island eating Tostitos chips and salsa.

"Want a margarita?" Ben asked, looking up, smiling. While he was trying to be cute, this enraged her. "Nice hair."

"What does that mean, *nice hair?*" she balked, patting the sides of it to tame down any frizz.

"Nothing," Ben recanted. "Sheesh. Can't a man give a woman a compliment these days without some sort of backlash?" Ada smirked at him and huffed away to open the refrigerator.

"Mom, what the heck? Dad is trying to be nice. What is up with you?" Lilly sneered while scrolling on her cell phone.

Well, Ada wanted to say, for starters, *it is three o'clock in the afternoon.* Why is Ben already drinking a margarita? *So, is this what he does all day, while I work my butt off in the grim office to support him?* She knew that construction was light in July, but it seemed like he was *never* working.

Every time she saw that he commented on Facebook or shared some ridiculous meme, it irked her.

"Isn't it a little early to be drinking?"

Ben ignored her, turning his head back toward the kids. She dropped her purse on the dining room chair, which was already cluttered with beach bags, towels, and bottles of sunscreen.

"Why are you home so early, Mom?" Lilly asked.

"I just felt like leaving. I hate being at work in the summer." She noticed her new Clinique sunscreen she had just gotten from Macy's was stowed in Lilly's beach bag. "I wish you would ask me before you went taking my things," Ada said, reclaiming the lotion.

"Jeez, chill, Mom," Lilly said. "Can we go to the mall then? I want to go to Sephora. I can get some sunscreen there."

"Lil, no. Not today. It's been a long day, and the last thing I want to do on a sunny afternoon off is drive to Hyannis." Truth be told, the Cape Cod Mall wasn't that bad, and there was always talk of it having a makeover. However, it hadn't made a comeback or been upgraded since the seventies. It felt dated and depressing, despite the new Target.

"Fine," Lilly said, sulking and texting her friend with one hand. "Can you drive me to Rachel's house then?"

"Sure, whatever," Ada said, exasperated.

"I'll take you," Ben interjected.

"Aren't you, like, drunk, Dad?" Lilly asked. "I don't want to die in the car."

"Oh my God, relax, Lilly," Ada said. "Your father had one margarita. I think he's fine." She wasn't sure if this was in fact true, but she sure as hell didn't want to drive her. She wanted to go pout upstairs in her bed. Or maybe take a bath with her new foaming bath balls.

"Well, two, but that's okay. Same difference."

"And a Coors Light!" Lilly chimed.

What exactly is going on here? Ada wondered. *Why is Ben home boozing all day? It is summer and all, but three drinks by three o'clock.*

"I'll take her," Ada huffed, storming past Ben. "I kind of just wanted to relax after work, but whatever." She knew she was being passive-aggressive, but she didn't care. She was angry—angry at herself for falling for Mack, angry at Ben for sitting on his ass, and angry at her lot in life. When Ada got in the car, she took twelve deep breaths in and out, closing her eyes, trying to count her blessings. She heeded the advice of her therapists, telling herself it was going to be a great day, even though the day, as far as she could tell, was plain old shitty. When she opened her eyes, she saw an Angry Birds stuffed animal in her center console. She remembered when she and Mack got it at the Stop & Shop that rainy afternoon. They went inside afterward to grab a sandwich from the deli, and on the way out, he won it for her in the claw machine by the registers.

Perhaps Mack wasn't terrible after all. Sure, maybe he'd had some dalliances, but he had something special with Ada. She wanted to believe so. It could have just been a misunderstanding. Their connection was undeniable. She felt it. It was real.

When Lilly jumped out of the car at Rachel's house, Ada set out to do something impetuous, perhaps reckless. She decided to drive to see Mack at Nana's house and confront him. *Why not?* she thought. She had nothing to lose at this point. Clearly, he didn't really care for her. And it was over between them now that the cat was out of the bag that he was having sex with all three of them. Right? *Disgusting*, she thought. *He needs to pay.* She pressed her foot on the gas, backing out of Rachel's driveway so quickly that the tires screeched. Her passenger side mirror swiped the rhododendron bush. Lilly looked back at her, giving her a faint wave and a look of surprise.

Ada drove down Quisset Avenue up to Woods Hole Road leading to Route 28. Eventually, she made it to Scraggy Neck. Cyclists hogged the road causing her to swerve in and out.

"That's what the bike path is for," she muttered to herself. "Stupid tourists."

Ada rolled down her window, hair blowing in her face and sticking to her freshly applied lip gloss. She looked in the rearview mirror. She wondered if she should pull over and put on some more under-eye concealer. Ever since she turned forty, it was like she had been punched in the face with dark circles each morning. She chuckled about the time Lilly said she thought she was pretty except for "those dark lines under your eyes." At the time, Ada didn't understand what she meant, thinking her eyeliner had run all over her face. It wasn't until later she realized her daughter was referring to the shadows of age, poor sleep, and depression.

As she approached Nana's driveway, she squinted to see the numbers on the mailbox. Yep, this was it. She had googled the address since she had not been there before. She turned on her blinker and slowly drove up the driveway, noticing the clay tennis courts to her left and the gazebo on her right. After parking, she opened the car door slowly and carefully, trying not to make noise. She wanted to surprise him. She was hoping this whole mess could be cleared up and that he would reassure her with his warm kisses and strong hugs that she was the one he loved. But then reality hit. He most likely was with Sadie or Charlotte.

She tiptoed on the balls of her feet over the gravel driveway and up to the front screen door. She could hear Mack's deep, raspy voice talking inside. She wondered if he was on the phone. She leaned her ear closer to the screen, and her cheek rested on the wiry mesh. Then she heard laughter—high-pitched female laughter. Ada couldn't identify the laugh.

Who could it be? Charlotte's laugh was deeper than that, and Sadie's was louder. Maybe one of them was trying to play coy or seduce him with a fake, flirtatious laugh? Ada's bravery took over, and she pushed the screen door open, lobbing herself awkwardly into the front foyer. She could hear the voices in the other room. Nana's old black-and-white photos framed the walls in the hallway. It looked like a Kennedy house in Hyannisport.

Creeping slowly past the kitchen, Ada spotted two wine glasses and an open bottle of Veuve Clicquot on the counter. What the hell was going on here, she wondered, a celebration? The laughter continued to echo from the living room. She stumbled over something on the floor: a Chanel flip-flop. *Charlotte had Chanel flip-flops,* Ada thought. She recalled the time one of them was missing on the beach. They scoured the sand looking for it for twenty minutes before finding it next to a German shepherd. She remembered Sadie telling her the stories about Charlotte's childhood when she was called a cow and teased by the boys. Now, she was just oozing for male attention wherever she went! And what a fraud to say that she was ending things with Mack when, in fact, she wasn't at all.

Ada kicked the Chanel flip-flop to the corner of the baseboard heater and powered through, slowing down right before the living room. She inhaled deeply, ready to spring on them like a trapdoor spider. Her stomach was in knots and her heart leapt bounds. She approached the living room and peeked around the corner to see who it was. Mack sat on the end of the white coach. And next to him, with one of her legs resting on his was . . . not Charlotte.

Holy shit, Ada thought. She squinted to make sure, but who she was seeing was someone she might never have anticipated.

It wasn't Sadie either.

It was . . . Caroline Wall, her tennis partner, Little Miss Perfect and *happily married* Caroline Wall.

Chapter Twenty-Four

RAGE ROVER

SADIE

Sadie and Caroline Wall had just finished a round of tennis at the club when they decided to grab lunch on the patio.

"Hello, Mrs. Wall," greeted Frank, the general manager. "Is Mr. Wall here with you this afternoon?"

"Hi, Frank. No, he's working," Caroline said.

"Ah, I understand," Frank replied. "Mr. Wall is a very important businessman." Sadie noticed he had not mentioned that Chip was an important businessman.

"Right," Caroline chuckled. "Well, he seems to think so, at least." Frank lowered his head and organized the menus at the host stand with his white-gloved hands.

"Good afternoon, Mrs. Cooper. How is Mr. Cooper today?"

"He's just dandy!" Sadie replied. "And he won't be joining us either."

"Very well. Enjoy your lunch, ladies," Frank said, scurrying off.

Sadie and Caroline made their way to the front porch overlooking the putting green. Sadie sat on the wire lawn chair and sunk into the floral plush cushion. She looked on as a group of four children dressed in golf club gear clumsily putted the balls into the hole. One girl dragged the flag along the green and made a mess of it in her patent leather shoes. Her mother scampered up on the balls of her toes, so as not to also puncture the pristine green with her kitten heels.

"Clarice, you need to put that down now," the mother begged. "Now."

Clarice just stood there staring at her mother, who looked impeccable in her Lilly Pulitzer ruffled dress. The little girl began to tap dance on the green in her patent leather shoes.

"It's time for bed, Clarice. Casey will take you home, and Mommy and Daddy will be home later to give you a kiss night-night when you're asleep." The mother ripped the flagpole out of Clarice's hand and grabbed the middle of her forearm, dragging her off the green as she winced.

"Oh, there's Charlotte!" Caroline chirped. "Should we ask her to join?"

Sadie looked across the porch and saw Charlotte sitting alone. For a moment, she felt bad for her best friend and wanted to run over to hug her and tell her everything that had happened to her.

"Um, no. Let's just keep it to the two of us," Sadie said, sweeping a Burt's Bees facial wipe across her sweaty brow. She hadn't exercised in at least two weeks since her fight with the ladies, and her physical atrophy really showed when she lost to Caroline by ten points.

"Did something happen between you and Charlotte?" Caroline asked.

"Long story, but let's just say we aren't speaking right now."

"Oh, that's too bad." Caroline frowned. "Let's put a pin in that, and I'll just go say a quick hello," Caroline said. Sadie hated the phrase "put a pin in it." It wasn't even a thing anymore to put notes with a pin on a bulletin board, since the invention of iPhones. Caroline probably had designer Post-its pinned symmetrically on a flowery bulletin board in her kitchen, like something you'd see on Pinterest.

Sadie watched from the corner of her eye as Caroline skipped across the patio to Charlotte's table. She grabbed her phone from her purse to see if she had any missed messages from the kids or Chip and tried not to think about what Charlotte was saying to Caroline while kibitzing in the corner. Charlotte chuckled loudly, a familiar sound that Sadie had so many times enjoyed, that now made her feel like she was in eighth grade and left out on the loser side of the lunchroom. She thought about the time when she and Charlotte laughed so hard that she wet her pants while lunching at Añejo. She had to go buy a new pair before heading to a work meeting.

Sadie shifted her attention to the harbor in the distance. She was trying to remain steadfast in her disdain for Charlotte. The view from the patio was stunning on a clear day. The rolling green hills of the golf course led down to the sandy shore and a small hidden beach next to a long finger pier. Locals called this the Sea Glass Beach where, if you were lucky, you could collect red and blue pieces of sea glass along the shore. Motorboats whirred by, and Sadie sighed, longing for simpler and more joyous times. She recalled the time that she and Chip had a romantic evening on the Knob, walking hand in hand up the woodsy trail to the summit. He carried a backpack with two plastic wineglasses, a cutting board, a chilled charcuterie, and a bottle of French rosé. They sat on the stone bench at the top that had the name of a couple inscribed on it with the dates. She and Chip joked that they would someday have their own bench up there, and a young couple like themselves would be toasting to their fifth wedding anniversary.

"Did you order?" Caroline asked, taking a seat.

"No, no one has come over yet," Sadie said. She desperately wanted to know if Charlotte had said anything to Caroline about their fight or about Mack, but she dared not ask. Perhaps she'd bring it up organically later.

"I think I'll just get the kale salad with chicken," Caroline said. "I feel like an Arnold Palmer too!"

"Oooh, riskee!" Sadie joked. "Hard day?"

"So, tell me about the fight with you and Char," Caroline said. A black fly landed on her water glass. "Eww!" she said, shooing it away. "Yuck."

"I don't know. It's kind of a long story," Sadie said, not sure she could trust Caroline with information about Mack. They were friends, but not close friends. In fact, Caroline Wall didn't have any close friends that she knew of. She kept everyone at arm's length and her circles tight with just her husband and kids. *Probably a smart move*, Sadie thought. Friendships just led to drama. She was going to circle the wagons, focus on her and Chip and the kids, and shut it down for the remainder of the summer.

"You know Mack Taylor, right?" Sadie asked. "You showed him a house or something awhile back when we played last?" She tried to seem nonchalant, even though she clearly remembered the seething jealousy she experienced when learning that Mack would be with Caroline, even if just for real estate business.

"Um, yeah, sure," Caroline said. "He was looking to buy on Sippewissett. Just returned home after a divorce or something?"

"Yeah, well . . . I don't know, forget it, it's too complicated," Sadie said.

But Caroline pressed on, wanting more details and listening with an intensity Sadie hadn't seen before.

"No, I want to know. Tell me. Did you date him in the past or something? He's very attractive, I mean for an older man. And not that I'm looking." She chuckled.

Oh, what the heck, Sadie thought. She would just spill the beans. Perhaps some objective perspective would be helpful. Maybe Caroline could offer sound advice.

But when she finished telling the long, sordid tale of Mack's antics and the fight between her and Charlotte and Ada, Caroline Wall's face looked wan, like she too had been in the argument.

"So, he's just a rotten player, like the rest of them," Sadie said affirmatively, putting a cap on the story.

"Wow, I . . . can't . . . believe that . . ." Caroline said. She seemed deflated.

"Oh my God," Sadie said. "It's like you lost your best friend too! Are you okay?"

Caroline shook her head affirmatively and excused herself to visit the bathroom. Sadie observed Charlotte, who was paying her bill, and for a moment, their eyes met. She focused back on the table and straightened the knife and fork slanted on the corner of her plate. By the time she checked again, Charlotte had gone, and Sadie could see her making her way to her car in the parking lot below. She was texting someone. Perhaps it was Mack? Maybe she was still seeing him? Caroline rejoined the table, a plastic smile across her face.

"Sorry about that!" she said. "Should we grab the check?"

"I got this one," Sadie said. "You good?"

Caroline nodded, but Sadie sensed this was a lie. What had happened? she wondered.

"I think I just need a break from the sun," Caroline said. "I'm sure I'll be fine. Maybe a little heat stroke."

The women walked to their cars and hugged goodbye. Sadie watched as Caroline sat in her Range Rover texting furiously, her perfectly shaped brows now furrowed. Then she picked up the phone and started yelling—screaming, in fact. Sadie tried to avert her gaze but couldn't help but stare. Caroline was gesturing, hitting the dashboard, angry, mouth agape, a complete 180 from the woman she'd just lunched with. This was not the perfect Caroline she knew.

The next day Sadie texted Mack that she wanted to talk to him and asked to meet in Cotuit at Kettle Ho. She initially thought about meeting him somewhere private or in her car, but prior meetings there had ended with them entangled and pawing at each other's flesh. No, she wanted to keep this strictly business. It was an inquisition, after all, a come-to-Jesus moment. She would demand answers.

When Mack arrived at K-Ho, he hunkered down in a corner booth next to Sadie and slid closer to her on the maroon cracked leather bench.

"Too close," she said. "I'm moving to the other side."

Mack laughed. "Aw, come on, girl. No love for your old pal?"

Old pal? Is this what she was now to him? An old chum? This further enraged her, and she could feel the lava inside her bubbling just below the surface. One step out of line and she might explode, another reason to meet in a public place. She didn't trust her rage.

"Let's get on with it, Mack," Sadie said, grabbing the salt and pepper shakers and moving them like chess pieces in front of her on the table between them.

"Get on with what?"

"You know what."

"Um, no, I don't." Mack smiled.

"Oh really? You don't know about leading me on all summer while you were fucking not only one but TWO of my friends? Oh, wait, I didn't count Caroline, so that makes three. You were fucking THREE of my friends AND ME this summer. How do you explain that?" She lobbed a saltshaker across the table, and it landed in his lap.

"Sadie, honey,"

"Don't call me honey." She groaned.

"I never promised you anything. I am sorry you are hurt, and I can tell that you are, but I honestly was just having fun. You know I care for you!"

Sadie refused to meet his gaze. She grabbed the bottle of hot sauce now, opening and closing the cap.

"You're just so cool and a blast to hang with," Mack continued, "and I got carried away. But you're married, and Chip is a good guy, and I started to feel terrible. I know if I were him, I'd hate to lose you. Plus, I just got divorced myself, so . . ."

Mack reached for her hand. Sadie pulled hers back.

"What about all those proclamations of how you couldn't stop thinking about me? And the wishes that we had gotten married the first time around? Was that all just for *fun*? Because, to me, that is pretty sick, and not fun. It is sociopathic, which I now know you are."

Mack took off his baseball cap and put it on the table, as if he were singing the anthem at a baseball game.

"You have forever destroyed any trust or faith I have in you, Mack," Sadie said. "You are filthy. God knows what sort of STD you passed along to me. I feel like I need a complete panel at the gynecologist."

"Can you stop?" Mack chided. "And, not for nothing, but I had sex with your *friends*. Are you saying they have STDs?"

This enraged Sadie.

"Are you serious?" Sadie said louder, now alerting some of the old-timers at the bar. The bald one in jean overalls and a Budweiser T-shirt turned around and gave her a look of disdain. "So now you can tell me how to act? Priceless."

"Sadie, I don't know what you want from me."

"I don't want anything from you." She started to gather her things, zipping up her purse, trying to swallow and stop from crying.

"Then why am I here? So you can scold me and throw a saltshaker at my face?"

"It didn't hit your face . . ."

Mack laughed. "True."

"I was just hoping to get an answer from you, some sort of clarity about what you were thinking. What we had meant something to me. I am literally—" Sadie stopped short of finishing her thought and looked down. Her voice broke and she started to cry. Her shoulders began shaking uncontrollably.

"What?" Mack said, moving to sit next to her.

"*Crushed*," she said, weeping, and she lay her head on his broad shoulder, the same shoulder she had lain her head on the multiple times they'd lay in bed talking and caressing each other.

"Look at me," Mack said, grabbing her chin.

"What?"

"I am sorry, Sadie," Mack said. "I truly am. I didn't mean to hurt you. I care so deeply for you, and the last thing I'd want to do is make you upset." He caressed her shoulders and went in for a hug. She couldn't help herself. She embraced him wholeheartedly, crying. He smelled so good and familiar. She wanted to forget it all and be with him.

Mack pulled back, gazing at her. "We have known each other our whole lives," he said. "That's not going to change."

Frank Sinatra's "Summer Wind" began to play overhead. She and Mack had danced to that long ago, the first time she met his parents in her white dress. It was Mack's father's favorite song. Sadie pointed her finger up in the air toward the ceiling.

"Your dad," she said.

Mack nodded. "You remember."

"That was a good time," she said.

"Sadie . . ."

She stood up, grabbing her purse and straightening out her pants.

"Nah," she said, shooing him away with her hand. "I have to go."

She walked out of the bar, feeling the weight of his stare at her back.

Will he miss me?

Did he ever love me?

Am I not enough?

She closed the door behind her. She would never know the answer.

Chapter Twenty-Five
SURF DRIVE

CHARLOTTE

Charlotte was ready to have it out with her friends once and for all. She texted them asking to meet at Surf Drive Beach at 5 o'clock. By that time, the beachgoers would have gone home to shower and get ready for dinner, and the sunset drinkers wouldn't have arrived yet. There were always at least ten cars at sunset parked in the beach parking lot at Surf Drive, surrounded by seagulls gaming for snacks and leftover picnic debris.

Charlotte arrived first. She looked in the rearview mirror and puckered her lips coated in frosted brownie lipstick, the same color lipstick she'd worn in her twenties when she went out clubbing in Soho. She was modeling then and smoked cigarettes—and an occasional cigar—instead of eating. Her diet then consisted of coffee and cigarettes, with an occasional late-night omelet at Empire Diner that she would promptly throw up in the bathroom.

Sadie pulled in next to Charlotte and parked. She gave a feeble wave through the window with wilted fingers. Her hair was pin straight, like she'd had a blowout, and she'd dressed in platform sandals and a white sarong, as if she was planning to go somewhere other than to hash out some drama with her two best friends.

"Your hair looks good," Charlotte said, walking toward her, extending the first olive branch. "Did you just get it done?"

"Yeah, I'm heading out with Chip, and I hadn't had it colored in a while."

Ada pulled up in her minivan and emerged holding some form of travel coffee mug. Charlotte chuckled and gave her a "cheers" with her thermos.

"Nothing like a hot java at five!" she joked. Ada and Sadie laughed, perhaps too hard, to ease the anguish in the salty, humid air. "Do you want some?" Charlotte asked.

"Nah, I'm good. I'll wait till dinner," she said. "I haven't eaten much today."

The women took off their shoes and walked barefoot through the parking lot onto the sand on the beach, dodging seaweed and rocks, over to the jetty. The tide was high and the water a darker shade of green, even at the sand bar, which was typically a bright green midday. It was nearing sundown and the air had cooled, but it was still sticky. Nights were much hotter these days with climate change.

"So, I'll go first since I called this meeting," Charlotte said.

"You sound so officious!" Sadie said. "Should we take minutes?"

Charlotte and Ada giggled, and Charlotte kicked her foot out in Sadie's direction, touching her forearm. Sadie moved back and swept the sand off her arm.

"So, anyway . . . I just wanted to say, first and foremost, that I miss you guys," Charlotte continued. "And I wish we had not gotten to this point."

Ada and Sadie nodded in agreement.

"However, I will also say that I am very disappointed that you both were dishonest with me, and I guess, I wasn't so honest with you either."

Sadie's face grimaced. "Yes, that is correct. I'm glad you're taking some responsibility for it now."

"I always took responsibility for it, Sadie," Charlotte retorted. "But you said some pretty shitty things to me at lunch that day, some things that went below the belt. Like talking about my eating disorder? Not cool."

"What does that have to do with your dishonesty? See? Here you go again throwing a red herring out and dodging the fact that you lied about you and Mack."

"I didn't lie!" Charlotte clamored, her voice raising an octave.

"Fact! You did!" Sadie said.

Ada stood up from the jetty. "Okay, can I have a say here, ladies? You two always seem to leave me out. I know I am the 'new' one to this little clique of yours since like forever ago, since you always seem to bring that up, *Charlotte*, but I have a stake in this fight too." Charlotte turned her head off to the side, sulking. Why was Ada so meek and the victim? This is why she always emphasized that Ada was the odd man out, because she was weak and annoying.

"Fine. Go ahead," Charlotte said. The waves started to slap against the jetty, spraying ocean droplets onto her legs. The tide was rising. She spotted a crab between the large rocks headed for a snail.

"I forget what I was going to say," Ada said.

"Touché."

"Charlotte, don't be rude," Sadie scolded.

"Why do you always come to her rescue? She's a big girl."

"Shut up, Charlotte," Ada said. "You know, I can't imagine Mack actually liked you, since you're so angry and bitter all the time. It's super unattractive."

"Oh really? And being anorexic and coy is?" Charlotte replied, standing up, moving closer to Ada off the jetty. Some seagulls nearby flew away, flapping their wings loudly and cawing.

"You cannot be serious talking to me about an eating disorder, Miss

Chew My Food and Spit It Out, can you?" This was not going how she had planned. She wanted to make up with these women, but it was impossible.

"How dare you suggest I still do that! As if you would even know! You don't know anything about me! In fact, I don't even really like you, Ada, and that is why I don't tell you anything," Charlotte shouted.

"Well, guess what? I never liked you either! I was being nice because I was friends with Sadie!"

Sadie now stood up, stretching out her arms. "Okay, guys, let's take this down a notch. I thought we were trying to talk through something."

"Oh, okay, *Switzerland,*" Charlotte piped in. "You know what? You are a liar, and you are desperate. You reek of it. Mack knew you were not over him, and he probably pity fucked you, since you were grandfathered in from when you were twenty."

"Pity fucked me? You have got to be kidding. At least he did fuck me—*many times,* for that matter!"

"You guys! This has gone too far. Enough is enough!" Ada shouted, moving backward and tripping on a sandcastle behind her. She fell onto a mote lined with dead crab carcasses and seashells and shrieked.

"I can't breathe," Ada yelped. "I feel like I'm having a panic attack." She began to inhale and exhale, wheezing and coughing. She then got down on all fours and lay down on her stomach in the sand. Charlotte peered across the beach at the onlookers. She recognized Carl Smith from Town Hall, whom she regularly visited with to pay her parking tickets, and Laura Lowenstein, a librarian at the Falmouth Library.

"Grab your popcorn and tickets!" Charlotte exclaimed. "Or just take a picture; it lasts longer!"

Sadie erupted in laughter. "Oh my God, we haven't said that since seventh grade!"

Charlotte broke down giggling uncontrollably. The release felt good. She was emotionally and physically beaten and exhausted. "I can't do this anymore," she said.

"Me either," Sadie replied.

"Agreed," Ada mumbled, pulling dried seaweed from her skirt.

"What the hell do we do now?" Charlotte asked.

"You got me," Sadie said, shaking her head. "This is a disaster."

"Oh! I remembered what I was going to say!"

"What's that?" Charlotte laughed.

"Mack is banging Caroline Wall too! I saw them!" Ada exclaimed.

Charlotte stood up from the sand. "Wait, say that again?"

"Yeah, Caroline Wall. Mack's having sex with Caroline Wall too."

Charlotte and Sadie exchanged glances. Then they peered over at Ada.

"Wow," Charlotte muttered under her breath, in disbelief.

"He's a player," Ada said. "And we all fell for it."

"We sure did, didn't we?" Charlotte said, reaching down and grabbing a load of brown seaweed, the kind that has the rubbery nubs on it, like erasers. "I feel like such an idiot."

"I can't believe it," Sadie said. "Caroline Wall? I thought she and Dave were good!"

"We all did," Ada said. "But obviously, nothing is what it seems now, is it?"

The three women sat down next to each other on the beach, exhausted. A lame seagull hopped nearby. His wing seemed to be broken. The air was thick and still as the tide crept in, dragging lady slipper seashells and rocks onto the foamy shore. None of the women spoke. Taking in the moment, the sound of waves breaking filled the silence. Charlotte was happy to have some peace, just a tad, in this calm before the storm. The women were silent, but not for long.

Chapter Twenty-Six

DRY, DIRTY, AND STRAIGHT UP

ADA

Ada's leg wouldn't stop shaking as she drove north from Surf Drive. *What if someone from work had seen her fighting in public,* she thought. She had worked too hard to let this summer threaten her career. It seemed like just yesterday that she had showed up to her first interview out of college at the Museum of Fine Arts in Boston wearing her Ann Taylor navy-blue suit and Forever 21 crisp white blouse underneath. She remembered her horror when she leapt up the stairs, running late from riding the T. Coffee droplets jettisoned out of the sippy lid on her Starbucks cup and stained her blouse right before the interview.

Ada had moved her way up the nonprofit ladder in a variety of different jobs since then and found she loved fundraising the most, except for making the actual ask for money. First she was a development associate, then the annual fund manager, and she finally landed the executive directorship. If it all went to pot because of Mack, she thought, it would be even more reason to clear things up, which is what had brought her to Nana's cottage. She and the women decided they would confront him together that evening and put an end to his shenanigans. A player can play for only so long before he, too, is played.

At seven p.m., Ada arrived at Nana's from Surf Drive. She parked flush next to several plump bushes of blooming purple and pink hydrangeas and waited for Sadie and Charlotte. *Only the proper amount of shade and soil acidity could produce such brilliant shades of color on these sensitive flowers, and Nana was just the type to research how to accurately care for them,* Ada thought. Before she had passed, she had probably attended horticulture classes at the Osterville Library in the evenings and spent weekday afternoons at Mahoney's Garden Center kibitzing with the staff about how to best care for her rosa rugosa and orchids.

Ada imagined how the confrontation with Mack would go down: she, Sadie, and Charlotte would barge in through the screen door and storm into the living room. Mack would surely be with Caroline Wall or another one of his victims who would stand up, confused. Mack would then pretend he had no idea what they were talking about and lob out words like "unrequited," "crazy," and "infatuated"—typical gaslighting. She'd learned about this gaslighting behavior while reading in the self-help section of the Eight Cousins bookstore for an hour. Gaslighting, she learned, was common for narcissists like Mack.

Ada consulted the rearview mirror and attempted to clean up her smeared eyeliner with the edge of her index finger. She then foraged around her Kate Spade tote bag to find some lipstick and mascara to reapply.

"Can I help you, dear?" Nana inquired, knocking on the passenger side window of Ada's car.

Startled, Ada dropped her lipstick on the floor mat and screeched, "Nana?" What the hell? Wait, no. It couldn't be. She was *dead*. But here she was in front of her. Ada shuddered. "Oh, um . . . hi," she said, rolling down the window. "Sorry. I was looking for Mack. I was told this was his address?"

"Oh! Mackey! He's my grandson! Is he one of your friends?" Nana smiled widely. She had a Kennedy smile.

"Yes! Well, no. I mean, kind of?" Ada stammered. She glanced behind her to see if the girls were pulling into the driveway to rescue her. All she could think was "SOS." *Was she dreaming?*

"Well, which is it, dear?" Nana implored.

"Neither. I mean, BOTH! Sorry, I am making no sense."

"It's hot out," Nana said. "Would you like to come in while you wait? Can I offer you some water or maybe a glass of fresh lemonade?" Nana was dressed in a pink and green flowered dress, with a white apron over it, as if she had just baked fresh cookies. And her short nails were painted a bright poppy red, which matched her lipstick. Her lips were thin with scalloped lines along the upper one, revealing her age. Yet, she didn't look a day over sixty-five, even though math told Ada she must be closer to eighty.

Nana, whose real name was Peggy Clark, was a town socialite. Everyone knew her. She volunteered weekly at the Hand in Hand Thrift Shop, and her name was always featured with thanks in various giving societies and on gala programs. Peggy was passionate about several causes, mostly Cape Cod Healthcare and the Marine Biological Laboratories, where she served on the board. Peggy planned to go to medical school before she married, but she quickly became pregnant with Mack's mother, Catherine, and her dreams of becoming a physician were squashed.

"Lemonade would be lovely," Ada said. "Thank you." She brushed the sand off her arms and pulled back her hair into a knot. She felt so disheveled and out of place.

"Do you need a towel to wipe off that sand, too?" Nana asked.

"Oh, sorry! God, I am so embarrassed," Ada said. "I was just at the beach with my friends, and they should be here momentarily." She checked behind her again. "You see, we met at Surf Drive to, um, celebrate. We celebrated, um, the fact that our kids were going back to school in the fall, and summer was nearing an end. You know how crazy summer can be with kids, and no school and stuff. Right?"

Nana nodded, trying to keep up with Ada's frenetic tone and pace.

"Oh, and then we were like, 'We should go see Mack! Yes, we should ask Mack how he's doing!' You know, because of the divorce and all? And maybe he was sad this time of year, not being with his kids? I don't know. You know what I mean? My friends really are coming . . ."

"Yes, you said that," Nana replied. She too looked behind Ada down the driveway, as if she suspected a prank. "What is it I can do for you gals?"

"Well, see, we are friends with Mack," Ada began.

"Right, so you said." Nana laughed. She was known to be a bit of a spitfire, while always maintaining dignity and class. She was one of those women who was raised with etiquette and civility, the opposite of her kids, who wouldn't know how to craft a thank-you letter or pick out a salad fork if you shoved it in front of their faces. Mack told stories about Nana's various "rules," such as never asking a woman her age, always crediting your neighbor instead of yourself, and listening is the art of good conversation. Ada could feel herself flailing in front of this matriarch.

Just then, Sadie and Charlotte pulled in and got out of the car.

"See? I told you they'd be here!" Ada piped up, grateful for the out.

The two women quickly approached, passing rows and rows of blooming tiger lilies, black-eyed Susans, and daisies. Their arms swung vehemently by their sides, as if they were going on some sort of aerobic exercise walk.

"Well, I'll be!" Nana said with a huge grin. "It's Sadie!" Sadie reached out her hand from afar and grinned. "Well, hello there, Miss Sadie!" Nana outstretched her long, thin arms.

Sadie stopped dead in her tracks. Startled, Sadie responded warmly, welcoming the woman's feeble embrace.

Nana continued, "Perhaps *you* might tell me who this fine *sandy* young woman is in my driveway!" She winked at Ada, who got out of her car to join them.

"Nana, this is my friend Ada," Sadie said. "Oh, and you remember Charlotte, right?"

"Charlotte? Or wait—I thought you said your name was Pammy. Yes, we saw each other in . . . where was it? Windfall Market! That's right!" Nana seemed pleased with her recall but confused. Sadie glared sideways at Charlotte.

"Yes," Charlotte said, peering down as if she were a child who had spilled on the carpet. "I actually go by Charlotte." Nana didn't seem to catch on.

"Well, to what do I deserve, *or does Mack deserve*, this honor of three fine women?" she said, raising an eyebrow. "Jeez, I knew he was a looker, but three of you!" Nana laughed, not recognizing the severity and veracity of her implication.

The women giggled a little too loudly. Ada wasn't sure if she should pipe in, if they should shove off to discuss, or if they should just make a run for it, like when they were children playing a neighborhood game of ding-dong dash.

"Funny you say that," Charlotte said. Ada felt like she was going to have the runs. *No,* she thought. *Charlotte, no, this is not the time for you to whip out your New Yorker on us!* But Charlotte persisted. "Thing is, we do in fact all have a relationship with Mack. You're spot-on!"

"Yes, and we just were looking to see if we might say hello," Sadie interjected, pushing Charlotte aside so that she tripped, almost twisting an ankle in her espadrilles off the stone walkway. "Is Mack here, Nana? Or do you know where we might find him?"

Nana squinted her eyes like a serpent ready to pounce on a mouse.

"Oh, the jig is up," she said.

"What's that?" Sadie whimpered. She started itching her arms up and down, rabidly. Ada still wanted to make a run for the bathroom. This was beyond her level of comfort, and she was beginning to feel faint.

"Sadie, honey, I am almost eighty-five years old; this is not my first rodeo."

"What do you mean by that?" Sadie asked.

"She *means*," Charlotte interjected, "that she knows Mack is a scoundrel!"

Sadie and Ada gasped. Nana snickered.

"Well! Well! Miss Charlotte here seems to be the only honest one of the bunch!" Nana said. "Come on in, Charlotte. I'd love to hear your tale." She pushed the screen door open all the way, and in a sweeping motion invited the women inside.

"I think I will," Charlotte said. Ada and Sadie looked at each other and back at Charlotte, who followed Nana. Ada couldn't believe they were all there in that house. That same house in which Mack had had sex with them! She wanted to exit, rapidly. And what if Ben found out? She would be mortified. Her marriage would be over! She would be fired from her job, and her kids would hate her for the rest of their lives. This was not going to end well.

Ada hustled in behind Charlotte. "I think it's best if we go," she said, tugging at Charlotte's sleeve. "We wouldn't want to upset Peggy, and these old-time pranks are wearing thin."

"What are you even talking about?" Charlotte said, whipping her head around and scowling like a mean girl in the eighth grade.

"It's okay, Ada," Sadie said. "Nana is one of us." She smiled warmly at Nana, who returned the grin.

"Listen, dear. Whatever you must tell me stays here," Nana reassured her. "Now, take that lemonade I offered you a few minutes ago, add some bourbon to it—bottom shelf on the right in the kitchen—" as if Ada didn't already know this "—and sit your fanny down. It's not too often an old bag like me gets a good story."

Ada was shocked and followed directions, something she was apt to do. "Um, okay, well, thanks? And can I please use your ladies' room?"

"A lady doesn't ask," Nana said. "She just sneaks off."

Great, Ada thought. As if she didn't already feel like a trollop involved in a threesome, but now she had no etiquette either. She shuffled off to the bathroom. Along the way, she spotted various gold-framed photos, mostly black and white, hanging on the walls. They were of Nana and her husband Joe, her children, grandchildren, pets, and one in which Mack was in college wearing a Yale baseball hat and standing on the pitcher's mound. Her heart ached as she moved her face in closer to get a better look. He was so handsome, even back then. She continued down the hallway slowly, one foot in front of the other on the long-braided rug. She peered up the dark wooden staircase, where framed photos lined the wall leading up to what she presumed were Nana's children's bedrooms. The house had a musty smell, like an old house where spiders lurked in the corners of beams and moths lay dormant in sweaters for the winter.

Ada made her way to the bathroom and locked the door with a latch. There was a claw-foot tub in the corner with tiny pink soaps in the shapes of shells in it. Behind the toilet seat was a small wicker basket with three bottles of perfume that seemed as if they hadn't been sprayed in years: Chanel No 5, Jean Nate, and Estée Lauder White Linen. She lifted the Chanel up to her nose as she sat down to pee. Ada's nerves were calming, but she wanted out of there, and fast. She reached into her purse to get her phone. She had no texts. She secretly hoped there would be one from Mack. *Maybe I should take a photo of his nana's bathroom and send it to him*, she thought.

When Ada returned to the living room, she carried a short glass full of lemonade, ice, and two shots of Knob Creek bourbon. The women were seated. Mack's nana was on a floral armchair, and Sadie and Charlotte sat on the couch.

"So, get to it, Charlotte," Nana said. "Tell me everything now that Miss Ada has returned. Find everything okay, dear?"

Ada nodded.

Nana rubbed her knees and winced. "Are you okay?" Ada asked.

"Oh, yes, sweetie. Just played too many rounds of tennis this week is all. Damn joints are killing me. I'll be fine after a martini—or two!"

Sadie jetted to the kitchen to craft Nana a martini. "Dirty, dry, and up?"

"The memory of an elephant!" Nana called out. She then turned to Charlotte, who was staring directly at her from the couch, hands on her knees, ready for action. "So let me have it, Charlotte. And don't mince words."

"Well, as I said before, Nana . . . Can I call you Nana?"

Nana nodded.

"Your grandson Mack? He's a player."

"A what now?"

"A player. A scoundrel. A liar. A cheat," Charlotte said. "Shall I continue?"

Nana didn't chuckle, nor did she reply. The air was stifling, more so than on a typical summer day on Cape Cod. The furniture had a wet, mildew feel like it needed a good bout of dehumidifying.

"You're not telling me anything I haven't already heard," Nana finally replied. "But Mackey is still my grandson, so I reserve the right to defend him."

"Of course!" Sadie said, handing her the martini. "We love Mack! I mean . . ."

"We don't love Mack anymore," Ada said with unabashed bravado.

"She has risen!" Nana joked. Charlotte and Sadie laughed, but Ada did not. She was tired of being the weak one, preyed upon.

"Perhaps I have! And you know what? Your grandson is the one who needs to learn some manners! He should be ashamed of himself." She began to weep.

"Oh, Ada, a lady never shows her weakness. She stands proud, strong. She certainly doesn't let some man get under her skin. After all, men don't like weak women. They prey upon them, but they never fall for them."

Here was another one of Nana's lessons she had failed. And she began to wonder if maybe she would have had Mack all to herself had she seemed stronger. She was so meek, pathetic.

"So, now, let me guess," Nana said. She leaned closer to Charlotte and began to whisper. "He was dating all three of you at once, and he brought you to my house here, and he made you all fall desperately and madly in love with him, thinking you were the only ones to hold his gaze and heart." She pursed her scalloped, poppy-red lips and took a sip of her martini.

How could she know this to be true? Ada wondered. So, this was a pattern of his? Mack was worse than she could have imagined.

"Pretty much," Charlotte said. "You nailed it."

Nana sat back in her chair, like a queen who had just finished eating a delicious four-course meal. She was satiated.

"I can't believe this!" Ada shouted. "This is, like, a thing? A pattern? And you know about it?" Ada was livid. Mack would be hearing about this. No, actually, he would not. She would no longer grace him with her presence or ever talk to him again, as long as she lived. Ada vowed to hate Mack until she was in the grave. He was dead to her. She thought of poor Ben, who was home with the kids.

"Sweet Ada dear," Nana said, "my grandson is a wonderful man, and you are not the first women to fall head over heels for him. But he is also flawed, like his grandfather, *my Joe*. Joe was also handsome, charming, and quite the ladies' man. He was the apple of my eye, and many others' eyes too. I learned this too late in life, right as he lay dying. Women came in droves, saying their goodbyes, feeling the need to divulge their trysts while my husband lay by my side."

The women listened with intent, incredulously, as if they were watching a movie. Mack's nana sipped at her martini and continued.

"But I'm no dummy," she said. "I knew this all along! You think I wouldn't guess he was out getting his kicks with a bunch of broads when he'd show up at six in the morning, blitzed out of his mind, claiming he'd been palling around with his buddies?"

"I'm so sorry," Charlotte said.

"Oh, don't be! The joke was on him!" she said. "I kept my wits about me, my head on sharp, and I lived a good life, surrounded by my friends. A woman doesn't need a man to make her happy, that's for damn sure. I learned that the hard way. And you are learning that lesson now too, I suppose."

"I don't know about learning a lesson," Charlotte said. "But I do know I learned that Mack is an asshole!"

"Charlotte!" Sadie scolded.

"It's okay, Sadie," Nana said. "Mack is an asshole! He's been doing this for years! He's been a goddamned thorn in my side since before he married that poor young woman."

"He said she cheated on him!" Charlotte screeched.

"Well, now, perhaps only a small portion of what Mack tells you is the real truth," Nana said.

"Oh, and he also said you were dead," Charlotte replied. Nana leaned backwards in her chair, mouth agape, as if she, too, had seen a ghost.

"Now what in God's name?" Nana gasped. "Mack said I had passed?"

She glanced at Ada and Sadie, who nodded in agreement. Nana shook her head. "This is just too much. I thought he had lost his moral compass, but now it seems he's lost his mind!" She stood up and walked towards the window, peering out. She paused. Then, as if a lightbulb went on, she exclaimed, "And you know what? I'm tired of it. You're not the first to come crying to me, but you may be the last!"

"What do you mean?" Sadie asked.

"I'm done with this!" Nana declared. "He needs to pay the piper, that Mackey, and own up to his charlatan behavior. All these secrets and lies! It's disturbing. Very. He must be held accountable," she said. "If I do one more thing on this earth before I die," she continued, "It may be to right my grandson's behavior. He's lost his way. I need to guide him toward a better future. I need to make him a better man! I love my Mackey, and it's not too late to straighten his sorry ass out."

"I don't know about a better future, but he sure as hell deserves a piece of your mind!" Charlotte responded.

"Don't you worry, Charlotte. I know just the thing to do."

"What's that?" Ada asked.

"You women have to be strong. You're too weak, and this is what a strong woman would do."

"What's that?" Sadie asked.

"I don't know off the cuff. Let me think . . ."

Nana closed her eyes and took several deep breaths. Suddenly her eyes shot open. "I have it!" she exclaimed.

"What? The plan? What is it?" Ada asked.

"Oh, a lady never tells all!" Nana replied. "She is mysterious! She keeps it close to the vest. If I told you everything, you wouldn't come back for more now, would you?"

"Interesting," Sadie affirmed, as if she were taking mental notes.

"So, what should we do?" Ada asked.

"Just be patient and wait for my call," Nana said. "You dolls just put your chins up and trust me. I know what I'm doing. I was married to Mack's granddad, after all. Believe you me, we ladies always have the last laugh." Nana held up her martini glass as if to make a toast. "To the Mack Project!"

The women lifted their glasses, looking at each other for validation. They clinked glasses and called out, "To the Mack Project!" They snickered, the first real laugh since they'd arrived.

"Until then, you girls get some rest and go back to your husbands, if you have them. We all make mistakes, but we can also correct them. Take it from me. I've lived a long life, and that's one thing I know for sure. Don't look back. The more you do, the sooner you'll be going that way. Move forward, keep your head up high, and act like a lady . . . And keep this to yourselves. A lady never gossips or tells secrets."

Chapter Twenty-Seven
BEACON HELL AND KITTEN HEELS

CHARLOTTE

Charlotte tried to heed Nana's advice to act like a lady, but not for long. She was preparing dinner for her and John when she got a text that he was staying over in Boston for yet another "client dinner." She had just about had it with him and their charade of a marriage. One hot sex session on the kitchen floor a few weeks ago did not make up for the years of his indiscretions. She couldn't count how many times she'd received a text like this, but she could count the number of times she replied this way. One.

JOHN: *Gonna be a late client dinner. Will just stay up here tonight.*

CHARLOTTE: *Don't bother coming back at all. And when you do, I won't be here.*

After she hit "send," Charlotte went into John's contact information on her phone and hit "block caller." She didn't even want to see his reply or field a phone call, should he bother to make one. Maybe that trollop he was having a skirt steak dinner with at No. 9 Park on Beacon Hill could console him. Or maybe he actually didn't need consoling. Perhaps this is what he wanted, an out. Charlotte wondered if she'd just fallen right into his trap. He'd made *her* do it, instead of him. *In fact, yes, that's probably exactly what was going on here,* Charlotte thought. John was no dummy. He most likely was in love with someone else but too cowardly to initiate divorce, so he acted out repeatedly until Charlotte could no longer stand it or found someone else.

The problem now with that "someone else" Charlotte found was that it was Mack. And, if all went according to Nana's plan, he was about to be confronted. As much as Charlotte wanted to watch Mack squirm and struggle, she couldn't get past one thing. She was in love with him. Yes, she finally admitted to herself that she loved him. She knew it was wrong, but she couldn't help it. She liked assholes. John was case in point. But she and Mack had a genuine connection. Rolling around on Sandy Neck and making love, talking late into the night on the phone, and the secret last-minute trip to Nantucket were all amazing memories that she couldn't forget or imagine were lies. *I mean, she knew he was with Sadie and Ada too, but did they really have that same intimacy?* Charlotte doubted it. She started to get cold feet. Maybe she would reach out and warn Mack, or just talk to him alone and get an explanation. She thought maybe he'd confess that he was confused, rebounding from a divorce, sowing his wild oats, but had actually fallen in love with her and her alone. Wishful thinking? She didn't know.

Charlotte walked to the fridge and opened it, searching for snacks, but all she could find was red pepper hummus, a couple of lemons cut in half with hardened skin and brown edges, a bowl of tuna fish, and salad dressings. She knew she needed to go shopping, but it was such a hassle, and truthfully the less she had in the fridge, the better she could stick to her diet. She may have quelled her eating disorder since her modeling days, but she still didn't want to take any chances. Charlotte stuck to the outer aisles of the grocery store, only buying produce, lean proteins, legumes, and a bit of dairy for that occasional cheddar cheese craving. Her trainer had instructed her to eliminate dairy altogether, citing cheese as the devil, but she gave in to those cravings sometimes, usually on weekends.

"Do you ever consider anyone besides yourself when shopping?" John asked. "I mean, I need to eat too, you know. Not all of us are trying to relive our glory days modeling and being mistaken for Kate Moss."

Some support system John was, Charlotte thought. She grabbed a small handful of raw almonds and headed upstairs to grab her suitcase and start packing. "I'm outta here," she muttered.

Charlotte opened her closet and was overwhelmed. How could she pack all of it? Rows of color-coordinated expensive fashions hung neatly on hangers. She decided it was best to pack some for now, and the rest she could send movers to acquire. She started to panic and thought of calling Sadie but refrained. She didn't need to be convinced that she was acting impetuous, as usual, or that she wasn't making the right decision. When you know, you know. Charlotte needed to trust her gut. She'd heard the "whisper" that John wasn't right for her from the very beginning, but she'd panicked and pulled the trigger on the marriage anyway. That whisper had grown louder and louder over the years, and now it was an all-out scream, shattering her eardrum: *Get the hell out!*

Charlotte sat on the edge of the king-sized bed that was always too big for her. She preferred to cuddle and spoon while sleeping. She looked over at the mahogany bureau she and John shared, knowing she needed to make her way over there to pack her underwear, bras, and socks. John's box of important mementos sat on top of it: a ticket to his first concert, Pearl Jam at Great Woods in Boston; his Psi U fraternity pin; his wedding ring—which he refused to wear, despite Charlotte's pleas. And . . . wait . . . what was this? Charlotte peered closer, lifting something out of the box. It was a folded-up receipt for an overnight in Kennebunkport, Maine, at the Captain Lord Inn. She and John had never stayed there. No, when they went to Kennebunkport for her cousin's wedding, they had stayed at the White Barn Inn, not the Captain Lord Inn. She turned it over, and it had a note scribbled in windy cursive on the bottom of it: *Always Got You on My Mind. xx Kim.*

Charlotte stared at the note, reading it again and again, the windy cursive and the name "Kim." She held it in the palm of her hand and watched as her fingers slowly closed in on it, like a Venus flytrap catching its prey, crumpling the receipt into a tiny ball, which she put in her jeans pocket. She didn't want to think any more about this, because, well, it was no surprise. In fact, the worse things got, the less she felt. This was, she learned in therapy, her body's way of protecting itself from harm. It was a fight or flight. When the shit hit the fan, Charlotte became numb inside. However, it was the little things that sent her reeling, like being late for dinner or gaining a pound of water weight.

Charlotte opened her underwear drawer and took out enough pairs to last her a few weeks. Typically, she was the type of woman who matched her thong to her bra. But this time, she just tossed whichever bras she could find, even the ones where the hooks had been bent or the padded triangles had fallen out in the dryer. She threw them into her suitcase, then grabbed two pairs of heels and some sneakers and put those in a separate bag—dirty soles must be kept separate from clean underwear. Next, she headed for her makeup and jewelry. When she was finished packing, she wheeled her luggage down the stairs. It landed like a thud on each step, and she closed the front door behind her. She was getting the hell out. But where she would go, she had no idea.

Charlotte got the text from Sadie that they were scheduled to meet Nana and Mack for the "intervention" at The Quarterdeck on Main Street in Falmouth. The Quarterdeck was a staple restaurant for old-timers like Nana, offering Old Cape Cod favorites like the traditional fried fish sandwich and seafood Newburg drenched in butter and Ritz cracker breadcrumbs. Nana had her usual table in the back of the restaurant, away from the bar that was littered with men her age starting around one p.m. daily. The same crew often met up for cocktails, wearing ball caps, dock shoes, old khaki slacks, and sweaters. They were the former town clerks, landscapers, and fishermen, who were now retired. There were always a lot of laughs, and often a lot of men, which is why Nana, a lady, preferred to keep to herself in the back—with the other ladies around town.

Charlotte sat parked in her car behind the restaurant, chewing on her nails. One at a time, she bit them off and spit them out onto the center console. Her stomach was in knots, and she felt like her eye was twitching. This was not going to be easy. She opened the car door and stepped out, wearing her black espadrilles and a floral wrap dress. When she went into The Quarterdeck, she looked around anxiously, hoping she was the first to arrive. Various license plates hung on the brown wooden panels behind the bar. It had a familiar smell of clam chowder and warm, white dinner rolls, the kind you can only get nowadays if you ask for them along with your side salad. They were a staple for years before the Zone and keto diets emerged, forever ruining carbs for the millions who loved them.

"Howdy, Charlotte!" Rick called out. Rick had been a bartender at The Quarterdeck for as long as she could remember, and for at least as long as she'd lived in town. Rick knew what everyone liked to drink, and you never had to ask. He'd get it started for you with a smile and always a witty quip.

"Going with the Baby Sancerre today?" he asked, reaching for the bottle from the tiny fridge by his feet behind him.

"Oh, I'm actually meeting some people this time," Charlotte apologized. "Have you seen . . . er . . . *Nana*?" She felt embarrassed that she couldn't remember Nana's proper name. She was drawing a complete blank, perhaps from the stress of finding the receipt, her leaving John, and the impending intervention with Mack. She hadn't seen Mack, after all, in a few days, despite his pleas to meet up.

"You mean *Lady Taylor*?" Rick asked, lowering his voice and raising his brows.

Charlotte laughed. Nana sure was a "lady" about town, even by title now.

"Yes, have you seen her?"

"She's at her table in back, hon," he said, motioning with his finger toward the blue-carpeted room behind her. The bar was dark, and the overhead lighting in the back was much better for folks who actually liked to see the menu or needed readers.

Charlotte walked back past the bathrooms and the Frank Sinatra poster on the wall. Nana motioned for her to join her with a wave. She was wearing a sparkly diamond bobble ring on her middle finger that glistened as she moved her hand. And, seated to her left, was Mack.

"Charlotte," Nana called out, "you're the first of the gals to arrive." Charlotte's stomach turned. She didn't know what had transpired yet, but she wasn't looking forward to sitting through this. Mack looked despondent as if he'd been punched in the face. His complexion was flushed and his mouth downturned. She zoomed in on his beautiful, full lips that she remembered kissing. He stood up, like a gentleman, and pulled a chair out for her.

"Well, hello, Charlotte," he said, smirking.

"Hello," Charlotte squeaked. She cleared her throat and sat down without making eye contact.

"So! I just finished telling Mackey here that he will no longer be part of the Taylor Family Trust," Nana said, folding her blue linen napkin and putting it on her lap. "As of today, he is *cut off.* He cannot be trusted, and he has embarrassed me and our family name *for the last time.*" Nana seemed resolute and continued. "Until he can prove he's a better man to me, in time, he will be forced to get a real job and to work for his money. Nana's well has dried up for old Mackey here. It's *not* for cheaters and liars!"

Nana frowned in her bright peacock-blue dress with round gold buttons. Her hair was in a bun at the nape of her neck, and a tiny blue ribbon lay atop it. She had the look of a nun in a Catholic school who had just whipped her student with a ruler.

"Wow," Charlotte said. "I'm . . . sorry? To hear that?" She looked to Mack for a response.

"Charlotte," Mack said. "I am the one who is sorry. Unbelievably sorry."

"Thank you," Charlotte said. She looked down at her lap as she twisted her coaster, breaking it in half.

"Mack here realizes now the harm he's done to you three ladies—to your friendships, your marriages, your reputations, and, most importantly, your hearts."

"I didn't mean to—" Mack started to say, but Charlotte interrupted.

"I honestly don't want to hear it from you. Not now. Maybe at a later time, but this is enough for today," Charlotte said. "If you will excuse me, I don't think I would like to stay while the other ladies join in." She stood, and the lump in her throat seemed to grow so much that even a deep swallow would not quell the tears.

"Charlotte, dear, a lady doesn't—"

"Excuse me, Nana? I am so sorry, but I just am in no mood to hear what a lady would do right about now," Charlotte said. "A lady wouldn't have laid on her back on the beach and cheated on her husband. A lady wouldn't have broken the trust of her best friend since she was eleven. A LADY wouldn't stand to be treated this way but still be in love! Obviously, I'm not a lady!"

Her voice broke, and Charlotte could no longer continue speaking. Mack stood up and embraced her. She put her head on his shoulder and sobbed. She missed his smell. "*How could you?*" she asked.

"I don't know," Mack said. "I . . . just . . . I'm an idiot."

"Oh, Mack, that's not a great apology, dear. You have got to come up with something better than that. *What were you thinking,* she wants to know?" Nana urged. She tugged at Mack's Nantucket red pants from her seat.

"I wasn't thinking. That's the truth of it. I got carried awasy and swept up in the moment," Mack said, shrugging apologetically. "I truly hope you can forgive me, Charlotte, because you were the one that I really fell for." He stared at her intensely with his blue eyes.

"Okay, just stop right there," Charlotte said, holding her hand up like a crossing guard.

Just then, as if on cue, Ada and Sadie arrived.

"Hold it right here, ladies, we are having a moment," Nana said, lifting her martini glass as if she were making a wedding toast. "Mackey here says Charlotte is his *true love* of the bunch! Isn't that right, Mack?" Nana was outing him like she was getting back at her own Joe for all the years he abused her. All the cheating Joe did was now coming back to haunt Mack. He was going to pay for generations of Taylor men: his father, who cheated on his mother, and Grandpa Taylor, who cheated on Nana. *Perhaps this is why Mack cheated also,* Charlotte thought. No, it couldn't be genetic. That would be too easy of an out. He was scum, lower than low, the worst of the worst, a spoiled brat, and a trust fund douchebag.

"Yes, you were saying, Mack?" Charlotte said, fluttering her eyelashes and smirking at Mack.

Mack looked stunned, like a kid with his hand in the cookie jar. Then he inhaled and let out a huge exhale and began to talk.

"Yes, it is true," Mack said, now addressing Ada and Sadie. "I love Charlotte."

"You are pathetic," Sadie said, shaking her head. "Truly."

"I don't even have words," Ada scoffed. "I planned this big speech, but upon seeing you, I just . . . I'm not sure you're even worth the effort."

Mack's shoulders slumped. He looked to Charlotte to help him. *Hell no*, she thought. He was going to have to endure this pain by himself. She was certainly not his life raft, even though she wanted to be with every ounce of her body. It felt amazing to be told he loved her. She loved him too, desperately, and she wondered how that connection, which felt so amazing and true, could be false. Mack proved to her it was not. She wanted to run away with him in glee, but she knew better. He was pathetic. And she was pathetic. This whole group was pathetic! And here she was getting involved with yet *another* asshole, when she had finally left the first asshole, John. She hated herself.

Charlotte pulled off Storrow Drive in Boston onto Arlington Street, armpits sweating, gripping the steering wheel in a ten-two position. She'd made it to Beacon Hill and their apartment in an hour and ten minutes from leaving The Quarterdeck. In other words, she hauled ass.

She parked in front of 27 Phillips Street. The gas lamps lining the pristine brick sidewalks were aglow, as it was just past sunset. A young woman in her twenties walked by holding an orange tabby cat by the leash. She acknowledged Charlotte with a wave. People were friendly in Beacon Hill, even if they weren't familiar. Sharing a zip code was enough of an acquaintance to merit a smile or wave. The air was slightly muggy, as it always was once you drove over the Bourne Bridge. Charlotte inhaled the smell of the magnolia trees and headed straight for the front door. She wasn't sure what to expect inside, but she had a feeling it wasn't going to be good. She reached into her clutch and pulled out the key. It was on its own separate gold Cartier keychain, monogrammed with her initials. She turned the key, fiddling with it, as she rarely ever used it or came up to their Boston apartment. Upon unlocking the door, Charlotte stepped in.

"Can I help you?" Kimberly exclaimed, shuddering in the middle of the living room of Charlotte and John's apartment. She looked nothing like what Charlotte expected. She was a thin brunette with gold streaks in her long hair, and she was wearing some sort of soccer mom getup: a navy-blue and white striped shirt with an equestrian blazer, and tight boot-cut jeans with kitten heels. She did not appear to be the trashy minx Charlotte had imagined her to be when she was penning that note in Kennebunkport, donning John's bathrobe, and ordering room service on their credit card.

"Can I help *you?*" Charlotte retorted. "You are, of course, in *my* apartment." She threw her Louis Vuitton purse on the floor, the same floor that she and John had made love on, coming home drunk from The Sevens on Charles Street last year.

"I think you may be mistaken," Kimberly said. Her voice was meek, and she was far from threatening. It annoyed Charlotte. So, this is what John wanted? Someone more like Ada? Some mousy Talbots soccer mom?

"No, you are mistaken, KIMBERLY. That's your name, isn't it?"

Kimberly's face flushed and then turned a shade of white that matched her pearl earrings.

"Um . . . yes. How do you know my name?"

"Well," Charlotte said, reaching for the crumpled-up receipt in her back pocket, "I believe this note to my husband—John? I believe it's from you." She threw the note at Kimberly, who stepped backward, almost tripping on the Oriental carpet in her kitten heels. Kimberly unraveled the note.

"Where did you get this?" she asked.

"Are you, like, really ignorant?" Charlotte asked. "Or just hearing impaired? I got it from, *like I said, my husband*, John. Or should we refer to him as your lover, boyfriend, what?"

"John is my fiancé," she replied, furrowing her brow. Charlotte looked down at Kimberly's left ring finger. She was, in fact, sporting a large, shimmering emerald-cut solitaire diamond. "And I presume you are his ex?" she asked.

"His ex?" Charlotte threw her head back in the air, cackling like the Joker. "Now, that's a laugh riot. Where is that fucker?" She stormed off, past the kitchen, peeling around the corner to their bedroom. The apartment smelled of beef stew that had been braising in a crockpot all day long. There were candles lit and new décor with a more feminine touch. The photos of her and John were gone, replaced by ones of him and Kimberly in frames on the bookshelves.

"Wait!" Kimberly yelled, following her, clamping in her heels on the wood floor.

Charlotte busted open the bedroom door to find John, sitting in his bed, shirtless and working on his laptop.

"Charlotte!" he exclaimed. "What are you doing here?" He threw his laptop off to the side of the duvet cover and leapt out of the bed in his black silky boxer briefs.

"You are really something, John," Charlotte said. "So, this is your *fiancée?* Did we get a divorce I didn't know about?" She looked back at Kimberly, whose lips were pursed with consternation.

"Charlotte," he reached for her, grabbing her forearm. "I can explain—"

"Don't come near me," Charlotte said, pulling his wrist off her. "I'll save you the shock and surprise of getting served divorce papers. Consider it done. Hope you guys enjoy your wedding." Charlotte pushed past Kimberly and headed to the kitchen. John looked at Kimberly and followed her.

"What are you doing?" John said. Charlotte was riffling through various kitchen drawers, opening and closing them, searching for something in particular.

"These are my grandmother's," she said, holding up several crocheted coasters with images of New England on them. "And I'd like my Girl Scout doily back as well."

"Can you relax and please stop going through my drawers?"

"These are not your drawers, John. They are *our* drawers!" Charlotte screamed. "In fact, I think I was there when we picked out these cabinet fixtures at Pottery Barn!" She threw a sterling silver rounded fixture at his face. It bounced off his cheek.

"Ow!"

"Oh, and I believe this is the toaster oven that we got from our registry at Crate and Barrel. I mean, Kimberly? Maybe you want to check it out, so you don't buy the same one when you two register." Charlotte continued to forage, huffing and puffing and slamming cabinets open and shut.

"Charlotte, please," John said. "We need to talk."

"Do we?" Charlotte replied. "I've been trying to talk to you for years. Now is a little late. *Give me my fucking doily!*" She was on a tear, now moving to the living room. Suddenly, she felt a slight tap on her shoulder. It was Kimberly.

"Here you go," she said. "Is this your doily?"

Charlotte scowled, ripping the green Girl Scouts doily from Kimberly's hand and throwing it in her purse, along with an avocado masher and a coffee mug that read "Don't Feed the Models."

"Things weren't working!" John pleaded. "You know that!"

"Yes, I know that!" Charlotte shrieked. "But you could have had the decency to break it off with me before getting fucking ENGAGED to someone else! At least I just fucked somebody! Multiple times! And it was *good*!"

His face looked sallow, almost as if he was going to cry. For a moment, Charlotte wanted to reach out to him, to comfort him. She saw him as a little boy who needed a hug. But this sentiment faded quickly.

"Doesn't matter," Charlotte said. "And neither do you." She stormed off to the front door of the apartment and paused as she gripped the golden handle. She then turned back to Kimberly. "Be careful," she urged. "He's not what he seems. Oh, and neither is his penis, but I guess you already know that."

Charlotte got into her car, her chest heaving, sobbing uncontrollably. She looked at herself in the mirror on the sun visor, snot blowing out of her nose. Her blonde hair looked stringy now and had a halo of frizz around it. She was a far cry from the *Sports Illustrated* swimsuit model or even the heifer back in eighth grade. She had become a shell of the person she once was, someone lost and living on Cape Cod with no ambition, no family, and no life. She had thrown it all away for John and the hopes of being a "normal" person, one without an eating disorder or the drive to be on the cover of *Vogue*. She couldn't take any more hurt. First Mack, now this. She sped down Phillips Street, heading for Cambridge Street. She passed Massachusetts General Hospital and Finagle a Bagel, the Liberty Hotel, and the sign that reads, "If You Lived Here, You'd Be Home

Now." *But this was no longer my home,* Charlotte thought. She wasn't sure where home was anymore. Everything in Falmouth was a wreck, and she couldn't bear to look at Mack, Sadie, or Ada. And Boston and her life with John were completely over. What was the solution?

She reached for an Altoids in her center console, turned up the volume on Spotify, and asked Siri for help.

"Hey, Siri? Where is the closest liquor store near me?"

"The closest liquor store is off Massachusetts Avenue, Exit 2," Siri replied.

Just then, the Train song "Marry Me" started playing, which she vehemently rejected on Spotify and gave it a thumbs-down. "Ugh!" she yelled aloud, weaving in and out of lanes.

Charlotte felt crazed, lost, and reckless. But, as she drove farther down 93 South, something happened. A sense of calm washed over her, and she had a brilliant idea. She did not get off at exit 4, her regular exit toward Cape Cod. No, instead she continued on 93 South and headed to Interstate 90 South. Charlotte was going back to New York City. *Yes, Manhattan; that is where my home is,* she thought. What a terrible mistake she'd made all those years ago, moving here to be closer to Sadie and her own summer memories. She would go back to the city and make a new start of things, maybe work for Elite Models in casting or do staging for Manhattan apartment sales. She could start over and leave this terrible life behind. She would never run into Mack again, and she wouldn't have to wonder if John was sleeping in Boston. *What a dream!* she thought. A chance to start over . . .

Two hours later, Charlotte glanced at the digital clock on her dashboard and yawned: 9:54 p.m. She had two hours to go until she reached New

York City. What had initially seemed like a good idea was beginning to seem crazy. First and foremost, she worried about money. Renting an apartment in Manhattan was going to cost at least $2,500 a month, and she didn't want to live with roommates or in the outer boroughs. After all, she wasn't in her twenties, let alone her early thirties, anymore. Also, Charlotte had not had a real job in years, because John had been there for support. He paid all the bills and took care of everything. Her modeling career was definitely a thing of the past, and most casting agencies would probably not recognize her name, even though she used to be an industry favorite. And her body? Charlotte couldn't even bear the thought of how they'd examine her fat thighs and wrinkled face. She would have to start a crash-liquid diet immediately and get Botox. She thought back to the time she arrived in wardrobe for a commercial, and the only pants to choose from were size 3. She was a size 4. The head of wardrobe scolded her in front of everyone for gaining weight since her measurements had been taken. She definitely would be closer to a size 6 now.

"Fuck John," she whispered. "And that trashy tramp in kitten heels wearing that gaudy fucking engagement ring." Charlotte began to cry. In the rearview mirror, she saw her mascara trickling down her face, like a drawing of a river on a map. A man in a Dodge with a Friday the 13th sticker on his windshield tried to pass her. He swerved close and almost swiped the side of her car.

Charlotte wondered if she'd even be able to leave John, especially after what had happened with Mack. Venturing into the unknown and dating someone new was exhilarating. But when it blew up in her face and she lost her friends and dignity, she was apprehensive to dip her toes back in the water. In fact, she wanted to just retreat and hide behind her marriage and stay indoors. Maybe she was at fault, she wondered. She, too, had cheated. How could she blame John for being an asshole when she was just as bad? Was that hypocritical?

And maybe, just maybe, John knew about Mack. Maybe she had been obvious about it, and she'd driven him into the arms of Kimberly. Perhaps he was doing that for attention. Well, he surely got it. *Aw, wait,* she thought. She was definitely the jerk here. That was sort of romantic of John. He did this all to get her back, to win her attention, and get noticed. This marriage perhaps was not over. Maybe, in reality, it was just beginning, and this was the fresh start she'd wanted. Yes, maybe she would turn around and go back to Cape Cod. This was *insane* to think she could go to New York. A sense of calm washed over her body. She had been clenching her teeth in the ten-two driving position for hours, so she exhaled and could feel her shoulders lowering.

Charlotte peered at the dashboard clock again: ten thirty. She figured she'd stop for a coffee in New London, which was exactly halfway, and maybe even grab a hotel room at the Mystic Inn before turning around and heading back home. She pulled over on exit 86, near the Coast Guard and Connecticut College, and drove down Main Street looking for a diner. She passed the Amtrak station and circled around and around until she parked in front of Grafton Street Café, which was open till midnight. The "G" on the lightbulb on the sign had burnt out so it read "rafton Street Café," and there was a loud buzz coming from the alley HVAC system.

As Charlotte entered the diner, bells clamored. She shut the front glass door and noticed how alarmingly bright the place was inside, like a laboratory, particularly since she had been in the dark car for two hours. She smelled a combination of maple syrup, bacon, and French fries, almost as if she were in an IHOP. She grew self-conscious and extracted her blush case from her purse to wipe off the mascara under her eyes. A waitress was bussing tables who reminded Charlotte of Flo on the 80s sitcom *Alice*: beehive hairdo, gum-smacking, with an accent. She wore a light blue shirt, the color of doctor's scrubs, with "Grafton Street Café" stitched in white across her right breast. Charlotte sat on a cushioned stool at the counter and swiveled side to side, like a child. She reached for the table tent listing the specials: mammaw's slow-roasted brisket, French onion soup au Grafton, and roasted cod with mashed potatoes.

"Can I get you something to drink, hon?" the waitress asked, removing the pencil from behind her ear.

"Um, yes. Just a coffee? Black? Do you have dark roast?" Charlotte asked.

"We got whatever's on the burner," the waitress replied. Charlotte glanced at her nametag that read "Sonya."

"Thank you, Sonya. I'll have that," she said.

"No food?" Sonya replied. She looked like she'd worked the graveyard shift two nights in a row. The dark circles under her eyes and the creased smoker's lips hardened her look.

"No, thank you. That will be all," Charlotte said. She grabbed her cell phone to prevent herself from staring, so that she would not have to engage in awkward conversation. Sonya returned to the counter holding a white mug of coffee that was chipped around the edges from wear and tear. The thought of all the yucky teeth eroding away at the mug turned Charlotte's stomach, but she knew she had no other choice, so she sipped at it.

"Where you coming from?" Sonya asked, refilling the red squeezable ketchup bottles with the pointy tips.

"How do you know I'm not from here?" Charlotte asked playfully.

"Well, for starters, I saw you driving around in circles outside," Sonya said, chuckling. "And next, you just have this sad puppy look about you." This struck Charlotte, particularly since she was feeling the same way about Sonya. To elicit pity from someone who already looked pitiful seemed extra pathetic and alarming.

"Wow, is it that obvious?" Charlotte asked, softening to Sonya. "Did the Tammy Faye Bakker mascara streaming down my face give it away? I didn't have any wipes in the car," she said.

"I got some wipes in the back, if you want," Sonya said, jutting her thumb up and behind her like she was hitchhiking.

"What kind of wipes?" Charlotte asked.

"Fresh-Ups or something? I dunno. Some kinda wipes. Fran uses 'em in the kitchen."

"I'm okay," Charlotte replied, questioning what those wipes would actually look like.

"Suit yourself," Sonya said, returning to her side work. She placed the ketchup bottles under the counter in a gray plastic bin, similar to the ones used at airport security.

"Sorry, I don't mean to be rude," Charlotte said. "I've just had a long day."

"You're not bothering no one, hon," Sonya said. "No need for apologies. That's sure as hell something I've learned along the way. In fact, I learned the hard way."

"Oh yeah?" Charlotte asked, perking up. The saying "misery loves company" seemed opportune.

"Just ask my kids," she continued. "They watched it all go down, the abuse," Sonya said.

"Oh, I'm so sorry," Charlotte replied. "I can't imagine," she said, even though she very well could.

"Yep, my ex was a hitter," she said. "Pretty much every day for about fifteen years, till I smartened up and grew a pair and got the hell out of there."

Charlotte listened intently, sipping at her coffee.

"You see, he was nice at first. They all are—abusers. It's the old bait-and-switch." Charlotte shifted her head to the side. She didn't get it.

"The Prince Charming act?" Sonya continued. "Come on real strong, buy you things, make you feel like you can't do nothing wrong—like you're the best God-damned thing that ever walked through their door. You're on top of the world, shitting diamonds!" Sonya said, laughter erupting in a smoker's fluid-filled cough.

Then, she moved closer and squinted her eyes. Charlotte could smell the grease from the fryer on Sonya's clothes. It reminded her of when her hair smelled like home fries when she worked at the Coffee Shop in Union Square.

"But then, slowly, very slowly, they begin to scratch away at your confidence, at your soul, and you don't even know it's happening," she said, picking at the air with a fingernail for effect, just a touch of ketchup on the tip. "It's like that metaphor with the frog in the boiling water."

Charlotte shook her head. She wasn't familiar with the tale. She took another sip of coffee, and Sonya topped it off.

"Oh yeah, the frog." Sonya shook her head. "That damn frog, little old frog is all happy in the water. But slowly, as time goes by, the water gets a little hotter, each and every day. But the frog don't notice. He's happy, or so he thinks. Then, one day, one day, the frog realizes he's damn near boiling and his legs are burning. The water has gotten so hot, boiling hot, and he didn't even notice, until it was too late. He was almost frog legs!"

"Oh my God, that's awful!" Charlotte said. "The poor frog."

"Yeah, well, that's what them abusers do to you. Or what mine did to me, that's for sure. One day I wake up and I'm in boiling hot water. I was frog legs."

"So, what did you do?" Charlotte asked.

"I got the hell outta there," Sonya said, now folding napkins into triangles and rolling silverware in them. "But I planned carefully, for months. I stocked up on canned goods and toiletries—toothpaste, toilet paper, shampoo—storing them under my bed in a black duffel bag. I saved my tips and hid them from my husband. I packed luggage for me and the kids, left it in the trunk. Then, one night, when he was asleep, I grabbed the kids, the duffel bag, the clothes, and I hauled ass."

"Oh my God, that must have been so scary," Charlotte said, gripping both sides of the coffee mug.

"Refill?" Sonya asked.

"No, thanks."

"Well, yeah, I was scared outta my mind," Sonya said. "But know what?" She raised both brows high, her forehead wrinkles accentuated.

"What?"

"I ain't scared no more. And that, my friend, is freedom. That is living. I was dead. I was afraid."

Charlotte thought of her own situation with John. It certainly wasn't as terrible as Sonya's, but the idea that she was captive, not living, resonated. She had become someone she was not. A townie? Maybe. A cheater? Yes. A bad friend? Yes. A victim? Yes. Shame washed over her as she reached for the check to pay.

"Thank you for sharing that with me," Charlotte said. "I am happy you're free."

"You know, you can be free too," Sonya said.

"Oh, I don't have it that bad," Charlotte said.

"Do you feel the hot water surrounding you?" Sonya asked.

Charlotte pretended not to hear, as her hands tingled, and her face felt hot.

"Thank you. Keep the change," Charlotte said, smiling slightly and looking Sonya in the eye. "Have a good night."

"You too, hon. You take care," Sonya said, placing the heap of silverware roll-ups into another gray tub under the counter.

Charlotte left the diner and walked toward her car in the dark. It was close to midnight, so she shuffled quickly. The air was cooler than it had been. Charlotte thought about the oak tree on her front lawn on the Cape, about Sadie and Ada, and Mack. She didn't know who she was anymore. Perhaps it wasn't a good idea for her to go back. She didn't want to end up like Sonya. She wanted to be free. She was tired of living beneath John's thumb. She was tired of the lies. Maybe she should trust her instincts to move on, go back to New York, and start fresh. She was too young to throw in the towel and be complacent. But she wasn't sure. She needed her best friend for advice. This was what she'd done forever.

"Hello?" Sadie said on the other end of the call.

"Hi," Charlotte said, holding her cell phone close to her ear. She was locked in her parked car near the diner. "I'm glad you picked up."

"I'm glad you called," Sadie said with a softness in her voice. "Are you okay? What's going on? It's midnight."

"I don't know," Charlotte said. "I'm in New London on my way to New York."

"Oh," Sadie said. "So, what's happening?"

"Well, I just wanted to call to say that I miss you. And I miss your advice. I'm leaving John, and I'm moving back to New York," Charlotte said. She didn't feel the need to tell her about Kimberly, about the fight, about all of it. She just wanted to hear her voice. She needed her.

"I'm not surprised you're leaving him," Sadie replied. "He's an asshole."

"He is an asshole, isn't he?" Charlotte said, laughing. It felt good to laugh.

"I'm sorry. I've been an asshole too," Sadie said.

"Stop. We both have," Charlotte said. "Okay, well maybe you more than me," she laughed.

"Shut the fuck up!" Sadie said, joining her. "I wish you wouldn't go, but I understand why you have to."

"So, you don't think that's crazy?" Charlotte asked.

"Nah, it's you! You're crazy!" Sadie said. "And this Cape life never really suited you in the first place. You hate the ocean!"

"I do prefer pools."

"And you don't eat seafood, and you are still wearing black all the time!"

Charlotte began to cry. She wasn't sure if she should be happy to be talking to her best friend in the world again or to be sad that she had been leading the wrong life for so long. After hanging up the phone, Charlotte turned the car ignition on and headed toward the highway.

But, this time, instead of heading North to the Cape, she headed South to New York. She chose herself.

Chapter Twenty-Eight

FRIENDS WITH BOATS

SADIE

The end of summer on the Cape, marked by Labor Day, was always bittersweet. It was a blessing to see all the tourists leave, to not wait in traffic, and to get back to "normal." But it was also sad to say goodbye to August—a time of beaches, barbecues, night swimming, and summer friends.

But not this year. Sadie couldn't wait for the school year. The summer had been exhausting, to say the least, and she wanted to get on with her life. It was almost the shoulder season, the best time on the Cape when all the restaurants stayed open, and the beaches cleared out. Sadie thought often about Charlotte in New York and considered reaching out, but she never did. She needed space. She did know, however, that Charlotte was returning for the Farewell to Summer Fling at the club, because Scarlett Crane told her she'd seen a post about it on Instagram.

Sadie had not seen Ada either, since the Quarterdeck intervention. And she didn't have to wonder about Mack because he was the topic of conversation around town. Regarding Mack, ever since Nana cut him off from the family trust, people had begun to gossip. Friends who had invested in his resort clamored for a return and felt they'd been hoodwinked. She heard he hadn't made the payments on his dock slip, and he was in *The Enterprise* police logs for suspected drunk driving and a DUI. Chip said his friend Rob saw Mack day drinking at the Quahog Republic behind Walmart several times, trying to hide on a sunny day.

Sadie was relieved that her relationship with Mack was over. Hiding and deleting text messages, worrying about shaving and nice lingerie, and ditching her family for a quickie was debilitating and exhausting. It was easier to eat a box of Cheez-Its, not worry about matching her panties and bra, and let her armpit hair go for more than a day. She was tired, very tired. She begged Chip to go to counseling with her, but he seemed more inclined to watch football than to work on things. He wasn't a believer in therapy. But didn't he believe in their marriage?

It occurred to Sadie that maybe Chip, too, was doubting their marriage. Maybe she wasn't the hot commodity she once was, or thought she was. Perhaps he'd taken notice that she was shaving and matching her lingerie, and he knew something was up. Or, worse yet, what if he too had feelings for someone else? What if he was secretly messaging someone on Facebook or meeting some mom out on the DL and she hadn't noticed? Sadie's stomach churned, and she started to feel a sense of panic. It never occurred to her that Chip would leave her. It was always the other way around. But maybe she had taken him for granted. He was solid, her rock. And here she was throwing it all away for some momentary summer high.

She started to spiral out. Chip had been acting withdrawn, but she thought it was because he was setting up his fantasy football league, something he always did in September preseason. This was a big deal for Chip. He would watch every game with anticipation and emotional investment. She recalled the time they were in the grocery store, and Chip looked at his watch in a panic. They were going to have to leave the store, he said, immediately—with a cart full of groceries—to get home in time for the Patriots game. God forbid, he had to miss a game! And if his "guys" lost, that was a whole other story. He would pout for the rest of the evening and retreat to the basement for hours, reworking his lineup and hoping for trades. It was an obsession, one that Sadie couldn't understand. Seemed ridiculous, in fact, but she kept her mouth shut.

Sadie continued to worry when she heard a knock on the door. She panicked momentarily, as she'd been cleaning and had sweats on and no makeup.

"Just a minute," Sadie called out. She scurried to her dresser, applied a fresh coat of Chanel lip gloss, and threw on her Maxwell beach cover-up. When she got to the door, Scarlett Crane stared back at her through the mesh on the screen, gripping the straps on her pink Hermès Birkin bag hanging over her left shoulder.

"Well, hello there, honey!" Scarlett chirped. "I am sorry to barge in on you, but I was in the neighborhood and figured I'd swing by. It's been *for-ev-er!*"

"I know. I'm so sorry I haven't called," Sadie replied, unlatching the screen and letting Scarlett in. "Can I get you something to drink? Water, lemonade, a glass of wine?" Sadie laughed. It was only eleven o'clock in the morning.

"Ooh, I do like some pink lemonade, if you have it. If it's unsweetened, I'll pass," Scarlett said. "I've been around enough salt lately and can use the sweet."

"Tell me about it," Sadie said. "This summer can't end soon enough. It's funny, because we wait all year for it to arrive, and then we can't wait for it to be over. Is there a time where we can just be happy?"

Scarlett chuckled. "I do miss you," she said. Then she paused and leaned forward, at attention. "Now, tell me, what is going on with that Mack Taylor?"

And here it was, the real reason for Scarlett's pop-in. She didn't miss a beat.

"I mean, he's a *loooooser*," Scarlett said. "And I never got a good vibe from him. He always seemed a little off, and I'm not surprised it's come to this. He was handed a silver spoon, and he did absolutely nothing with it. Talk about failure to thrive."

Scarlett didn't mince words. When she wanted to eviscerate someone, she could do it better than most.

"But he wasn't always a loser," Sadie said, folding beach towels. Sadie wondered if Scarlett maybe was just jealous that Mack hadn't made a pass at her. He was overtly flirtatious at the club with all the women, except for her. To be fair, Scarlett had packed on a few pounds around her midsection from ladies' nights and girls' lunches, and she certainly wasn't the prom queen she'd been in her glory days as a Falmouth Clippers cheerleader.

"Sadie, honey, I know you have a soft spot for this character being your first love and all, but please. He needs to go back to where he came from. Plus, I heard he might be, you know, hooking up with some of the women in Falmouth. And, by *some*, I mean many."

Sadie stopped folding. "Oh, really? Like who?" She feigned ignorance and hoped to God her name was not going to come out of Scarlett's mouth.

"Well, I hate to gossip, 'cause you know me and that's not my thing. But I heard Caroline Wall was seen messing around with him on his boat one evening. I won't say how I found out, but let's just say *I have friends with boats.*"

It's always the women who said they didn't like to gossip that gossiped the most, Sadie thought.

Relieved, Sadie pushed for more information. "Messing around? What does that even mean?" Of course she knew about Caroline Wall, but it was amusing to see Scarlett light up when spilling the tea.

"I don't know, Sadie! I didn't ask for details! All I know is some kissing and canoodling happened on a boat, and Dave Wall sure as hell is not happy with her."

"He knows?" Sadie's eyes widened.

"Child, this town is teensy, as you know, especially in our circles." Scarlett was just getting started. This was her favorite topic: exclusivity and private wealth.

"I don't know that I'm in that circle, but . . . "

"Well, you know what I mean," Scarlett said. "The golf club, Wianno, FYC, our husbands, our friends, et cetera scene! And yes, you are, Little Orphan Annie. Puh-leaze."

"Have you reached out to Caroline?" Sadie asked.

"Are you kidding me? I don't want to be in the fray. I keep to myself and stay out of all that mess," Scarlett said. Sadie couldn't help but laugh. "Speaking of, now what is the story with you and Charlotte? I haven't seen you two palling around as usual. Did you have a falling out?"

Sadie was quick to reply and change the subject. "We're just doing different things, is all," she replied. "Maybe I should reach out to Caroline to see if she's okay."

"Suit yourself," Scarlett said. "But don't kill the messenger! You did not hear this from me. The only Hermes in this situation is my Hermès scarf!" She cracked herself up.

"Wow, Greek mythology humor? Who knew you were into the classics!" Sadie was fairly sure Scarlett had learned that from *Real Housewives* on Bravo, but she let it go.

"Scarlett, I hate to cut this short, but I am swamped with cleaning and errands I have to run. I only have a few hours before the kids and Chip get home, so I have to get back to it."

Scarlett downed the rest of her pink lemonade placing it dead center on the coffee table.

"No problem, dear. I'm just glad we could catch up! Don't be a stranger now!" Scarlett said.

"Definitely not. Let's try to have a girls' night at Estia in the next couple of weeks. Hey, even invite Caroline Wall." Sadie laughed, but she felt sort of queasy at the same time.

"Oohhh! Now you're talking! I like it!" Scarlett exclaimed, her eyes lighting up.

Scarlett made her way out, and Sadie locked the door behind her. She stood in the center of the living room surrounded by plastic bins, towels, clothes, and sheets to fold. What had she gotten herself into? she wondered. She had a life here. Kids. A family. This summer had been a terrible mistake, all of it with Mack and Charlotte and risking the marriage and family she had built with Chip. She had lost her best friend, might potentially be losing her husband, and all for what?

Chapter Twenty-Nine

CALL HER DADDY

ADA

Ada lay stretched out on the bed, stomach down, in her new Cosabella lingerie. It was black and lace. The thin black string of the thong crept up her perfect, tiny ass, which she could see bubbled up and round when she looked in the vanity mirror across from the bed. She kicked her back legs up in the air, crossing them, noticing her ruby red toenail polish. Her pillowy breasts were pushed against the mattress and slightly falling out the sides of the black lace bra. They were soft, small handfuls spilling onto the bed. She thought about the last time she'd worn this lingerie, and it was with Mack, not Ben. She wore it when they'd made love on the beach, rolling in the sand, crunchy seaweed wrapping its tendrils around her hair. She remembered he did this thing with his fingers when they had sex from behind, laying his sturdy frame over her back and rubbing her clit between his thumb and index finger. She got excited just thinking about it, clenching inside.

Ada had learned a few new tricks in bed with Mack, and she was excited to try them out on Ben. Maybe it would reinvigorate their sex life. It had been at least a couple of months since the last time they'd slept together, and she wanted to try the "twist and pull" blow job maneuver she'd learned. It had made Mack's eyes roll into the back of his head. She'd heard about it on a podcast one day while driving to pick Lilly up at a dance practice off-Cape. It was called *Call Her Daddy* by Barstool Sports, and this raunchy but hilarious show host talked at length about her sex life and gave women and men technique tips and advice. Ada couldn't stop laughing and tuned into the podcast on her drive to work each morning, often testing out the new tips on Mack's tip!

She looked at her watch. Ben was still not home. She wondered if he had stopped at the package store to grab some beers on his way or maybe snuck off for a cold one at Papa Jake's with the guys from work. She could always tell when he'd gone to Papa Jake's because he smelled of pizza and buffalo sauce. Or she'd find a Keno card in his jacket pocket. Guess there were worse things to find than keno, and Ada sure knew about that. She wondered if Ben would notice her lingerie. He was never that into lacy things or thongs. "Wear what's comfortable," he would say. "It's going to end up on the floor anyway." So, Ada never bothered to spend the money on lingerie, even though it made her feel sexy to wear it. This was the new Ada. She would do things for herself, not just for others. She was tired of being a pleaser.

Ada lay with her face on the duvet cover. It was cold and soothing against her warm cheek. She lifted her wrist to her nose and inhaled the Gucci Bloom perfume. It smelled of peonies, pink roses, and lavender, a bouquet of her favorite flowers. She thought back to her wedding when she walked down the aisle at the First Congregational Church in Nantucket holding a bouquet almost like that, with her best friends at her side. The wedding had been small, with about eighty-five close friends and family, and the reception was held under a Sperry Tent in her uncle Dick's backyard. She remembered how it was pouring rain that day. She had drops of mud all up the back of her wedding gown from dancing on the wet grass. She had implored Ben to spend money on creating a wooden dance floor, but he said he could build one himself—and never got around to it.

Ada started to think of the menagerie of things Ben never completed that he'd said he would. The door to the bedroom opened slightly, and his face appeared in the crack.

"Whoa, am I interrupting something?" Ben asked, now pushing the door forward, smiling. He held his keys and still had his work boots on. She smelled a whiff of buffalo sauce.

"Well, I missed something," Ada said. "Your dick . . . " She tried to look like a vixen, even though she was desperately uncomfortable.

"Well," Ben exclaimed. "Yikes, I didn't expect to ever hear that from you," he chuckled. Ada laughed, chagrined, hiding her face in her hands.

"Oh, God, I'm no good at this," Ada grumbled, turning over to face the ceiling. "I'm trying to be sexy, but I'm failing miserably."

"You *are* sexy," Ben said. He sat by her side and gave her a pat on the head, like a dog. It was not quite the gesture she was hoping for. "But you already know that."

"No, I don't," Ada exclaimed, shooting up off the bed. She shuffled to the mirror, grabbed a cotton ball from the small crystal jar, and began taking off her makeup.

"Honey, you can't just, like, force this upon me. I just got home from work. I'm tired," he said. "I don't mean to be insensitive here, but did you take your pill today?" By "pill," Ben was referring to the antidepressant she took daily for anxiety and depression. His inability to understand the depths of mental illness always irked Ada, in addition to him thinking that by taking a "pill," all would be well.

"Yes, Ben. I took *my pill*," she replied, putting on her terry cloth robe that screamed of being a mom and an old JCPenney ad. Ben retreated to the bathroom to change. He did this every night when he got home: take off his Carhartts, put on his flannel pajama bottoms, and then made himself a margarita before heading to the basement to watch sports. "Where are the kids?" he called out from the bathroom.

"They're at their friends' houses. I'm going downstairs. I assume you already ate at Papa Jake's?"

Ben emerged from the bathroom in his slippers and flannel pajamas, no shirt.

"What's going on? I don't get it. You're acting strange."

"Nothing. Forget it. I just want to go downstairs. I'll get dinner started."

"Jesus Christ, Ada. This is exactly what I mean when I say you take everything to the next level."

"What? What do you want me to do? How should I feel when I'm, like, naked, begging for your . . . cock . . . ," she whispered, as if she had stolen something, "and you put on your slippers and pajamas!"

Ada walked downstairs to the kitchen. The gray tiles were cold on her bare feet. *Typical,* she thought. Ben was terrible at communicating and couldn't handle it when she cried. And, no, this was not her being over-the-top and dramatic. Sure, she could be explosive, but who wouldn't be with two school-aged children and a full-time job? Apparently, *the pill* wasn't helping enough. Maybe she should up her dose.

Ada was first diagnosed with anxiety and depression after Lilly was born. She didn't realize it was postpartum at the time. She just thought, well, this is how it is when you have two toddlers and are home all day. She and Ben had sort of drifted apart, and she was in the thick of it between breastfeeding and entertaining a two-year-old. She missed working, and she felt desperately alone. Her "baby brain" left no room for creativity or drive to do anything, so she lay around in yoga pants, Henry cooing on a blanket on the floor, and Lilly watching episodes of *The Wiggles* and *Octonauts*. She didn't have many friends. She was too afraid to take the baby out to library groups like Mommy and Me or Lap Babies Sing Along because she worried the baby would get sick. Ada began fixating on germs and fretting about her own health, too. Daily, she would google her symptoms and even manifest other ones to align with diagnoses, like kidney failure and lupus. She'd google "fatigue," and when nearly fifty results came up, she'd convince herself she had each one of the diseases, many of them fatal. She would then burst into tears and call Ben at work to say she needed to go to the doctor.

It was on a cold, blustery day in February that Ada finally realized she had a problem, a mental problem. Most likely due to her anxiety, she'd had chest pains all day. A blizzard was raging, and she was home with the kids while Ben was working. The electricity and thus the heat had gone out, as it often does on the Cape in a Nor'easter with high winds. She was cold, as were the children. Her chest pains increased, and Ada began worrying that her left arm was going numb, and she was having a heart attack. She called Ben for help, but he was working and didn't answer. She then tried calling her parents but to no avail. So, eventually, she dialed 9-1-1 and had an ambulance take her and the children to the emergency room at Falmouth Hospital. Upon arrival, they asked about her symptoms and admitted her to the ER for an EKG and heart monitoring. When Ben arrived, they both spoke with the doctor, who diagnosed her with panic disorder and recommended that she see a clinical social worker on the unit. It had never occurred to Ada that she could have a psychological issue, and it scared the daylights out of her. But eventually, she felt at ease and reassured that there was a name for her problem, and she began taking the medication.

By the time Ada got to the kitchen, it was seven o'clock. Standing in front of the fridge in her mom robe, she reached for a glass of Chardonnay. *Fuck it,* she thought. *I'm going to get drunk and, to top it off, take a Xanax.* She was amped and jittery after Ben's rejection, an advance that Mack would have relished. How could Mack have been such a fraud? Maybe she had no clue what any man wanted. First Mack jilted her, and now Ben rejected her—even in Cosabella lingerie using porn-speak. She walked to the bathroom and opened the medicine cabinet, where she found her prescription for Xanax. As she popped one into her mouth, washing it down with wine, she looked at herself in the mirror.

"Dis-GUS-ting," Ada blurted out. "I am heinous. What happened to me?"

She tossed cold water on her face, dabbing it with the hand towel she'd bought at a Christmas tree shop with "Beach Time!" embroidered on it along with a scallop shell. Her entire bathroom was decorated in the traditional Cape motif: shades of blue and turquoise and framed beach art with references from sand in the toes to boating and beach life. There was the long white wooden sign hanging with a rope that read, "It's 5 o'clock Somewhere."

She walked back to check her phone. No text messages, no calls, not even from the kids. Ada missed her girlfriends and the text chain with banter that went back and forth all day, a welcome distraction from work. Normally, after a fight or even slight irritation with Ben, she would call or text Sadie to vent. But she still hadn't spoken to Sadie since the intervention at the Quarterdeck. She thought of calling her sister, Nora, but then thought better of it. The problem with telling Nora was that she would tell the rest of the family, and then everyone would be upset with Ben, even long after Ada had forgiven him.

She flipped on the kitchen TV instead. The nightly news was on, and she started banging the pots around searching for her frying pan to start dinner. This was something that irked Ben. "Why are you so loud?" he'd ask. "Everything you do is on decibel 500. It's deafening." She was going to make stir-fry with grilled shrimp, one of her favorite dishes. She had picked the shrimp up fresh from The Clam Man. This evening had taken a turn from her original plan—to lay around lazily in bed, post-"toss," and order in Chinese food.

"What're you making?" Ben asked, lingering in the kitchen doorway.

"Stir-fry. With shrimp. That okay?"

"Sure, whatever you like. But I could grab some takeout if you prefer, or we could order delivery. Or even go out."

Ada didn't say anything, just continued stirring the onions around with a wooden spatula.

"We haven't been out together in a long time," Ben continued. "How about the Lobster Trap? A good ol' spicy Trap-arita? That might do us some good!"

Ada lay the spatula down on the side of the oven. Her back remained turned to him. She drank the last sip of the Chardonnay in her glass.

"Sounds good," she said. "I'll get dressed."

"Honey, is everything okay?" Ben asked. Ada knew he was trying, that he was sorry. She was the one who should be sorry.

"Yes," Ada said. "Everything is okay." She started to move, but then felt a wave of dizziness and nausea, so she steadied herself, bending over the kitchen island with her arms outstretched for balance.

"Whoa, you good?" Ben said, grabbing her for support.

"I. Am. Fine," Ada slurred, her eyes half-mast.

"You don't look fine, honey."

"Oh yeah? Want to say anything else shitty to me tonight?"

"Honey—"

"Don't 'honey' me!" she exclaimed, moving away from Ben's hold, stumbling backward. She pointed her index finger at him. "You . . . You . . . are not good."

"What? I don't understand you. You're slurring."

"Go to hell," Ada yelled. "Now I have a drinking problem too?" Her eyes widened and she fell backward into the fridge. Her medication was not mixing well with the wine.

"Honey, please, you need to sit down. You're going to get hurt."

"Maybe you should have thought of that before when you re-JECTED me," she mumbled. She shuffled toward the stove, as the oil and onions were popping. The room smelled of fennel and lemon from her shrimp recipe.

"Let's turn the stove off. I can order in," Ben said.

Ada continued to stir. "But you said we are going out," she replied.

"Well, maybe it's not such a good idea," he said, approaching her and turning off the stove.

"I am making something! You . . . you are . . . unappreciative." She reached into the frying pan, grabbed a hot shrimp, and ate it, tail and all. Hot oil dripped down her glistening chin.

"Jeez, what is going on with you? Did you take some kind of pills? Maybe you shouldn't be drinking with your meds."

"I'm having a PAH-TAY!" Ada slurred, tossing shrimp, one after the other, all over the floor.

"You're out of control, honey! Stop it!" He reached for her, grabbing her wrists so she would stop throwing food.

"I love me a good food fight," she yelled, laughing. "Ow, you're hurting me! Let go of me!"

"You're going to bed," Ben affirmed. "You are done."

"No, you are done!" Ada growled. She ran to the fridge, grabbed her bottle of Chardonnay, and started for the back stairwell.

"Where are you going?"

"What do you care?" Ada shouted leaping up the steep wooden staircase, two steps at a time. "Go back to Papa Jake's!"

Just then, she tripped on the tie to her robe and smacked her face hard on the staircase. She let out a scream. Ben ran to her, turning her over. She had a cut above her eye that was bleeding profusely and a nosebleed.

"We are going to the hospital," he said. "You need stitches."

"Snitches need stitches!" she called out, laughing, blood all over her face.

Ben grabbed Ada, cradling her in his arms, and tossed her into the car. He then reached over her, belting her in like she was an infant.

"Stop it!" Ada said, trying to get out of the car. "I need to go shopping! Lilly needs new ballet slippers."

"Ada, just relax. I am going to take care of you," Ben replied, speeding down 28 to get to Falmouth Hospital.

"Oh, just like you took care of the wooden dance floor at our wedding?"

"Huh?"

"You heard me! You never put in the fucking dance floor! You said you would! You promised!" She was pointing at him from the passenger seat, her robe now open, revealing her lace bra and underwear.

"Honey, this isn't about the dance floor. Calm down."

"Oh, yes, it is. It's ALWAYS been about the dance floor," Ada slurred. "You. Are. Done!" she said, and then she closed her eyes and rested her head on the window. She passed out cold. Blackout.

Chapter Thirty
LABOR DAY

SADIE

Sadie woke up feeling terrible, coming to terms with the notion that her best friend in the entire world, Charlotte, had left her and moved to New York. On the one hand, she was sad for the time they had lost and spent fighting over Mack. What a waste. On the other hand, Sadie was envious that she, too, could not escape and start over. How wonderful it must be to pick up and begin anew, with a clean slate and no strings attached. She could get a job in publishing, and she would live on the Upper West Side, across from the Museum of Natural History. But then she wouldn't have her children. There was a price to pay for that. And it was a price she'd pay repeatedly.

Sadie decided to go for a walk in Woods Hole to decompress and get some fresh air. She parked in front of Pie in the Sky and went in to get a large dark roast coffee and a popover. She then walked down Water Street and stopped on the stone bench in front of Candy Go Nuts to have a bite. The sous chef from Quicks Hole Taqueria wrangled with a five-foot-tall plastic lobster sculpture as if he were a fisherman fighting a bull shark. He arduously dragged the lobster over the clam shells up the wooden patio step and into the restaurant. Soon, the Landfall would host the annual "Take Back the Beach" party and the locals would rejoice that the summer people were gone. Drinks flowed, the streets of Woods Hole closed, and Crooked Coast played on a floating barge in the harbor. All the twenty-somethings would attend, including the staff from the other restaurants, like The Captain Kidd and Shuckers. But Sadie and Charlotte would sit out back of the Landfall on the Adirondack chairs, just as they had in years past, taking in the sunset, the ocean, and a Cosmo.

Not this year.

This year, Sadie would be alone on the back deck, or with some of the regular barflies, like Lucy and Clarence, who sipped Zinfandel at the far corner of the bar and rode their bicycles to the restaurant, having lost their driver's licenses. Maybe she could ask Chip to come this time, she thought. And then she felt a pat on her shoulder.

"Well, well, well," Mack said, grinning like a handsome Kennedy. He sat down beside her, unkempt and unshaven. He was stress manifested.

"Oh, boy," Sadie said, smiling and rolling her eyes. "I was wondering when I'd run into you."

"Has enough time passed for you to stop hating me?"

"Um . . . no," Sadie said. She couldn't help but laugh.

"Okay, then," Mack said, rising to his feet. "I'll go." Sadie grabbed his pant leg like she would Charlie's.

"Sit down," she said. "It's fine. I'm over it." She wasn't in fact sure if this was the truth, but it was hard to stay mad at Mack, especially when he looked like shit. The rumors had been true, it seemed, the ones Scarlett Crane mentioned. Mack was drinking his face off every night at Liam Maguire's or Grumpy's, and it showed. He was bloated, like a dog tick, with a round, reddish face and grown-out facial hair. His clothes, too, looked disheveled and wrinkled, like he'd either worn them to fall asleep on the sofa or dusted them off from the floor of someone's bedroom. He had an old Woods Hole Yacht Club T-shirt on with a hole in the upper right shoulder and a pair of khaki shorts with some sort of blood on them, either from fishing or a drunken fall.

"So how have you been? Dare I ask?" Mack said. He wreaked of malt and old vodka. Sadie's stomach rumbled. She moved back a few inches.

"I've been better," she said. "Charlotte left. She's back in Manhattan."

"Really?" Mack said. "Wow, good for her." His blatant nonchalance was irritating but also sort of validating that maybe he was never, in fact, into Charlotte. "Is that coffee? Can I have a sip?" He reached for her cup, and she pushed him away.

"Eww, that's disgusting, especially with, like, morning breath!" Sadie scoffed. And stale vodka breath. She couldn't believe he would be so gross as to think that was okay. Was he always this foul, she wondered, or was she once wearing rose-colored glasses? What was it that hooked her in the first place? Maybe she had romanticized the memory of him. He'd hooked her like a bluefin tuna and thrown her back wounded.

"Sheesh!" Mack laughed. "Someone is grouchy!"

"I am *not* grouchy," Sadie snarled. "I merely don't want to swap spit with you or anyone for that matter."

"Not even Chip?" Mack asked.

"That's none of your business," Sadie said, turning her face in the other direction to watch the ferry boat leave the dock for Martha's Vineyard. It sounded its horn as it backed up, and she could smell the gasoline, a welcome break from his pungent breath.

"So, how's the resort coming along?" Sadie asked. She knew that the plans had been stalled, perhaps never even having been started.

"Uh . . . decent. We kind of hit a wall," he laughed, "with our investors."

Nana's trust had clearly dried up.

"That's too bad," Sadie lied. "So, what next? You sticking around for the winter?"

"I don't know. Maybe going to split my time between here and Boston. I got some verbal work commitments up there."

A verbal work commitment usually meant no commitment, from what Sadie had seen. And whenever folks on the Cape claimed they'd be going up to Boston a lot, it demonstrated their discomfort with their situation there. They were hiding from something, most often themselves.

A long silence ensued.

"How's Nana?" Sadie asked, fidgeting with her coffee sleeve.

"She's good," Mack replied. "You know Nana! She's back at the club golfing every weekend and getting ready to do her fall planters. She asked me to check out Mahoney's for some mums."

Sadie remembered she, too, had to get the planters going for the front of the house. She prided herself on having an immaculate home exterior, even if the inside was a mess.

"Well, I hate to jump, but . . ." Sadie said, rising. "It's good to see you, Mack."

"Yeah, you too," he said. "Don't be a stranger."

Sadie gave him a smirk and exhaled as she strolled away.

"Hey, you going to the Farewell to Summer Fling Saturday?" Mack called out.

"Yes, I think so," Sadie said. "You?"

"Sure thing," Mack said, winking. "I'll be Nana's guest."

His wink annoyed her. Sadie hated when men winked. It was so condescending. She even hated the "wink" emoji, when people would add it to an email right after saying something mildly offensive.

Sadie got back into her car and checked her phone. Charlie and Tina were still at their respective sleepovers, so she would have some time for herself. She peered down Water Street before leaving, where she saw Mack sitting alone, appearing deflated, on the steps of the Community Hall. She recalled when he first messaged her on Facebook, and then when he walked into the Lobster Trap. She had felt so much anticipation, so much hope. She teared up. It was all such a mess. Mack was a mess.

When Sadie arrived home, Chip was sitting on the front porch sipping a piña colada while seated in the white Adirondack chair.

"Drinking?" Sadie asked. "At eleven in the morning?"

"Eh, it's the weekend," Chip said. "And the kids are off with their friends, so . . . why not?"

"True. Wanna make me one?"

"Sure thing!" Chip said, laughing. He rose and went inside the house. Sadie sat down on the front stoop and exhaled. Labor Day weekend. The summer was officially over. It was time to move on; the ride was over. To her surprise, she was not rattled at all by seeing Mack. In fact, she was sort of glad she had, especially since he looked so downtrodden and pathetic. It just verified what she already knew deep down, then and now. He was no good for her.

Chip swung open the screen door, handing her a piña colada.

"Oh, I love how you put the whipped cream on it," she joked.

"Shh, don't emasculate me," Chip said. "I feel like my dick just shrunk."

They both started to crack up, almost too much.

"How *is* your dick?" Sadie asked.

"Wouldn't you like to know?" Chip exclaimed. "He is lonely, actually. He feels neglected and sad!"

"Well maybe we should do something about that," Sadie said, raising her eyebrows. For once, in an exceptionally long time, she actually meant it.

"You don't have to ask me twice," Chip said, darting up from his chair.

"I didn't mean now!"

"Oh! Sorry," Chip said, sitting back down.

"Oh, what the fuck," Sadie said, getting up. "Come on, let's go upstairs." She grabbed his hand, leading him up the stairs behind her. One foot after the other, slowly, making their way together.

Sadie looked at the photos that lined the stairwell as he walked in front of her. There was one of them in college, in sweatshirts, youthful and cherubic. Then, there was one of them at the Knob, overlooking Buzzards Bay, when they got engaged, him holding her ring finger to the camera. This was followed by the traditional wedding photo of them in front of St. Barnabas Church in Falmouth, and then them as a family with Tina and Charlie on either side of them. They had a lot of history, she and Chip. Some of it bad, some of it good. But it was history. It was perhaps something worth fighting for.

Chip stood at the top of the steps, looking down at Sadie below him.

"You alright?" he asked.

"Yeah," she said. "I am. All right. It's going to be all right."

She joined him on the top step, looking into his familiar eyes, and kissed him.

It was going to be all right.

Chapter Thirty-One

THE ACCIDENT

September 2019, The Day After the Farewell to Summer Fling

SADIE

At 9 a.m., Sadie's phone vibrated with a message from Scarlett Crane: Mack had been in a terrible car accident and was in the ICU at Falmouth Hospital. His truck was totaled, smashed to pieces, on the side of Route 151 and Currier Road. No one else was injured, but Mack's future was uncertain.

Dread, guilt, and shame coursed through Sadie's veins. She'd seen Mack peel away in his truck at the end of the Farewell to Summer Fling wondering if she should call him a cab or take his keys. He was drunk, very drunk, and in bad shape. She had watched as he tossed back at least five Moscow Mules and then switched to whiskey neat. His hair was wet with sweat as he moved about the dance floor, grabbing Sandra Pierce for a waltz and busting out 90s dance moves like the running man and the cabbage patch. He even slid on his stomach doing the worm at one point, to Nana's dismay, and that's when she tapped him out, her poppy-pink lips pursed with a scowl on her face.

Sadie continued to check her phone for details, refreshing Falmouth Discussion on Facebook, where she might see an update from the police or someone who had witnessed the accident. Then it happened. She received a call from Scarlett Crane around noon. Scarlett's neighbor, who was married to a male nurse from the ICU, relayed that Mack was speeding at 75 mph when he swerved to avoid hitting a coyote and slammed into a telephone pole. The coyote was safe, but Mack was not in the clear. It would be another 72 hours in critical care before they could determine if he would survive. He suffered from multiple fractures, crushed lungs, and a blood clot in his brain with swelling and excess spinal fluid. He was responsive when awake but needed to remain under sedation to keep from extreme agitation and irritability. They would continue to run CAT scans, but the outcome looked grim.

Sadie clenched her teeth, her mouth dry and parched, as she knelt in prayer. *Please God,* she thought. *Please have mercy on Mack. I know I wished him dead, but I didn't mean it. He is kind, deep down, and deserves forgiveness. Please also have mercy on me for sinning, God. I have been bad, but I will make up for it. I promise.*

Several tense days passed, and Sadie's phone blew up with texts and calls from her friends. But the one call she cared about the most was the group call with Charlotte and Ada.

"I can't believe it," Ada said. "I feel like it was just yesterday that we were cussing him out."

"He was plastered," Charlotte said. "And I hate him," she paused. "But I still don't want him to die. I wonder if we should reach out to Nana."

"I left her a voicemail," Sadie replied. "I haven't heard anything back. I wonder if she's with him at the hospital. And his children! I forgot about his poor children . . ."

"This is awful," Ada sighed. "I—just—I don't know."

A brief silence ensued.

"Listen, he's not our responsibility," Charlotte said. "I mean, they're doing what they can, and all we can do is wait."

"And pray," Sadie said.

"Yes, that too," Charlotte replied.

"Pray," Ada said.

Mack survived. He was transported to Mass General in Boston for surgery, and he'd been recovering for several weeks. He had broken bones, fractured ribs, brain swelling, and significant memory loss. *Would he even remember this summer?* Sadie wondered. Did she want him to remember?

As much as Sadie wanted to forget those sultry summer days with Mack, she couldn't. She and Chip were in therapy to work on forgiveness and trust after she came clean about the affair, and she was helping Ada pick up the pieces of her failing marriage to Ben.

But every now and then, in the stillness, Sadie would think of the good times with Mack: his soft touch, his pillowy lips, the laughter, and the passion. She would busy herself with organization, to-do lists, and the children, but the memories persisted. She would pack them away, like the summer clothes in bins, and she would move on with her life and be present. She had so much to be grateful for.

It was time to let him go.

ACKNOWLEDGMENTS

First and foremost, I need to thank Jamie Cat Callan, author and friend extraordinaire. She and I met every two weeks to exchange pages of our novels and to provide feedback. Without her, I would not have been able to write my book. She held me accountable and over the course of two and a half years, I was able to write this novel ten pages at a time. I am forever grateful for her encouragement, support, and love.

I would also like to thank Greenleaf Book Group for taking a chance on me as a debut novelist, and for the editors and my team there. In particular, I want to thank Sally Garland, Leah Pierre, Justin Branch, Tanya Hall, Brian Phillips, Tiffany Barrientos, and Madelyn Myers.

I wrote *Friends with Boats* while living on Cape Cod, and I want to acknowledge the establishments I mention for their kindness over the years.

I want to thank my parents, Bill Speck and Phoebe Office, for their eternal support with my various endeavors. I love you! I hope I've made you proud. I also want to recognize my siblings, Stasia, Stephanie, and Billy. I am so lucky we are close, and I love our phone calls.

I need to thank my husband, L.T. Slater, who is my best friend and partner. L.T., your love is something I could have never imagined. I am grateful for you every day. Thank you for bringing wonderful London and Farah into my life, for making me laugh, and for getting me back to Cleveland!

And, finally, I want to thank my children, James and Caroline, whom I live for, love with all my heart, and cherish. Mommy loves you more than you will ever know . . .

ABOUT THE AUTHOR

Alexandra Slater is an award-winning journalist and writer who received the Edward R. Murrow award for writing when she worked as a reporter for NPR. Alex graduated from Columbia University with a degree in English literature and attended Northwestern University's Medill Graduate School of Journalism. Since then, she's been an actress, a comedian with Upright Citizens Brigade, a drama and creative writing teacher, a clinical research assistant, a fundraiser, and a marketing advisor—all of which paid little but sound good. She splits her time between Boston and Cleveland with her husband, their children, and three dogs.

Made in the USA
Monee, IL
31 May 2023

35044961R00163